Pippo and Clara

Also by Diana Rosie

Alberto's Lost Birthday

Diana Rosie

Pippo and Clara

MANTLE

First published 2021 by Mantle
an imprint of Pan Macmillan
The Smithson, 6 Briset Street, London ECIM 5NR
Associated companies throughout the world
www.panmacmillan.com

ISBN 978-1-4472-9305-7

Copyright © Diana Rosie 2021

The right of Diana Rosie to be identified as the
author of this work has been asserted by her in accordance
with the Copyright, Designs and Patents Act 1988.

All rights reserved. No part of this publication may be reproduced,
stored in a retrieval system, or transmitted, in any form, or by any means
(electronic, mechanical, photocopying, recording or otherwise)
without the prior written permission of the publisher.

Pan Macmillan does not have any control over, or any responsibility for,
any author or third-party websites referred to in or on this book.

1 3 5 7 9 8 6 4 2

A CIP catalogue record for this book is available from the British Library.

Typeset by Palimpsest Book Production Ltd, Falkirk, Stirlingshire
Printed and bound by CPI Group (UK) Ltd, Croydon, CRO 4YY

This book is sold subject to the condition that it shall not, by way of
trade or otherwise, be lent, hired out, or otherwise circulated without
the publisher's prior consent in any form of binding or cover other than
that in which it is published and without a similar condition including
this condition being imposed on the subsequent purchaser.

Visit **www.panmacmillan.com** to read more about all our books
and to buy them. You will also find features, author interviews and
news of any author events, and you can sign up for e-newsletters
so that you're always first to hear about our new releases.

To my family:
old and new,
here and there,
lost and found.

PROLOGUE

A furious roar stopped the man in his tracks. Taking hold of his daughter's hand, he turned and looked along the dusty road.

Three men scowled and swaggered towards them.

'Hey, you!' shouted one, pointing a hefty finger. 'We don't want your kind around here.'

The others sneered in agreement.

The man stood still as the three walked slowly closer.

'You lot, you're all mosquitos,' said their leader. 'Good for' — he swatted the back of his hand with his palm, squashing an imaginary bug — 'nothing.'

One of the men guffawed and repeated the action, the sound of the slap ringing out over the cicadas' raucous evening song.

As he calmly watched, the man saw one of the group, the smallest, hold back for a moment so the others didn't see him. He reached up and pulled the skin beneath his right eye.

The man knew the message he was being given. Watch out.

He bent down towards the little girl and spoke quickly. Her dark hair shone as she leaned her head towards him and listened, her amber eyes flitting between her father and the three men. His daughter was only four, but his tone made her listen closely, a solemn look on her face.

When he finished speaking, the child hesitated, looking up at her papa nervously.

'Now, Clara,' her father said urgently.

That was enough. She snapped her head up and began running, away from Papa and the men, her bare feet kicking up tiny puffs of dust.

Clara ran as fast as she could. She did not turn her head when she heard gruff voices shouting. She did not blink at the unkind words spat at her father. She did not even slow as the sounds of a scuffling fight began. She did as she had been told.

Turning off the lane, she raced down a path through the downy oaks and pine trees. As her legs began to slow a little, a break in the woodland up ahead appeared, giving her the push she needed to speed up again – she was nearly home.

The door was open, so she ran up the steps and inside to where her mother stood attentive, almost as if she had been waiting for her. Listening as her daughter spoke quickly, the woman grabbed her shawl and instructed the girl to take care of the baby.

Clara saw her mamma run down the steps, calling to family, neighbours and friends. She heard her mother say her husband was in trouble. She didn't mention the bad men that Clara had just told her had followed them, or that they used nasty words. Mamma just said Papa needed help. But that was enough. Men quickly gathered around, asking where he was. Her mother pointed to the path that led to the road. With shouts to others, they headed into the wood at a dash — a few women, including Clara's mother, following behind.

As the excitement died down, the girl turned and crossed to where her brother lay sleeping, gurgling noisily, unaware of the danger his father was in.

The boy was still asleep when they returned. They walked so slowly and silently that if Clara hadn't been sitting on the steps waiting, she might not have known they were back.

Twilight had settled over the sky and the child had to squint to see the men's faces. Then her eyes rested on an outline — a large, long, heavy load the group carried between them, then gently lowered to the ground.

A whimper made her pull her gaze upwards towards her mother, who, while Clara watched, sank to her knees, dropping her face to the dark shape. Clara noticed then that part of the form had been covered by a shawl, which her mother began to unwrap. As her papa's face was exposed, Clara's breath caught. Blood lay black on his swollen skin and soaked his white collar.

The men stood as watchmen while her mother leaned over her husband, gripping his shoulder and resting her nose in his neck as the girl had seen her do so many times, her sobs lost in the woollen shawl. Clara waited for what seemed like forever before her mamma, wiping her face with the heel of her hand, sat back on her heels. Then slowly and carefully, as if to avoid hurting him further, she reached to her husband's kerchief and untied it from his neck. Pulling it gently towards her, she stood. With a glance at the men, she nodded and turned away from her husband, walking towards her home.

Clara's gaze didn't leave her mother, but she was aware that the men had picked up her father and were carrying him into the darkness. Her mother's face was pale, her steps hesitant as she stared at the red patterned cloth in her hand. Just as Mamma's dusty shoe reached to the first step, her brother let out a wail, making mother and daughter turn in unison towards the noise.

Without a word, the woman went to the child, lifting him up and kissing the soft hair on his head, whispering soothing words into his ear. With a jut of her chin, she indicated for her daughter to sit and, when she did, placed the baby into her lap. He was big and heavy for the four-year-old, but she rocked him in her arms and played with his fingers as he chattered happily to himself.

Mamma quietly sat at the table opposite them and reached for her sewing box. Laying the square of fabric out flat, she took up a pair of scissors, pausing, a tremor in her hand, before making the first snip. Carefully, she cut the fabric into thin strips.

Then the girl watched intently as her mother, murmuring words quietly to herself, plucked a dark hair from her own head. Then another. And another, until six black hairs lay on top of each strip of her father's kerchief.

Deftly threading her needle, the woman folded the first length of cloth around the hair and, her fingers pushing and tucking, she sewed the thin strip of fabric to safely encase the hair. Her lips didn't stop moving until all six were finished and she put down her needle.

Gathering three red strips, she tied them together at one end, then quickly braided them tightly. Repeating her actions with the second set, she was soon knotting the end securely.

Resting her hands on her thighs, Clara's mamma sat back, contemplating her work. The boy watched, occasionally chirruping to himself. The woman smiled briefly, her honey-coloured eyes lacking their usual light, before picking up the braided strips and standing.

Taking her son's arm gently, she wrapped the fabric around his left wrist — once, twice, three times, whispering words the girl did not understand. Tying it tightly, she then turned to her daughter.

'This will protect you,' she said, lifting the second braided band. The girl placed her brother on her chair, where he sat chattering, and lifted her right hand.

Her mother wrapped it tightly around her wrist twice, muttering her secret words as she did. Knotting the ends, she turned to her daughter's light eyes. 'It is a circle of love that will tie you to me and Papa, and also to your brother.' They both glanced at the boy.

'Wherever you go, whatever you do, your mamma and papa will always be with you. Even when we are not with you.' Her mother's voice cracked as she carried on. 'And if I cannot, you must take care of your brother.'

Clara nodded, contemplating the red bracelet on her wrist.

Holding her chin in her hand, her mother gently raised her daughter's head upwards. 'You must look after your brother,' she repeated.

The little girl turned to look at the small boy, playing with his podgy toes and yattering in his own unknowing language. She loved the little chatty bird and would do everything she could to protect him.

'I promise, Mamma,' the girl replied, and the woman wrapped her arms around the child's small frame. Clara's hands crept to her mother's neck, and as the hoo-hooing of an owls' conversation seeped into the room, they held each other.

I know the Communists.
I know them because some of them are my children . . .
Benito Mussolini

CLARA

1938

Clara Turns Right

'But I don't like it here, Mamma.'

We both look around the bare room. My brother lies sleeping on a dirty mattress, while my mother and I sit on top of a blanket heaped on bare floorboards. A tattered cloth hangs over the only window's cracked panes, and in the corner of the empty room is a filthy sink that a tap drips into. Our small pile of possessions, all we have in the world, has been carefully placed by the wall. Despite it being late in the night, the street outside is noisy.

I feel Mamma take a deep breath.

'Tomorrow we will begin to make this a home. Our castle.' She pulls me into a hug.

'With a proper bed?' I ask.

'With sheets of silk,' she nods.

'And a kitchen?'

'We'll have our own chef. He'll cook us all of our favourite meals.'

'Pasta al forno!' I whisper loudly.

'Mountains of it!' says Mamma.

'And pizza for Pippo?'

'Hundreds of them!' laughs Mamma, her golden eyes shining. 'And he'll want a different topping on every one.'

'And he'll tell everyone what he's eating and why he likes it,' I add.

'Of course. Our chatty bird.'

We both look at the little boy, quiet in sleep. Mamma says he was born chattering like a tiny sparrow with lots to say. I don't recall him being born, just over seven years ago now, but I know that for as long as I can remember, my brother has talked and talked and talked. He constantly tells us what he is doing and why he is doing it, and when he draws breath, his hands continue the conversation for him.

People have tried to hush him, scolding him to stop the endless babbling, but Mamma tells him to talk if he wishes. All those thoughts and words need to come out, she says. And I find I can listen when I want, but at other times I let his voice breeze over me, like a small bird swooping around my head, the air from his wings occasionally wafting against my face. I find it comforting, a constant background noise to my day.

I curl into the blanket as my mother strokes my hair. Then she seems to notice the red band tied around my right wrist. Taking it in her fingers, she turns it round and round, in the same way that Pippo plays with his.

'Never forget that these bracelets connect us,' she whispers. 'You and Pippo and me and Papa.'

'I won't, Mamma.'

She shifts her body, moving to get up.

'Where are you going?'

Mamma is already pulling her black scarf over her hair and tying it at the nape of her neck.

'I'm going to meet someone. The landlord told me about a lady who may have some sewing work.'

'Can't you go in the morning?' I ask, hearing the whine in my voice.

'She's going on a trip tomorrow. She wants someone to do the alterations while she's away. Now,' she leans towards me and strokes my hair, 'go to sleep. I'll be back before you know I'm gone.'

Snuggling down, I feel sleep drifting near me like gently lapping waves.

'Sweet dreams, Clara,' she whispers, giving the top of my head a kiss. 'Sweet dreams.'

I let my eyes shut and hear a door quietly close.

When I wake, stiff and aching, I do what I always do and gently rub the bracelet on my wrist between my thumb and forefinger. It's my way of starting the day with Mamma and Papa. Opening my eyes a little, I stretch and peer around the room.

My mother is not here. The sun is trying to force its way through the dirt on the window and the rag that hangs over it. My brother sleeps on, curled in a ball, his thumb tucked into his mouth.

Yawning, I turn and look at the closed door. Perhaps Mamma has gone to the toilet.

I wait for her, listening to the sounds of a city awakening; horses clip-clopping over cobbles, while men and women shout their wares. 'Milk! Fresh milk!' 'Cornetto!'

I have only had cornetto a few times, but the thought of the buttery, flaky pastry melting in my mouth makes my stomach gurgle and groan. After travelling all day, we arrived in the city exhausted. Pippo and I sat with our bags in the street while Mamma found somewhere to stay, then she brought us here to this room. There was no supper.

Perhaps she has gone out to get us some breakfast.

I realize that I need to go to the toilet at the bottom of the stairs, so, trying not to wake my brother, I climb out of the blanket and pull on my shoes. As I turn the handle on the door, it creaks and Pippo stirs a little, but he doesn't wake and I slip through the doorway, quietly pulling it shut behind me.

The stairwell smells unpleasant and I trot down the steps quickly. The bathroom is shared with other occupants in this building so I am as fast as I can be.

When I come out, drying my hands on my skirt, I turn to the main entrance. A tall, wooden door stands between me and an unknown city, but I want to look for Mamma, so I walk over and heave it open.

Sunshine hits my face and warms me instantly. I hadn't realized I was chilled. The entrance to our new home is down a long street. Drying sheets hang between buildings on both sides, and sounds of cooking, nattering women and crying babies waterfall out of the open windows. People bustle past, going to work, or carrying bread and pastries back to their homes for breakfast.

I look to the left. People are working all along the pavement. A line of men and boys are cutting cardboard to the shape of soles, and hammering them onto shoes.

I turn my head to the right. Nearby, a woman sits beside two huge baskets filled with flowers: bunches of giant daisies, roses and lavender. Scent rises from her buds and mingles with the street's smell of food and rubbish.

I glance left again, trying to decide which way my mother would have turned. The street bends, tall buildings blocking the sunlight and casting dark shadows over the thinning path. Looking to the right, I decide the flowers would have persuaded my mother, as they do me, to walk past their bright colours and delicious perfumes.

I step down onto the pavement and turn right, towards the small woman who sits wrapping twine around a thick bunch of lavender stalks. I won't go far, just a little way up the road, and if Mamma's not there, I'll go back to Pippo and wait for her return.

A sound up ahead grabs my attention and I see a woman throw a bucket of water over the cobblestones outside her door. Bright light reflects and glistens, transforming the water into a rainbow for a moment. Then I see her.

Mamma!

Blinking, I squint at her dark shape. It disappears behind a horse that is slowly pulling a heavy cart filled with fruit. I stand on my tiptoes, peering past the produce and watching for her tall, familiar outline to reappear. When she does, I'm sure it is Mamma. She wears black from head to toe, unlike the other women who wear blue, or brown, or green. The way she pulls her black shawl tighter over her hair, the way she walks — purposefully, her head held high — it is my mamma.

I call to her, but she is too far away to hear me so I break into a run, spurring my still sleepy legs into action and congratulating myself on deciding to turn right. As I reach the junction with the main road, though, Mamma has disappeared into the crowds. For a moment, I let myself be distracted by the noise and energy. Horses pulling small carriages trot past briskly. Cars navigate around them and the carts loaded with food that are parked on the edge of the road. Then I notice two boys, not much older than me, standing at the corner, smoking. I feel their eyes on me, and a thin shiver runs down my spine.

I turn my head to search for Mamma again, trying to peer over the swarm of people, looking for her slender silhouette. There are shops and cafes on both sides of the road, and I spot one with a sign that says simply: *Pane.*

Just as a plump woman bustles past me, knocking me sideways, I see the top of a black headscarf that I know is my mamma's disappear into the doorway of the bread shop. I dash across the road, running around the cars that have drawn to a stop, horns blaring at a cart that has spilled its load of wicker baskets.

I notice as I run up the steps that the window is stacked with loaves of all shapes and sizes, as well as boxes of biscuits and cakes. The smell is wonderful, and I skid into the small shop breathing in the warm, yeasty scent.

There are two women waiting to be served and one

of them is Mamma. Except, even as I reach out to touch her arm, I know it is not. The woman's dress, shoes and scarf are all black like my mother always wears, but now I am close, I realize this woman's figure is plumper, less elegant. She turns and I see a face that I do not know.

The woman smiles at my confused face and says, '*Sì, bambina?*'

'I, I . . .' I stumble. 'I thought you were my mother.'

The woman shakes her head, and is about to say something when the girl behind the counter interrupts.

'What do you want?' she says rudely to the woman who is not my mother. 'I hope you have money to pay.'

As the lady in black quietly pulls out a purse from her pocket and orders her bread, I turn to go, embarrassed.

'Have you lost your mother?' asks a more friendly voice.

I turn to see the other customer, a woman dressed in a smart green suit, her hair elegantly styled in large chestnut-coloured rolls. As she speaks to me, she tucks two long loaves of bread into her shopping basket, which already holds a selection of fruit.

I nod, but remain silent.

The woman guides me out of the shop, and as we take the steps down to the street, she says, 'When did you last see her?'

'Last night, when I went to sleep,' I reply shyly. 'When I woke this morning, she was gone.'

'Does she usually go out and leave you?'

I shake my head. This woman seems both kind and concerned, but experience cautions me against telling anyone too much about my family. My mother's words, warning Pippo and me to be wary of those who aren't like us, who don't understand our ways, echo in my mind.

The woman in black then steps out of the shop, nodding her head to the two of us before carrying on down the street I have just come up, a loaf wrapped in paper under her arm.

'Your mother was dressed like her?'

I look at the woman's black shawl covering her head and shoulders, the black skirt that stops just above her ankles, the worn black shoes, and I nod again.

The kind woman's brow furrows.

'Perhaps she has gone home,' she says, 'and is waiting for you to return.' Something about the ways she speaks makes me think she does not really believe what she is saying, but I nod.

'Come,' she says with a sudden determination. 'Let me accompany you home. If she is not there, we can look for her together.'

Despite my uneasiness with strangers, I feel a sense of relief as I point down the street, and follow the woman's confident stride. As we walk, she asks me my name.

'C-ca-ca . . .' I say, suddenly stuttering.

The lady slows and turns to me.

I take a deep breath as my mamma has told me to when I am nervous.

'Clara,' I say clearly, looking at the woman's face with all the courage I can command.

'And how old are you, Clara?' she asks.

'Ten.'

'Well, come along Clara who's ten. Let's find your mother.'

I guide her down the turning towards our building, noticing this time that the smoking boys' eyes glance from me to the woman, taking in her smart clothes and sophisticated hair. It is clear they have not seen women like her on this street often.

As we trot briskly on, I spot the flower seller and, gently pulling on the woman's sleeve, I point to the doorway beside her. Together, we walk into the building's entrance, where the woman takes a handkerchief from her jacket pocket and holds it to her nose.

I lead her up the stairs, wishing with all my might that when I open the door, we will see Mamma and Pippo playing, the smell of fresh coffee and crispy pastries filling the room. In my mind, my mother looks at me, at first delighted and relieved to see me; then something quizzical crosses her face as she sees the smartly dressed woman behind me. She would, of course, be gracious and ask the lady in for coffee, despite her embarrassment at our surroundings. And as my hand reaches up for the door handle, I briefly wonder if the woman will stay to have breakfast with us.

Pushing the door slowly open, I close my eyes, hoping to smell the coffee first, before I see Mamma. But all I smell is the damp. I open my eyes slowly and look around the dirty room. My mother is not there.

'Hmmm,' says the woman standing beside me, as she glances around the room.

I ignore her, unable to take my eyes off the empty

blanket lying on the bare floorboards. My breath catches in my throat in a silent gasp of horror.

I barely notice the woman's hand rest gently on my right shoulder.

My brother is gone.

PIPPO

1938

Pippo Turns Left

Pippo's mother always said that chattering birds like him talked from the moment they woke up. To prove her right, every morning, as he squirmed and squinted from his slumber, he would croak with a sleepy voice, *'Buongiorno a tutti!* How did you sleep? I slept very well.'

Whatever they were doing, Clara and Mamma would reply cheerfully, *'Buongiorno,* little bird!'

And so it was that day. The boy writhed in his blanket and, with half a yawn, called out, 'Good morning everyone!'

But no one responded.

He tried again, rubbing his eyes with the palms of his hands.

'Buongiorrrrrrno a tutti!'

Silence replied.

He sat up and looked around a room he'd never seen before. He remembered that he and Mamma and Clara had come to a new city after travelling for days. They'd arrived late last night, and he had sat with Clara until his mother had carried him and her heavy bags up flights of stairs. His eyes had already been shutting as she'd pulled a blanket from the bundle his sister carried, piled it onto the floor, and he'd gratefully climbed in.

It was morning now, but the room was grey.

And empty.

No Mamma. No Clara.

Twisting the red fabric band around his wrist, he called his mother in a dry rasp.

'Mamma. Mamma. Maaaammmmaaa! Mamma?'

He listened for a moment but heard no response. He kneeled on the blanket but didn't dare step out of its island of safety.

'Clara. Clara. Clara. Clara. Claaaaarrrrraaaa!' he called.

He waited. But there was no reply.

The silence made his tummy flip over in fear — they wouldn't have left him alone, would they?

'Where could they have gone?' he asked himself, frightened, but finding courage in the sound of his own voice. Without waiting for a reply, he said, 'Maybe they are out buying breakfast. I hope so. I am very hungry. Pippo's hungry, Mamma!'

When he stopped to listen for a response, at first all he heard was the unsettling silence. But then other sounds began to appear to him — doors banging, children crying, women shouting. He listened for Mamma's voice but it wasn't there.

'I don't understand,' he said aloud, twisting the band on his wrist. 'Usually, when I wake up, Clara is in bed beside me. Mamma always appears, it seems a moment after I open my eyes, with a drink. Clara and I sit up and sip the hot milk. "With a splash of coffee for flavour," Mamma says.'

The sound of his voice echoed in the empty room.

People always said that he talked too much. That he was never quiet, that he twittered like an opinionated little bird.

But Mamma said she liked nothing better than to wake to the sound of a happy sparrow telling her all about his day.

'And on special days,' he continued his monologue, 'Mamma makes hot chocolate. "Start the day in the right way," she always says. I have seen Mamma make it. She grates a piece of chocolate into the hot milk and stirs it. It is delicious!' he told the empty room, his eyes alight at the memory.

'And when you get to the bottom of the cup, there are little tiny lumps of chocolate, and me and my sister use our fingers to eat them. Mmmm!'

The thought of it made Pippo's eyes tingle with tears. Annoyed, he shook his head to dispel his fear and climbed out of the blanket.

'I will go out and find Mamma and Clara!' he announced to no one.

He found his shoes and, sitting down, carefully buckled them on. Then, pulling the door open, he looked out into the stairwell. Although there was a door like theirs on every level, they were all shut and no one was about.

Slowly, holding on to the iron banister, he walked down the stairs, hoping that his mother would appear before he reached the bottom. But when the steps finished and he was still alone, he crossed to the large wooden door and pulled it open.

At first, the sunlight blinded him and he heard the people outside before he saw them. Then he peered around. Opposite the door was a horse and fruit cart, a man standing beside it handing oranges to a gentleman in a hat. The seller didn't spot them, but Pippo watched two boys creep up to the cart and sneakily slip a couple of apples in their pockets before dashing away laughing.

Pippo's dark eyes searched the busy street, but he couldn't see his mother and sister anywhere. As he stood in the sunlight, he looked left and right, wondering whether he should go and search for them, or return to the room and wait.

To the right, past a lady selling flowers, the road became busier. To the left, past men and boys fixing shoes, the street became quieter.

'This way or that way? This way or that way?' Pippo asked himself quietly.

He was still thinking when he suddenly stopped and said to himself, 'What would Mamma say?'

He tapped his chin with a finger. 'Hmmm. She might tell me to return to the room and wait until she came back.'

Pippo glanced back and regarded the gloomy stairwell. Then he turned his face to the sunshine that was starting to warm him and shook his head. 'No. She would ask, "What does your heart say, Chatty Bird?"'

He closed his eyes and took an exaggerated deep breath. After a moment of brief contemplation, his eyes flicked open again.

'This way,' he announced to the world, holding out

his left hand, his wristband casting a flash of red, and marching down the steps onto the pavement. '*Sì!*' He nodded as he turned left and started to walk along the street, glancing around the people bustling past him to check they knew he'd made the right decision.

Then, up ahead, weaving through the busy road with a loaf of bread tucked under one arm, he saw his mother. He didn't ask himself why she was walking away from their new home, he just shouted.

'MAMMA! MAMMA! I'm here, Mamma! Wait!'

He broke into a run but, as he skirted around a stack of cardboard beside one of the cobblers, a small dog excitedly bounded up to him, yapping.

'Uh!' cried the surprised boy, as he tripped and fell heavily to the cobbles. Sitting up, he looked at his scraped knees.

'*Ohiii!*' he cried, watching the small beads of blood rise above the skin and feeling the sting of pain.

The little black dog jumped happily beside him, still yapping.

'Silly dog,' Pippo scolded, but when the pup eagerly licked his face, he had to forgive him and pat the dog's head. He couldn't stay and play, though; he had to find his mother, and he quickly stood to look for her in the crowd.

But she was gone.

'No!' he cried, as a fear that he wouldn't be able to find her bubbled up inside him. He ran to where he had seen her last. Ducking between passers-by, he looked for her cinnamon-coloured ankles and worn black shoes striding along the road.

The black dog followed him, skittering around his

feet, thrilled to be on an adventure, but Pippo ignored him. He stopped and stood on his tiptoes to try and spot his mother's tall outline, but he couldn't see past the people in front of him.

Looking around, he saw a crate on the side of the road, a woman sitting beside it.

'There!' he gasped and quickly ran over to it, climbing onto its wooden edge to get a better view of the street.

'Hey,' said the woman, and when Pippo looked down, he saw a baby swaddled in a blanket snuggled in the box.

'*Scusi!*' said the little boy breathlessly, as he searched the crowds for a familiar head.

'What do you think you're doing?' the woman asked, annoyed, as she picked up the baby.

'I'm looking for Mamma,' Pippo replied. 'I saw her. Just now. But the dog made me fall, and when I got up, she was gone.'

'What dog?' asked the woman.

Pippo took a moment to look down for the dog, but it too had vanished.

'Everyone is disappearing,' he said, more to himself than the lady who sat beside him, swaying her baby gently on her hip.

'Everyone?'

'Yes,' said the boy, raising his hand to his eyes as he knew the sailors did when they were on the lookout for pirates. 'Mamma. Clara. Even that dog. All gone.'

'Clara?'

'My sister.'

'And your papa?'

'He died,' said Pippo, searching for his mother's black scarfed head.

'Ah,' said the woman. 'I'm sorry to hear that.'

'I was just a baby. I have the same name as him. Filippo. But everyone calls me Pippo. And I am seven years old. And—'

'And where is your home, Pippo?'

'We don't have one.'

'No?'

'We move around.'

'Ah.'

'But Mamma said we would make our home here. In this city. She said she would find work here. She sews – she makes things seem like new. Look,' he pointed at an invisible patch on his jacket sleeve, 'it's like magic. She said the places we've been were fun to visit, but now Clara and I are old enough for school, we should settle down.

'So, now we live there.' Pippo pointed back the way he had run. 'It's not very nice. It smells. We only arrived last night so Mamma hasn't had a chance to make it more like our home. She's very good at that. But I woke up this morning and she was gone. Mamma and Clara. They were both gone. And I didn't know where they were. So I went looking for them, and I saw Mamma. And I chased her. But then I fell over the dog that is not here any more, and I lost her.'

Pippo looked down at the woman and realized that tears were welling in his eyes.

'I lost her,' he repeated.

The woman looked at him tenderly. Placing the baby back into the blanketed box, she held out her hand and helped Pippo back onto the ground. Then she pulled him to her and held him tightly as he cried into her apron.

'It's all right,' she hushed. 'We'll find your mamma.'

Pippo sat in the chair and took a bite of his breakfast. The fried egg sat on top of tomato sauce that was smeared over a crunchy baton of bread. When the bright yellow yolk predictably burst and ran down his chin, he used a finger to push it back up and into his mouth.

'Does it taste good?' asked the woman, rocking the baby as it suckled noisily on her breast.

'Hmmm,' nodded Pippo, chewing the bread hungrily.

'When you've finished eating, we'll go back to your home. Maybe by then, your mamma will have returned.'

'And Clara,' added the boy through his full mouth. 'She's bigger than me. She has had more birthdays.'

'And Clara,' agreed the woman. 'Tell me, Pippo, where did you live before yesterday?'

'We lived in a wood.'

'Ah. You lived in the country.'

'Yes. I've never been to a city before. It's very fast and noisy. Everybody is rushing here and there. Rush, rush, rush. That's all they do. Why are they in such a hurry?'

'Well, everyone is busy. They have to go to work, to make the money to pay their rent. No rent, no home.'

'No rent, no home,' repeated Pippo, not really understanding.

'Gino's papa is out at work now,' said the woman, nodding down at the breakfasting baby. 'He works on a building site. He leaves early and works all day. He only comes home in time for his meal.'

'What is he building?' asked Pippo, taking another bite of egg and tomato-soaked bread.

'New offices for people to work in.'

'Offices?'

'Yes. For the bureaucrats, no doubt.'

'Bureaucrats?'

'The people who do what Il Duce tells them to do.'

Pippo wiped his mouth with the base of his palm.

'Doesn't everyone do what Il Duce tells them to do?' He didn't really know who Il Duce was, but he'd heard enough from people who spoke to his mother to know that he was a bossy man.

'Not quite everyone.' The woman plucked her nipple out of the baby's mouth and pulled her shirt up. Indignant, little Gino burst into tears and squirmed in his mother's arms until she nudged her knuckle into his pink gums.

'Finished?' she asked the boy. 'Then let's go and see if your mother is at home.'

'Sì, Signora,' said Pippo, quickly slurping some water from the cup he'd been given.

'Donna,' said the woman. 'Everyone is equal in this world, Pippo. You may call me Donna.'

'Donna. Donna. Donnnna.' The boy practised the word, following the woman as she left the small kitchen, pulling a blue scarf over her and the baby.

Scampering to keep up, Pippo threw questions at the woman as they walked down the road.

'Why do the eggs taste different here? How do they

27

make the buildings so tall? Who were those men in the black shirts? Where do the cows and pigs live?'

The woman looked down at him.

'How does your mother answer all these questions?'

'She only answers the last one,' replied Pippo with a smile.

'Fine. The cows and pigs live outside the city on farms. Now, where is the building you came from earlier?'

'Ummm,' said the little boy, as he looked up at the tall blocks on either side of the road.

'Which way did you turn out of the door?'

Pippo stopped and closed his eyes. He remembered looking out of the building entrance and turning his head one way, then another.

'This way,' he said confidently, holding out his left hand.

'So the building was on this side of the road,' said the woman. 'And do you remember what the people outside the door were selling?'

'Flowers!' cried Pippo, thinking of the large baskets of colourful bunches.

'Like this?' asked the woman, pointing to the yellow, white and purple blooms of a flower seller.

'Yes,' nodded the boy, running towards them, then looking up at the tall doorway behind. 'This is it!' he cried excitedly, running up the front steps.

'Wait for me,' called the woman, hitching Gino up on her hip as she stepped into the cool hallway.

'Up here,' called Pippo, as he took the stairs two at a time. 'Mamma will be here now, I am certain. And

Clara too. They must have thought I would sleep for longer. But now they will be back. You can meet them. You will like my mamma. Everyone loves my mamma . . .'

The little boy stopped in front of a door.

'Is it this one?' asked the woman, huffing up the steps towards him.

'I think so.'

'You're not sure?'

'It might be up more stairs.'

'Up there?' The woman pointed to the floor above.

'No,' said the boy confidently, pulling down on the door handle. 'It's this one.'

The door was locked.

'Knock,' instructed the woman, and Pippo banged on the metal door.

There was a shuffling noise on the other side, before the sound of a lock turning and a stiff handle being pulled down.

As the door opened, the small boy gasped at the sight of a fat man, wearing a vest and trousers held up by braces. A cigarette hung from his lips and he peered grumpily through the smoke that floated into his face.

'What do you want?' he gnarled.

'Wrong floor,' said the woman, grabbing Pippo's hand and pulling him up the stairs. '*Scusi*,' she called as the man slammed the door shut.

'That was not Mamma,' said the boy.

'Let's try upstairs.'

'Yes. I'm sure now,' said Pippo, as he saw the half-open door which looked exactly the same as the one below. 'This is it. Mamma will be here. Mamma! Clara! I am here!'

As he pushed the door ajar, the woman stood and watched him. He stepped into the middle of the empty room and looked into every corner of the damp apartment. When he had turned a full circle, he stopped. The woman frowned.

Crouching down, she put the baby on the floor, propping him up against the door. Then she looked at the small boy and opened her arms.

Pippo let out a sob and ran to her.

CLARA

1938

Filomena's Right Eye

The smell in the kitchen makes my stomach growl hungrily. Garlic, onions and tomatoes hit my senses first, but as I look around the room, I see a large wooden block on the table, covered with freshly minced meat. It is more meat than Mamma would have cooked in a month.

When we enter, a heavy-set woman wearing a white apron and a white scarf over her hair turns to us. She looks me up and down, as if I am a chicken in the market whose owner is asking for hundreds of lire more than I am worth.

'Filomena,' says the woman in green, who stands beside me, 'this is Clara.'

Filomena nods her head to me.

'Clara will be staying with us for a few days while we try to find her mother.'

'And my brother,' I whisper, though Filomena ignores me.

'And her brother,' nods the lady. 'If it's not inconvenient, would you please give her something to eat.'

This is not a question, and Filomena and I both know that I will soon be eating whether it is convenient or not.

'Of course, Signora Salvadori,' she says, and her voice, like her manner, is austere.

'Clara.'

My head snaps up to face the woman whose name I have just discovered.

'I'm going to visit my sister. She has a daughter who is a little older than you. With luck, she'll have some clothes that are suitable for you to wear.'

I look down at what I am wearing: a once-white shirt, its elbows and collar now as fine as lace, and a long black skirt with a faded red border that my mother made from a dress she had been given.

'We'll wash your clothes,' says the Signora to me. There is a soft edge to her voice, and I feel gratitude.

Filomena clears her throat.

'I'll be back soon.' Signora Salvadori gives me a smile, her ruby red lipstick making her teeth dazzle.

I watch her leave, then turn back to Filomena, who stands looking at me, arms crossed across her large bosom.

I wait. And wait. Until eventually, Filomena sniffs loudly and points at a chair beside the large oak table in the centre of the room.

Sitting without a word, I observe her crossing the kitchen to the stove and, using a cloth, lifting the lid off a large iron pot. She stirs its contents briefly, before reaching above her head for a dish and spooning what looks like stew into it. She picks up a spoon and walks towards me, her severe face softened by the steam rising from the bowl.

She puts it in front of me and I peer in, spotting beans, cabbage, carrots and onion. The smell that rises from it reminds me that I haven't eaten for a day, and I hungrily pick up the spoon.

But Filomena raises her hand and I stop, my spoon hovering above the dish. I watch as she picks up a bottle from the middle of the table and, quickly placing a wide thumb over its end, tips it, drizzling a golden-green liquid into my stew.

I look at her, unsure if I am permitted to eat yet.

'Are you from around here?' she asks.

I shake my head.

'Then this,' she replies, nodding to the bottle placed back on the table, 'is the best olive oil you will ever taste.'

I nod, convinced she is right.

'*Mangia!*' She points her chin at my food.

I obey, and although the liquid burns my tongue, the taste is incredible. I realize that this is, in fact, the same stew that I have eaten all my life. But where my mother's soup was thick with bread, scattered with whatever ingredients she had to spare, the bread in this dish is merely a soft cushion for a wealth of beans and vegetables. With each mouthful I taste more – tomato and garlic in this, celery and carrot the next, the subtle warmth of chilli in the next.

And yes, the oil is different from any I have tasted before. I let it lie for a moment in my mouth, and feel its fresh, sage-like flavour. But when I swallow, it is gone, leaving no hint that an oil has ever been in my mouth.

I look at Filomena.

She stares into my eyes and, seeing that I have

become a devotee of her cooking — and her oil — softens a little.

'It is the best,' she says firmly, before turning to the meat-covered block.

As I noisily slurp the stew, my eyes follow her, and she notices.

'Hare,' she says. 'The Signore's favourite.'

I watch as she lifts a heavy pan onto the top of the oven, slides the meat into it and listen as its contents begin to sizzle. She stirs it with a large wooden spoon, and I see the concentration on her face.

Older than my mamma, wisps of black and grey hair escape her headscarf and float around her face. Her skin is the colour of a milky coffee, and I notice lines around her eyes and mouth that suggest she laughs more than she would like others to know.

She glances to me, catching me watching her, and my eyes quickly dart back to my bowl.

'Where are you from?' she asks, wiping her forehead with the back of her hand.

I shrug, unsure how to answer.

'You travel a lot?'

I nod.

'Hmmph,' she snorts.

I scrape the dish with my spoon, trying to collect all the splashes of soup left to eke out the best meal I can remember.

When I look up, Filomena is standing over me, making me feel very small.

'I am watching you, girl,' she says sternly, pointing to her right eye.

'This family,' she continues, 'I care for them. The

Signore may have some stupid ideas, but he and the Signora are good people. He's not even a true Fascist.' She shakes her head at me. 'He just joined the party to get a meal ticket — a job with the government.'

I hold my breath, unsure if I should respond, but she carries on.

'I have seen them battle through difficult times, and I vowed that I would do all that I could to protect them from more trouble.'

The large woman takes a deep breath, making her white-clothed body appear even bigger.

'I don't know why you're here, but if you have any ideas of taking advantage of them, think again.'

I shake my head the tiniest amount.

'Perhaps,' she says, looming over me even more, 'you should think about returning to where you came from, now — while the Signora is out. I could tell her that you disappeared while I wasn't looking. What do you think about that?'

I nod.

Then, slinking off my seat, I step away from her. As I do, I notice the thick steam coming out of the pan on the oven.

Filomena follows my eyes and shouts, *'Al diavolo!'* as she dashes to rescue the ragù.

I take the opportunity to sneak out of the kitchen and along the hall to the front door. My fingers are wrapping around the handle when a shape appears outside the frosted glass and the door swings open.

Stepping backwards quickly, I see the Signora before she sees me, but I am unable to hide from her.

'Clara!' she says, surprised.

I stand still, unsure what to do. There's a commotion behind us, and the Signora and I both turn to see Filomena lurch through the kitchen door, wooden spoon in hand.

'Signora,' she says, quickly composing herself.

The lady in the green suit looks at Filomena, then at me.

'What is going on?' she asks.

She waits for an answer, but neither of us speaks.

'Filomena, I believe lunch will need attending to,' she says, waving her away.

'Come,' she says to me, steering me with her hand on my shoulder towards the stairs. 'I have some clothes for you. But you'll need a bath first.'

As I let her lead me up the stairs, I glance at Filomena. She looks at me, and points to her right eye again. I press the red band on my wrist tightly between my thumb and forefinger.

Lifting the back of my hand to my nose, I sniff quietly. Yes, it's still there. Hours after my bath, where steaming hot water flowed out of the taps and a million bubbles gently soaked the dirt off my body, my skin still carries the scent of roses.

I sat, watching the pulsing water push bubbles against my raised knees, while Signora Salvadori, the sleeves of her blouse rolled up, massaged creamy soap into my hair.

'This evening, we'll talk to the Signore about your mother,' she said. 'Yes,' she went on, more to herself than to me, 'he will know what to do.'

I didn't reply. My search for Mamma, the feeling that

I had lost Pippo, my fear of Filomena, were all too much to contemplate, and so instead I concentrated on the scented suds.

'That man was no help at all — just taking your mother's money like that and asking no questions. He was only interested in whether the room was empty so he could let it again. Heartless,' she said, trying to untangle the knots in my hair.

I nodded a little, not wanting to think about the moment we had left the room. We'd waited a while. But then the woman had suggested we find the landlord and ask if he knew where my mother had gone, about the work she'd left in search of. We found him and he was not a nice man.

He told us where the woman Mamma had gone to meet lived, but when we got there the house was empty, and I remembered Mamma saying the woman was going away.

Perhaps if we'd stayed in that room just a little longer, Mamma and Pippo might have returned, I thought. Perhaps.

Sitting in the bath, I felt anxiety rise from the pit of my stomach and my head swirl with questions. Why did Pippo disappear? He had been asleep. Why hadn't he stayed and waited for me for return?

And where could our mother have gone? Of course she had gone out late at night, but people don't just disappear. I thought of my father, fearing for a moment that something similar had happened to my mother.

People would know she was different. One look at her clothes, her tinkling jewellery, even her golden eyes would tell them that. But she was convinced that people in the city would be more tolerant, more accepting of those who were different. And from what I had seen and experienced so far, this was true. Look at the Signora – taking me into her home, feeding me, bathing me, giving me clean clothes to wear.

So where was Mamma?

Confused, my mind swam. Maybe my mother had simply taken the wrong turning and become lost. Maybe she had been in an accident and was in a hospital somewhere.

And what of Pippo? Perhaps our mother had come back and found him by himself, then taken him to go and look for me? Surely she would have returned to the room and waited? Or, even worse, had my brother woken alone and gone to look for Mamma and me? Was he still on his own – wandering the streets of the city? My stomach lurched at the thought.

I held the wet wristband tight between my fingers and closed my eyes. Feeling a hand rest gently on my bare shoulder, I heard the Signora's voice.

'The Signore works for the *governo* – he'll know which officials to speak to about missing people. Perhaps your mother and brother are together. Or perhaps your brother was found by someone else. He may have been taken to an orphanage.'

At that, I turned my head to the Signora.

'Orphanage?'

'*Sì*. While they look for his family.'

I couldn't sit soaking in the warm water a moment longer. I didn't know what to do but I had to do something.

I made a move to climb out of the bath, but the

Signora, seeing my distress, laid her hand on my wet arm.

'Sit down,' she said, quietly but firmly. 'There is no point running around the streets looking for him yourself. The best thing to do is get others to do the job for you. My husband will do everything to find him.'

I looked at the woman in green, into her eyes, searching.

'Always trust your heart.' Mamma's words floated inside my head. This lady was beautifully dressed and spoke well, and I knew we came from places that were so different it was as if we didn't speak the same language. But from the first moment, my heart had felt this woman was good.

I sat back down in the bath. If I had to trust someone, it would be the Signora.

Now, sitting on a chair in a large room, wearing a stiff white blouse and brown skirt that are both a little too large, my hair plaited in long pigtails, I am waiting for the Signore to return home from work. His wife bustles about the house, rearranging long curtains that hang at the hallway windows, sorting letters on a desk beside the door, and bringing a vase of flowers to the table beside me – reminding me of the flower seller outside our new home. Was that only this morning?

I look around, taking in the soft pink walls, elegant paintings framed in gold hanging on one long wall, the opposite wall lined with bookshelves. Small tables and chairs have been placed around the room, but I have no idea what this room is for. I wonder if the rich have so many rooms to simply fill them with expensive things.

Standing, I drift towards the shelves, drawn by the

books. Many are old, their edges scuffed and faded, but scattered among them are newer ones, their covers bearing strong colours and letters. I see Mussolini's name written on the spine of many of them. I've heard of him and I've seen his picture on posters. I know he leads our country, but Mamma never spoke of him. Perhaps she thought he had no importance to our lives.

'Can you read?' interrupts a nasal voice.

I turn quickly to see a thin man with an equally thin moustache. He wears a suit and immediately I notice a green, white, gold and red pin on his lapel.

'A little,' I reply, worried he will ask me to read to him.

The man nods and runs his finger along a line of books. It stops on one and he pulls it out. A picture of Il Duce sits under the words *Italy Advances!*

He hands it to me, saying, 'This tells the story of what Il Duce is doing for you – in pictures.'

As I flick through it carefully, I see images of huge constructions, soldiers marching, and vast fields of crops.

'This,' he points at the photos, 'is how Il Duce will make Italy a nation that will be the envy of others. Did you know' – I watch the man's face light up as he speaks – 'that Il Duce has saved Europe from a war.'

I look at him blankly. I am not sure what Europe is.

'Germany and Britain were about to start fighting each other,' he explains.

I nod. These are names I think I may have heard of.

'But,' he continues, animated, 'Mussolini made them sign a deal which will stop all the countries in Europe from going to war.'

I give a small smile. I have heard unkind things said about Il Duce, but this news makes me wonder if he is a better person than others think.

'When he returned to Rome, thousands, millions maybe, lined the streets to cheer him. "Duce! Duce! Duce!" they shouted.' The Signore raises his arm above his head in salute.

He falls silent, looking at his raised hand, and I know he wishes he were there, in Rome, cheering the leader as he passes by.

'So,' he says, lowering his arm and turning back to me, 'the Signora tells me you have lost your family.'

I nod again.

'You will give me their details and I will investigate their whereabouts.'

'Details?' I ask, closing the book I'm holding.

'Their names, ages, and so on,' the man says curtly, pulling a small black book and pencil from his shirt pocket.

'My mamma's name is Maria. My brother's name is Pip—' I stop myself and correct, 'Filippo.'

The Signore writes.

'Surname?'

I look at him.

'Family name,' he says impatiently.

'Di Rocco,' I reply, after thinking for a moment.

'Ages?'

I look at him.

'My brother is seven.'

He nods. 'And your mother?'

I shrug.

'Twenties? Thirties?'

'Twenties,' I reply quietly, embarrassed that I don't know.

'And where do you live?'

'We moved to this city last night.'

'From where?'

'The country.'

The man sighs and shakes his head. 'Can you describe them?'

I close my eyes and picture Pippo. His face is animated and cheery, his eyes bright with excitement.

'My brother has dark hair and dark eyes. He is always talking — like a little chatty bird.'

And now I think of Mamma.

'My mother is very beautiful. She has long, dark hair like mine, but she wears a scarf to cover it. She was wearing a black dress and necklaces.'

'Necklaces?'

'When we moved away from our family, they gave her jewellery. She wears it all, gold necklaces mainly.'

I open my eyes and see that the Signora is standing beside her husband, whispering into his ear.

He frowns and closes his book, quickly placing it back into his pocket with the pencil. Without looking at me, he turns and, grasping the lady in green by the elbow, leads her out of the room.

I hear the duet of their murmured conversation — the Signore abrupt and annoyed, the Signora reasoned and calming, until it reaches its crescendo and the man's voice shouts, 'No!'

Then there is silence.

I strain to hear the lady in green, but instead I hear Signor Salvadori again. His voice is gentle now, apologetic.

I hear the Signora's muffled sob and, as their discussion resumes, I reach to put the book in my hands back on the shelf it came from.

Shoes click across the wooden floor. I turn my head to the right to see the man looking at me, a wary expression on his face.

'On my wife's insistence, you will stay with us while we try to find your family. In return, you must enrol in both the school and GIL.'

I hold my breath. A fist grips my stomach and tightens as a wave of fear washes over me. My mother is missing and I have lost my brother. I am living with people I do not know, and it seems the Signore does not like me. And now this. I breathe out a shaky sigh.

'Sì, Signore,' I say, as he turns on his heel and leaves the room.

I have never been to school and have no idea what GIL is.

PIPPO

1938

Mario's Song

Pippo adored Mario from the first moment he saw him. Flinging open the door of the house and stepping into the room, the swarthy young man called, 'I love my wife more than life itself!'

Donna, kneading dough on the table, turned to him laughing and, placing floury hands on his bearded face, cried in response, 'I will love my husband until the end of all days!'

The little boy watched them kiss passionately, and then, while they still embraced, whisper sweet words into each other's ears. Sitting on the wooden chair, he swung his legs excitedly, waiting to meet the man who had just entered his life.

'Mario,' said his wife, 'may I present to you, Pippo.'

'Welcome, Pippo,' said the man, striding towards him and shaking his hand enthusiastically. 'Are you here for a visit? Are you family?'

'I have lost my mamma and my Clara,' said the boy, trying to sound sad, but in fact thrilled that he was now an acquaintance of the wonderful Mario.

'We looked for them today,' said Donna to her frowning husband. 'We went to where they were living and asked some of the neighbours, but they only arrived here yesterday and no one knows them.'

'We asked lots of people — the grumpy man downstairs, the flower lady, the men fixing shoes — and none of them had seen my mamma or Clara. I told them what they look like, because Signora Donna doesn't know them,' Pippo said, shaking his head. 'She doesn't know that my mamma is tall and thin like a cypress tree, and more beautiful than any lady I have ever met.

'And my sister,' he took a breath before continuing, 'she is like me. But she has gold eyes — like Mamma.'

'Gold eyes?' repeats the man, a touch bemused.

'Yes. And she doesn't talk as much as me. Mamma calls me a chatty bird because—'

'I think I know why,' interrupted Mario, laughing.

The boy laughed loudly too, releasing a bit of the excitement welled up inside him.

'Pippo.' Mario bowed and, with a flourish, waved an arm around the room, '*Mi casa es tu casa*, as they say in *España*.'

'What does that mean? And what's *España*?'

'It means my home is your home — we have little, but we want you to be comfortable as long as you stay here.'

Mario pulled the cork from a bottle of wine and poured a glass as he sat down at the table, facing Pippo. 'And *España* is another country not far from here. I fought the Fascists there.'

'Mario,' hissed his wife in warning.

'What?' questioned the man with an upturned hand. 'He's a child.'

'You know nothing of his family,' Donna whispered.

Mario turned to face the little boy. 'Pippo,' he said seriously, 'are you a dirty, good-for-nothing Fascist?'

'No,' said Pippo, shaking his head violently to confirm his words.

Pippo didn't know what a Fascist really was, except they were a different kind of people – he supposed like the difference between a horse and a mule. But Mario clearly didn't like the Fascists, so he didn't either.

'There. That's good enough for me,' said Mario to Donna, who turned away in exasperation.

'Why did you go to another country when there are Fascists here?' Pippo asked.

'Ha! Good question, little one. The Fascists are more serious there – more dangerous. At least they were then. I wanted to stop Fascism growing, make them less powerful.'

'And did you?'

Mario took a drink and carefully placed the glass back on the wooden table. 'The war is still going on.'

'But you came home?'

'With difficulty, yes. War taught me a great deal, but most importantly,' he said, reaching out to Donna and taking her hand, 'I learned that I had to be with this beautiful woman.'

'Are you going to go to war with the Fascists here? Are you going to war with Il Duce?' asked the boy, frowning.

'Well . . .' Mario kissed his wife's hand, letting go to sip his wine.

'No, he is not,' said Donna, pounding her fist into the dough.

'It depends what he does next,' Mario spoke to Pippo but smiled at his wife.

'You have already done enough for the party,' said Donna, as the bread took another thumping.

'The party?' asked the boy, his heart jumping at the thought of a *festa*.

'A political party,' said Mario. 'It's a group of people. They meet and they talk, discuss issues, debate . . .'

'Just talking? No music? No dancing?'

'No dancing, no,' chuckled the man. 'But music — yes. Our political party has a song that we all sing at the beginning.'

Mario pushed back his chair, rose to his feet, and began singing with a deep voice: '*Avanti popolo, alla riscossa, Bandiera Rossa, Bandiera Rossa!*'

Donna joined in, holding her dough-covered fist over her heart.

'Forward people, towards redemption, Red Flag, Red Flag!'

As they continued, Pippo joined in, shouting, 'Red Flag! Red Flag!'

When they reached the end of the song — 'Long live Communism and freedom' — they all cheered, waking little Gino, who had been sleeping soundly in an old wooden cot.

'Why is the song about a flag?' asked the boy, as Donna picked the baby up and rocked him. 'And why is it red? The Italian flag is red *and* green *and* white.'

'Ah,' said Mario, sitting down, 'that's because it's the flag of the Communist Party of Italy. And it's red — just like all the other Communist Party flags in countries around the world.'

'Red like this.' Pippo held out the silk band tied around his wrist to Mario. 'But what is it? Why does it have a party? And why will it give us freedom?'

Mario took a deep breath. 'We Communists believe that we should share everything—'

'Mamma says I must always share with Clara,' interrupted Pippo.

'And she's right. But we must also share the work and share the food. So, we all look after the cow, then we all share the milk. Same with the crops in the fields, the things made in factories — everything. *Capisci?*'

'Of course! It's easy. If I work, I eat.'

'*Molto bene!*' cheered Mario, making Pippo grin. 'When we are all equal there will be freedom from hunger for you and your family.'

'I want to come to your party! I want to be a Comm . . . a Comm . . .'

'A Communist,' finished Mario, as Donna tutted and shook her head.

'*Sì*,' nodded Pippo.

'You cannot.'

'What? Why not? You are. Why can't I be? I can sing the song. I know all about it and the Red Flag.'

'Because Mussolini has banned it. The Communist Party of Italy does not exist.'

'But . . . but . . .' stammered the boy, confused.

'I'll tell you something not many people know, Pippo,' said Mario, leaning towards him to whisper in his ear.

The boy leaned in to him, waiting to hear his now beloved friend speak.

'We meet in secret.'

Pippo clutched both hands to his mouth and grinned. 'In secret?'

Mario nodded seriously. 'This is important, Pippo. If you are to stay with us, you must never speak of it. Never say the word "Communism". Never sing our song. Never mention the Red Flag. Do you understand?'

'Il Duce would be mad?'

'We don't call him Il Duce — he's not our leader. But yes, Mussolini, and all the people who like him would be mad.'

'Lots of people like him. There are pictures of him everywhere.'

'That's right. And sometimes you don't know if people like him or not. So, better to say nothing that might make them mad.'

'What would happen if I said something?'

Mario breathed out heavily and leaned back.

'We would go to prison,' said Donna seriously.

Pippo's eyes grew large and his mouth opened. 'Prison?'

Mario nodded. 'I have been to prison before, Pippo. It is not a nice place. They do terrible things to you.'

'Like what?' murmured the boy.

The man stared at him for a moment, then glanced at Donna, who nodded. Slowly, Mario lifted his dirty grey shirt. There on his chest lay a long, raised pink scar.

'They used an iron bar. It had been sitting in the

fire. It was so hot it was white. And they put it here, on my chest.'

Pippo stared at the scar wide-eyed, twisting the red band round and round his wrist.

'Why did they do that?' he asked, whisper quiet.

'Because they wanted to know who my friends were. The other Communists. So they could put them in prison too.'

'Did you tell them?'

'No,' said Mario, pulling down his shirt and tucking it in. 'But that's why you must never say a word of any of this to anyone. Understand?'

Pippo nodded. He understood.

The little boy scuttled through the dark streets, the fresh night air cool on his face. Further ahead, just in sight, was Mario. Pippo had been following him since he had heard the man rise quietly from bed, whisper a few words to his sleepy wife, dress and leave the house.

Pippo had guessed Mario was going to a meeting of his party and he wanted to go too. But from everything the couple had told him, he knew he would not be allowed. So he decided to go by himself, and become the secret viewer of a secret meeting.

The streets were quiet with few people about, so he hid in doorways, watching Mario striding confidently ahead of him, sucking on a cigarette.

Up ahead, his new friend made a sharp turn down a dark alley, so Pippo dragged deeply on an imaginary cigarette before dashing along the pavement. When he reached the corner of the street, he leaned his back against the wall, and peered around the edge into the gloom. He saw Mario silhouetted by a shaft of yellow light before disappearing into an open doorway. The door was then shut and the brightness extinguished.

Creeping down the alley, he stepped around the debris from the day's food stalls and businesses to the doorway. Placing his ear on the thick wood, he strained to hear Mario's voice, but the only sound was a low murmuring of men talking.

A weak light shone from a dirty window above his head, so Pippo pulled a wooden crate against the wall and climbed onto it. From there, standing on tiptoes, he could just see over the window frame and into a small room where a wide man guarded another door.

'Mario is in there,' Pippo hissed to himself, 'I know it. But how . . .'

Just then, a rat scuttled over his ankle, chattering as it went.

'*Aiiiyeee!*' screamed the boy in reply, jumping up to avoid the rat running over his other foot. As he landed, his heel caught the edge of the crate and, with a clatter, he and the wooden box fell.

Scrabbling to his feet, he was about to run when the door was flung open and the wide man stepped out.

'What are you doing?' he boomed at the startled child.

Pippo blinked for a moment before replying, 'I was looking for my papa. My mamma needs him.' He was surprised at how easily the lie came to him.

'Who is your papa?'

The man was both tall and fat, and the light from inside the room caught a strange mark on his cheek. Pippo stared for a moment and saw it was a birthmark.

A purple colour – the boy thought how like the moon it looked, and how odd it would be to have a small crescent on your face all day.

Distracted, Pippo paused and thought about his reply.

'I can't say,' he said, remembering Mario's refusal to talk of the other members of his party.

'What do you mean you can't say?' blustered the large man, a thin line of sweat on his top lip glistening.

'How do I know that it is safe to tell you?' asked the boy.

The man stared at Pippo, then snorted. 'Ha!' he laughed, leaning over and clapping the boy on the shoulder, steering him through the door. 'Well done, *bambino*. Your papa will be proud of you.'

Pippo grinned, pleased with himself, as he looked around the small room with just a table and two chairs in it. But when the fat man stepped over to the second door and, grabbing the boy's shirt, pulled him through it, his smile quickly dropped.

'Somebody is looking for their papa,' he heard, as more than twenty faces turned to look at him.

The boy looked around for the only familiar face he knew in the small, stuffy, windowless room.

'What are you doing here?' said Mario, stepping forward.

'I . . . I . . .' stammered Pippo, unsure how to go on.

Mario stood over him, his hands on his hips, his face dark.

'*Avanti* . . .' the little boy whispered.

'What?' Mario demanded, leaning forward.

'*Avanti popolo*,' Pippo sang quietly.

A twitch at the corner of Mario's mouth gave Pippo the courage to carry on a bit louder. '*Alla riscossa!*'

'*Bandiera Rossa,*' sang a baritone from behind Mario, who turned his head to make out the singer.

'*Bandiera Rossa!*' continued the boy, as more voices from around the room joined in.

Mario turned back to look at Pippo as the chorus of singers swelled, and soon the anthem was reverberating around the stone room. Pippo sang with all his heart, grinning at Mario, who grudgingly began to sing too.

As the song finished with a rousing cheer, the man gently pulled the boy beside him and the two listened as a curly haired man began to speak. Pippo didn't understand what he was saying, but he watched the men and women ask questions and talk, at times heatedly, shaking their fists.

Eventually, the wide man standing guard opened the door to the smaller room, the one with the table and two chairs, marking the end of the meeting. People began to file out, some stopping for a glass of wine, before the doorman opened the main door, letting cool, fresh air enter the warm room and a few party members slip out into the alley.

Mario bent over to talk quietly to him.

'Pippo, you shouldn't have come,' he said. 'I thought you understood – this is dangerous.'

'But I want to be a Communist,' said Pippo loudly.

'Aha! A new recruit,' said the curly haired man, approaching with his hand outstretched. 'Welcome, Comrade.'

Pippo took his hand and shook it firmly.

'I'm sorry, Bruno,' Mario began, but the man raised his hand to stop him and turned to the boy.

'How did you find this place?' he asked.

Pippo tugged at his lip with his teeth before confessing quietly, 'I followed Mario.'

'And did anyone follow you?'

'I don't think so.'

'And what would you have said if someone had asked what you were doing out, late at night?'

'I would have said I was looking for my papa,' said Pippo quickly. 'I would have said my papa was a drunk, that he was out drinking somewhere and if I didn't find him, my mamma would throw him out of the house.'

Mario raised an eyebrow as the boy continued, 'Mamma always says she will throw him out, and I always find him and bring him home and he begs for forgiveness.' Pippo clasped his hands together in a display of pleading. 'And there is screaming and fighting, and Mamma throws a plate or a cup at him, and then there is kissing.' The boy flung his arms around his body and cuddled himself to demonstrate. 'And Mamma never throws him out.'

The two men chuckled as Pippo finished, 'I would say I do not have time to talk because I need to find my papa.'

'What is your name, little man?' said Bruno.

'Pippo, Signore.'

'Call me Comrade, Pippo – we are all equal here.'

'Comrade,' said the boy with a delighted nod. 'Does that mean that I'm a Communist now?'

'Not quite,' said the man thoughtfully.

'What do I have to do to be a Communist? I know

the song – I can sing it again . . .' Pippo took a large breath to launch into '*Bandiera Rossa*'.

'That's not necessary,' said Bruno, raising his left hand. 'But there is perhaps a job you could do for us.'

Pippo began to jig excitedly. He did not see Mario turn to Bruno with a frown.

CLARA

1938

Saluting the Fallen

Glass doors tower above me as I look up at the lofty white building. I am surrounded by girls dressed exactly the same as me: white smocks with navy collars and a blue beret on my head. We all stand silently.

The boys are gathered in a crowd behind us, their teachers casting an eye over them, watching out for the boisterous ones. Pippo would find it impossible to stand as properly and quietly as they do; his body would compel him to flitter and chirrup excitedly.

I notice the ache inside whenever I think of my brother or Mamma. It is always there, but during the ten days since I lost them, the only time I have the opportunity to miss them is when I am in bed, at the end of another busy day.

Signora Salvadori had quickly taken me to enrol at the school. A stern woman gave me tests to do – reading, writing and numbers. I found it very difficult, but the Signora was kind and told me the results didn't matter – they would just show which class I should be put into.

The teacher was not so generous as she said I would

have to go into a class for younger children. But she admitted my skills were not as bad as expected, given my lack of education.

'My mother taught us,' I ventured, but the stern woman ignored me and spoke to the Signora directly.

'She will need the full uniform as well as gym clothes – Il Duce believes strongly in the benefit of physical exercise.'

'Yes, of course,' the Signora nodded.

'Here is a list of books,' she said, handing over a list. 'She can start as soon as you have all these items. Just telephone my assistant to let me know which day she will be coming, and we will allocate a desk and a peg for her hat and coat.'

And so we visited the school uniform shop, where we bought all the items of clothing I would need. Then the Signora led me to a leather store, where she chose a satchel. It was dark brown with a single strap and made of soft leather. She hung it over my shoulder, and I carefully opened it and lifted it towards my face. Breathing in the warm leathery scent reminded me of running my hand down a horse's neck, feeling its warmth and the tickle of its tangled mane on my skin.

I am unsure if it is a true memory or my mother's retelling of it so often it has become my own, but I think I remember the first time my father set me on the back of a horse. I wriggled my fingers through its long mane and squeezed its body with plump legs, giggling in delight. I can still hear my father's laugh at my happiness.

'Do you like it?' The saleswoman broke through the memory.

Yes, I nodded. I liked it.

'Then we'd better fill it with books,' the Signora smiled. 'And pencils, and a ruler . . .'

After a morning of shopping, spending more money than I had ever seen, she insisted that we pause for a coffee. We visited a small cafe filled with steam and people where, bustling to the front, she ordered a coffee for herself and an orzo for me.

When the drinks were delivered to the counter in front of us, the Signora moved mine towards me. I looked at it.

'Have you had this before?' she asked.

I nodded. Of course I'd had the barley drink, we all had. Mamma rarely bought real coffee — it was too expensive. But I'd never been in a cafe, standing by a counter to drink it.

'I'm sure,' she commented, taking a drink from her tiny cup, leaving red lipstick imprinted on its rim. 'All the children drink it.'

I picked up the cup and took a sip. The Signora finished her coffee and opened her bag, pulling out a mirror and checking her lipstick, while I carried on sipping.

Other people nudged and bumped us, a constant stream of customers arriving to order, drink their measure of coffee and leave. Some lingered a few minutes longer to eat a pastry and chat to their companions, but most simply took two or three gulps to finish their drinks before heading out of the door. I watched, mesmerized. Workmen in overalls, elegant women in hats, men in suits — they all entered the tiny bar and left again within minutes.

'Are you going to finish that?'

I looked at the Signora, realizing that I was not following the order of things. Nodding, I swallowed down the hot drink, sad that I hadn't been able to savour both my drink and the experience for longer. I'd barely placed my cup back on its saucer when we were out of the door, shopping again.

After that, the Signora worked with me on my books to prepare me for starting school, helping with words I did not know, reading some of the history books to me, and showing me on a map where Italy and other countries are in the world.

The Signore took me to the police station, where everyone stood and saluted when we entered. We went into a small room with an officer, who sombrely asked about Mamma and Pippo. I answered the questions I could while the Signore added details about where exactly the Signora had met me, and the place where I had last seen my family.

'And can you describe her, please.'

'She has . . .' I paused. 'Dark hair.'

'Lots of people have dark hair,' the Signore dismissed.

'No. It's very dark. Some say it is pure black. And her skin is a different colour to mine. It's more brown . . .' I remembered what Mamma called the tone. 'Like cinnamon.'

'Mmm,' the policeman said, frowning and writing in his small book.

'But her eyes are like mine.'

The officer paused and, for the first time, looked directly at me.

'Ah,' he said, a little lost for words. 'And what colour would you call that?'

I shrugged.

'Signore?' the policeman asked, peering at me.

The Signore leaned towards me, staring closely into my eyes.

'Light brown?' he ventured. 'Amber, maybe?'

'Gold,' the officer said quietly.

Of course, many people have said Mamma and I have golden eyes. Mamma thought mine were less noticeable, because my skin was fairer. But hers shone out from her face like shimmering stars.

'Any other distinguishing features?' he asked.

I looked at the Signore, confused.

'Is there anything about your mother that is different from most people,' he explained.

I thought of all the times Mamma and Pippo and I had been called different. All the times we had been called names and spurned. The times we had moved, from one village to the next, looking for a place to call home. To be accepted.

'Her necklaces,' I replied. 'She wears lots of gold necklaces.'

Both men looked at me.

'My family gave them to her,' I whispered, 'when we left . . .' My voice disappeared to nothing.

The policeman glanced at the Signore, who simply nodded. The officer made notes in his small black book with surprisingly elegant writing, and eventually he snapped it shut to let us know the meeting was over. I followed the Signore out of the door and stood beside him while he graciously thanked the senior officers. As we left, I glanced over my shoulder and saw the policeman who had interviewed me drop his notebook onto a nearby table and walk away.

At the house, I ate my meals in the kitchen, Filomena serving me begrudgingly at first, but as I devoured every plate of food she prepared, she softened a little. I quietly asked her how she prepared her focaccia — oily, salty and spongy, it was the best I had ever tasted. And the trick to her minestrone, she told me, was lard — and lots of it. I listened and learned, eager to tell Mamma about the recipes I had gained from a wonderful cook.

But every night, when I went to bed in a small room at the top of the house, I curled into a ball under the stiff white sheets and cried. I cried for the arms of my mother, her soft voice singing and telling tales. I sobbed when I thought of Pippo, missing his twittering talking. Terrible guilt tugged at my insides — I had promised to look after my brother and I had failed. I missed my family, and bubble-filled baths and mouth-watering food could not replace them.

Now, as I wait for the school doors to open, I see the large poster of Il Duce that hangs on the wall and read the familiar motto: *Better to live one day as a lion than a hundred years as a sheep.* I think again of how a lion must live — chasing and killing other creatures to eat, roaring loudly, being confident that all other animals fear it. I wonder how our lives would be if everyone behaved like that. The streets would be full of people shouting and arguing and demanding to be treated with respect.

No, I conclude, as I have every day I have stood here, it is better to be the sheep. Live quietly among those like you, take what grows naturally all about and, most importantly, avoid the lions.

A shrill bell rings and the doors swing open. I let myself be swept through the entrance and up the first flight of stairs along with dozens of other girls. Although sitting in a room for hours on end is alien to me, after four days at school, I'm starting to understand the routine. The roof over my head, the food in my stomach, depends on doing what is expected of me. The swarm thins as we reach the second flight, and at the top I peel off, along with girls whose faces I recognize. We walk quickly down the corridor, pausing briefly to hang our hats on named hooks.

Passing through our classroom door, we greet our teacher, '*Buongiorno, Signorina*,' before taking our seats. Mine is at the back, in the corner, furthest from the window. I feel safe here.

The room fills quickly, and when our teacher stands at the front and says, 'Girls . . .' we all know what to do. In unison, we stand and raise our arms, pointing our fingers forward. A salute seems to me a strange greeting, but it is expected in a Fascist school.

The Signorina then nods to one of the girls seated in the front row. She stands and turns to us. Following her lead, we cross ourselves and say a short prayer – our first duty is to the Almighty.

Then, in one movement, we swivel on our heels to face the image of a young man. His black-and-white photograph hangs on the wall between two windows, surrounded by silk flowers. A small plaque beneath it has words etched onto it: *Caporale Arturo Bianchi 1898–1917*.

After a moment's pause, we raise our right arms in salute, dedicating ourselves to those who have fallen for our beloved country. Looking at the young man's face, I am sad. Yesterday, I wrote the dates of his birth and death in my book and, using subtraction as Signora Salvadori has shown me, calculated that Arturo was nineteen when he died. I wonder if he went to school, if he had the chance to marry, have children, a job.

I wonder how I would feel if Pippo were sent to war. Would I feel proud that my brother was fighting for my leader, my country, my God? If he were killed, would I call him a hero? Would I expect children in classrooms across Italy to honour him?

No, I decide. If the army were like school, they would not like his chattering. They would want him to stop talking and listen. He would hate it, and I would like Pippo to do what he wanted to do. Perhaps he will grow up to be a storyteller, surrounded by children and adults hanging on his every word. Perhaps he could become one of the voices I hear on the radio, when the Signora invites me to sit with her and listen to a show.

Whatever he decides, I want him to live a long and happy life. To have a wife and children of his own. To die an old man. Not a young man, far from home and all who love him.

The thought of him makes me sob, and I realize suddenly that the other girls are all sitting looking at me. Embarrassed, I drop quickly into my seat, my head lowered.

'Clara,' says the Signorina, and I look up, past rows of girls' faces staring at me.

'*Sì, Signorina*,' I say, standing.

'I am sure Il Duce would appreciate your dedication to our fallen heroes.'

I lower my head, ashamed that my teacher thinks I am upset about the man in the photo.

'Now, everyone, open your books at page seventy-five.'

I gratefully pull my textbook from my satchel, relieved that the moment is over. As the Signorina begins to talk about a place called Ethiopia, I peer up to see if the other girls have forgotten me. They all sit silently, looking at either their book or our teacher. All except Emilia, who stares at me, her mouth stern and her brown eyes hard.

The music begins and I reach both arms up to the sky. I have worked hard to learn the routine in the three weeks since I began school, and now I must match perfectly the girls on either side of me, in front and behind.

I swing my right arm around in a full circle, then hold it up high while I swing my left arm. Then, placing both hands on my waist, I pull my feet together and bend my knees, lowering myself as deep as I can without losing my balance.

The band of the National Fascist Party's youth section plays loudly. Boys blow their trumpets and bang their drums to the anthem, and we do our physical exercises to the music. Stretching my arms forward, I take a moment to inspect my gloves. They are still white, as are the long sleeves of my shirt. I know there is a mark on one of my long white stockings, but I will try to keep it out of the sight of the head teachers when they come and inspect us at the end of our display. I do not like this uniform, especially the black, silk knitted cap that covers my hair and clings tightly to my head. But I am proud to be part of a group, creating an impressive show in the name of Il Duce.

Glancing around, I see a small crowd has stopped to watch. They stand, leaning against railings at the edge of a raised road, while we stretch and bend in the expansive gardens beneath them. I imagine if I had been passing, I too might stop and watch nearly a hundred girls aged between eight and fourteen perform their exercises to the music.

Suddenly, just as I jump, arms and legs outstretched, I feel a tingle through my body. Landing a little clumsily, I notice that the tiny hairs all over my body seem to be standing alert. I miss the beat of the next movement and, as I try to catch up, I see Emilia, a few girls away, turn and sneer angrily at me.

I force myself to concentrate on the next move and am just beginning to regain my rhythm when I hear him. Far away, from the crowd standing on the roadside watching, I hear laughter — the high, silly giggle of an overexcited little boy.

It is Pippo, I know it.

And I know I must be with him. Turning towards the cluster of spectators, I run along the line of girls. They continue their movements and I have to duck to avoid arms that thrust out at me. I turn right down another line to where I know the steps up to the pavement are, and I begin to shout, 'Pippo! PIPPO!'

Just then, a series of legs are stuck out and I trip over a shiny black shoe. As I stumble, I knock into another girl, who loses her balance and grabs at the girl beside her, trying not to fall.

I manage to regain my footing and begin running

again, staggering a bit and bumping into another two members of the group. They in turn wobble, while the girls ahead of me stop their routine and back away, letting me lurch forwards, still calling my brother's name.

Finally, I reach the wall and take the steps two at a time. When I get to the top, I look around at the crowd, who look back at me, puzzled. Frantically, I push past the men and women at the front, searching for a little boy with big brown eyes and an irrepressible smile. I have stopped shouting and am, instead, listening for a chatty bird, perhaps even that wonderful giggle.

But I cannot hear him. And I cannot see him. The group of people dissipate, some beginning to drift away; it is obvious that Pippo is not here. I sink to my knees without a care for my white stockings.

Filomena carefully lays long sheets of pasta along the table. She is preparing the Signore's favourite, lasagne, and prides herself on its numerous layers which give the final dish its impressive height and structure.

I watch, occasionally sipping my glass of water, a dish of half-eaten soup beside me. It was delicious; shreds of chicken and quickly chopped vegetables swirling around large dumplings that slowly soaked in the herby broth's flavours. But I am unable to finish even Filomena's food.

The cook slides her knife through the thinly rolled dough, making four evenly sized rectangles of pale pasta. She picks them up and drops them into a saucepan of gently boiling water. They cook for just a few seconds before she lifts them out with a spoon, immediately lowering them into cold water. She then removes them and lays them on a towel, before returning to the table to cut more sheets.

As she repeats the process, she looks up at me and frowns.

'What's wrong?' she asks.

'Nothing,' I reply.

'You're even quieter than usual. Has something happened?'

I shake my head.

Filomena puts the black-handled knife down on the table and steps towards me. She says nothing. She simply stands, her face without expression, waiting.

I look down at the bowl of food and say nothing, the silence becoming uncomfortable.

She does not move a muscle, but I feel her looking at me and it makes me squirm in my seat.

Glancing up, I clear my throat and say quietly, 'I think I heard my brother.'

'What?' She leans towards me to hear better.

'Yesterday. I was doing exercises with the GIL—'

'GIL? That Fascism for Children group?' she asks with a sneer.

'It's a movement,' I correct, repeating what I have been told. 'The Gioventù Italiana del Littorio.'

'Pah,' she said. 'ONB, Piccola Italiana . . . it's all the same thing. They're teaching you to be Fascists and preparing you for the army.'

I look up at her, shocked.

'Not you. You're a girl. You won't go into the army. No, they want you to have babies for the party. More little Fascists for the future.' She scoffs again.

'You don't like the Fascists?' I whisper, surprised.

'I did not say that.' She shakes her finger at me. 'Did you hear me say that? No! Not in this house. But I listen. I listen to people who know more than me about these things. And I remember. Remember how things were before Mussolini. Remember a time when we left people in Africa to look after themselves.' Her voice tails off and she shakes her head, clearly annoyed at Il Duce.

I have only just learned that my country has invaded Ethiopia — a place I discovered was in Africa. And that Germany has just become our new neighbour because of something called Anschluss. My world had always revolved around my mamma and my brother. Now I am discovering it is a much larger and more complicated place.

'Your brother,' Filomena prompts me. 'What is his name again?'

'Filippo. But we call him Pippo.'

'Yes. Go on.'

'I thought I heard him while we were doing our performance. I ran to find him, but he wasn't there.' I hang my head again.

'Maybe he was, maybe he wasn't,' she shrugs.

'I wish he had been,' I murmur.

'Of course,' she nods. 'The Signore has had no success finding your mamma either?'

I shake my head.

She sighs.

Pulling up a chair, she sits down and looks into my face. I turn to her and see a kinder, softer person.

'It is sad, yes. We all need our family. And whatever

type of family you have, it is better that you are with them. But while you are not, do not forget how lucky you are to be here. The Signora cares for you a great deal. Perhaps more than she should,' she adds gently.

I give her a quizzical look.

'I will tell you something – something you must never repeat.'

I nod my head.

'Good. I have worked for them since they were first married, and the Signora has always wanted children. But God has not been kind to them. She lost baby after baby. Not one has had the chance to grow properly in her womb. The doctors cannot help and there is nothing she can do.'

This news makes me feel unbearably sad for the woman who has taken me in and shown me such kindness. I realize at that moment why she has been so compassionate.

'Yes,' nods Filomena, seeing the thought cross my face. 'For now, you are the daughter she never had.'

'But I have a mother,' I whisper.

'She knows,' replies the cook. 'But let her enjoy it – enjoy you – for this short time.'

I take a deep breath, absorbing this news. I wish, once again, that Pippo had been with me when she found me. She could have taken us both in and Pippo would have been safe and warm, and she could have a complete, if temporary, family.

'Now,' says Filomena, 'I have not told you this – you know nothing of the Signora's life.'

I shake my head.

Thinking about the Signora, I take a deep breath and

start rolling the sleeves of my tunic up. I will help make the pasta.

Filomena is standing up when she looks at my arms and says suddenly, 'Che . . .'

I glance at my arms too, seeing the red marks that cover them. Quickly pulling both sleeves down, I get up from my chair, ready to leave the kitchen.

'Sit,' says the cook firmly.

I sit.

'Tell me.'

I wonder how to explain it. I don't want anyone to think I am trouble. While I am in this house, I am safe.

'I ruined the routine,' I begin.

'Routine?'

'Our exercise display. When I heard . . .' I pause. 'Thought I heard Pippo. I left my place. I ran to find him and knocked into some other girls.'

'Mmmm?'

'When I returned to my place, I was told I had ruined the whole performance. Everyone had to stay late to practise again. Because of me.'

'And the other girls were angry? They punished you?' she guesses, shaking her head.

I nod slowly, remembering the ugly look on Emilia's face. I tried to apologize, to explain, but she and the other girls turned their backs on me. It was only later, when we had collected our things and were returning to our homes, that I realized they were following me.

I turned to see Emilia and six of her friends just a short distance behind me on the quiet road. I looked around, wondering if I could escape them, and had seen an alley up ahead on the right. Hoping that speed would be on my side, I broke into a sprint, dashing down the side street.

I heard them shout and give chase, and looked ahead to the end of the alley. There I could see a road, busy with people that maybe I could disappear amongst. At least I didn't think they'd try to harm me in the view of other people.

But while looking to the end of the alley, I hadn't seen the wooden crate. My foot caught its edge and, with a thud, I fell to the dirty ground. The girls were on me in no time, pinching my skin with sharp fingers. They nipped and squeezed me all over, and I could do nothing but squirm under the weight of them all. I knew better than to call out.

'*Zingara*,' Emilia had hissed. 'Dirty thief,' sneered another.

Just when I thought they would never finish, a door beside us opened and a large man looked out.

'What are you doing?' he boomed, and the girls ran away, giggling.

'Are you all right?' the man asked, helping me get to my feet. Looking up at him, I noticed he had a purple birthmark on his face in the shape of a moon. Distracted from the pain, I wondered if his mother had been a woman of the night, or had he been born under the light of a magical blue moon? It must be a symbol of an important event or person in his life – Mamma would have known.

I nodded, pulling my skirt straight and picking up my hat. But I was not all right. I had experienced it before. The hate. Not just anger about the routine, but a desire to bully, to torment, to intimidate someone who was different. I thought fleetingly of my father. I was frightened. My legs shook a little.

I turned my head to the right, looked at the wide man and, from somewhere, found a smile.

The man with the moon on his face nodded as if I'd asked him a question, and his stare softened. 'Take care,' he said gently, and I fought back the tears that his kindness brought to my eyes.

PIPPO

1938

A Letter for Ernesto

Pippo had always loved running. So, when Bruno asked if he would do some running for him, he was delighted. Mario didn't seem so happy about it, but when the boy asked if he could, he reluctantly agreed.

'You will have to learn your way around the city, as well as some important places,' said Mario the next morning. 'I'll show you after breakfast.'

Pippo didn't notice that he kept his voice low, and excitedly asked, 'Where shall we go running first?'

'Running?' asked Donna. 'What running is this?'

'Nothing,' said Mario, shaking his head. 'I'm going to try to tire this little puppy – maybe we'll go to the gardens to burn off some energy.'

Pippo wondered what Mario was talking about, then realized that he was hiding the truth from his wife. The boy frowned, wondering why it had to be a secret, even from her. He would ask Mario later.

'The gardens?' pondered Donna. 'Maybe we should all go. I would like to get my hands out of dirty water, and my mind thinking about something other than cleaning and cooking.'

'*Fantastico!*' agreed Mario. 'We'll all go. Gino will love it.' As he turned to pick up the baby, he gave Pippo a wink. The little boy nodded quickly to show he understood. *A secret!* he thought. *Mario and I have a very important secret.*

They strolled through the city, past busy shops and bustling streets. Walking down one quiet road, they stopped for an elderly woman who shuffled past them and into a squat brick church. The boy watched the old lady, bent almost double by her twisted bones, disappear into the gloomy entrance.

'Do you go to church?' Pippo asked as they walked, skipping along between Mario and Donna, who carried Gino on her hip. 'I've been,' continued the little boy, without waiting for an answer. 'We don't go every week, but I've been. Mamma washed behind our ears and took us. Clara said she liked the smell. She said . . .'

Pippo trailed off.

'What is it?' asked Mario, looking at the boy's face.

'I wish she was with me. Clara. My sister. I wish she were here with me now. And Mamma. My mamma. I wish . . . I wish . . .'

Mario and Donna both stopped walking. Donna quickly passed Gino to her husband, kneeled down and pulled Pippo into an enveloping hug.

The child scrunched his eyes shut, fighting back the tears. But the hurt and missing feelings that bubbled inside him were too strong, and he buried his face into the warmth of the woman's neck and sobbed. She shushed and rocked him until the crying abated, then gently prised him away and looked into his pink-rimmed eyes.

'We are searching for them, *passerotto*, little sparrow,' she said softly. 'Aren't we, Mario?'

Pippo looked up at Mario, noticing that Gino's expression of concern echoed his father's. For a moment, he wished that Mario were *his* father. He didn't remember his papa, but his mamma had said he was a kind and honest man. She'd said she was sad that they hadn't had the chance to know each other, and Pippo sometimes wondered if his papa had liked to talk as much as he did.

'Of course, Pippo,' Mario nodded. 'We are asking everyone we know if they have seen your mother and your sister. Your description has been helpful, and we've checked with our neighbours and friends . . .'

'But not the police?' asked Pippo.

'No,' Donna shook her head. 'The police only work for the Fascists now, not for people like us.'

The boy looked up at Mario again, who nodded sadly.

'And if we go to the police,' continued Donna, 'we are worried that they might take you away from us, perhaps make you live in an orphanage.'

Pippo's eyebrows knitted.

'What is an orphanage?'

'It's where they take children who have no parents. They are not nice places . . .' Donna stopped herself from saying more.

'I have a mamma, and a sister. I have a family.'

'But they're not here, Pippo. The authorities will say that Mario and I are not your mamma and papa. They'll say we're not the ones who should be looking after you. We don't want them to take you away, *bambino*. We want to take care of you until we can find your mamma and Clara.'

'I don't want to go away,' cried Pippo, panic in his voice.

'No one is taking you anywhere,' said Mario, his tone calming.

'Breathe, little one,' said Donna gently, rubbing her hand in a circle on his back.

Pippo took a big breath, gulping in air.

'We want you to stay with us,' she said, wiping the tears from his cheeks. 'While you're with us, you are part of our family. Gino is your little brother' — Pippo glanced up at the baby, who grinned a one-toothed smile at him — 'and we will continue to look for your mamma and sister.'

The small boy sniffed and wiped his nose with his sleeve.

'If that's what you want . . .' Donna added.

'Yes,' nodded Pippo quickly.

'I know what you need,' said Mario seriously.

The boy looked up at him.

'*Gelato!*' beamed the man.

'Yes, *gelato!*' said Donna, holding Pippo's hand as they continued walking down the road.

'*Gelato!*' repeated Pippo. He had only tasted it a few times, but he knew he liked it.

'What flavour shall we have?' Mario said.

'*Limone,*' said his wife, smiling at him.

'Ah, *sì* — as refreshing as a beautiful woman,' he grinned. 'But perhaps a little sharp for the boys. Pistachio?'

'Too green for Gino,' laughed his wife.

'Too green for you?' the baby's father asked him, looking into his round face.

'What shall we have? I don't know all the different kinds. I've only ever had panna. Can we see all the different ones?' quizzed Pippo.

'Panna is good,' agreed Mario. 'Plain, but creamy and delicious.'

'No, I don't want panna!' cried the boy. 'I want to try something new. Something I've never had before. So long as you think I will like it. I don't want something I don't like.'

'But how will you know you don't like it if you don't try it?' asked Donna, though she was distracted. Her gaze had been drawn to where a small crowd was gathering. She peered over a wall down to the gardens below, where a large group of girls were performing synchronized exercises.

Pippo saw her look and dashed to the wall but, even on tiptoes, he couldn't see.

Mario ambled over too and cast a glance down.

'Fascists,' he said with a sneer and turned away.

'Hmmm,' said Donna.

'Can I see? Lift me up, please,' pleaded Pippo. But Mario and Donna were already walking in the other direction.

'Come on,' said Mario.

'But, but . . .' said Pippo, looking back at the wall as he followed them.

'This way to *gelato*.'

'Oh yes,' he grinned. 'But what flavour will we have?'

'Cream of sardine,' said Mario.

'What?' said the boy, confused.

'Or chicken risotto flavour,' continued Mario, ignoring him.

'No!' cried Pippo. 'You can't have those flavours — they're disgusting.'

'Have you tried them?' asked Mario, lifting Gino onto his shoulder and holding the baby steady with his strong hands.

'No . . .'

'Well then, you don't know, do you?'

'But I just—'

'Pippo,' said Donna.

When the boy looked up at her, he saw she was chuckling.

'He's teasing you.'

Then he saw the twinkle in Mario's dark eyes.

'Ahhh. Then I would like . . .' Pippo thought for a moment. 'I would like pizza flavour!'

'Mmmm!' grinned Mario. 'How delicious. With extra mozzarella?'

Pippo giggled loudly. 'Yes! And olives.'

'Black olives,' added Donna.

'Mushrooms,' cheered Pippo, skipping beside the family as they headed towards a shop with a picture of an enormous ice-cream cone hanging over it.

Pippo pulled his cap more firmly onto his head as he ran along the busy pavement. Nobody knew what he was doing, he thought, grinning to himself, dodging a mother with a baby carriage.

Turning sharply, he pushed open a door and came to a stop just inside it.

'*Buongiorno*, Signor Ferrari,' shouted Pippo across the

noise of the busy restaurant. Almost all of the small round tables were occupied by people eating, drinking and talking loudly. The smell of rich tomato sauce, fresh garlic and basil filled the air, and the boy sniffed deeply.

Behind the bar, an elderly man with wispy white hair was pouring a clear liquid from a long, thin bottle into an elegant glass.

'*Buongiorno!*' the boy called again, running up to the bar. This time the man heard him, looking up and jerking his head towards the end of the bar.

Pippo winked, badly. It was a trick Mario had taught him and he practised as much as he could but, having watched himself in the mirror, even he could tell it was slow and obvious — he didn't have the did-you-see-it speed of Mario. He vowed to keep practising as he ran around the bar, under the serving hatch and through into the kitchen.

'*Buongiorno*, Signora!' he called to the old woman who stood by the stove, slowly dropping fresh ravioli into a pan of boiling water.

'*Buongiorno*, Pippo,' she replied without looking up.

He ran through the kitchen and out of the open door on the other side. Noisily dashing up the wooden stairs, he pulled his cap off his head and, when he reached the door, he stood holding it for a moment while he caught his breath.

Knock, knock. Knock, knock. Knock.

It was the special sequence that Mario had taught him.

'*Avanti!*'

Pippo pulled the handle down and went into the room. There, a young man was sitting at a desk surrounded by books and piles of papers. Ernesto, the

Ferraris' son, was writing, his pen making a scratching sound. Without looking at the boy, he held his hand up, wordlessly telling him to wait.

The little boy stood as still as he could. Finally, the young man turned to Pippo, peeling his glasses from behind his ears and placing them carefully on the table.

'Aha. The postman has arrived,' he smiled, waving Pippo towards him.

'From Bruno,' said the boy, slipping a finger into the special lining in his cap and pulling out a few sheets of thin, finely folded paper.

'*Grazie, compagno*,' murmured the man, taking them and putting his glasses back on to read them.

He had only read the first line when he let out a groan.

'What is it? What's happened?' asked Pippo.

'The International Brigades have been ordered to pull out of the war in Spain.'

'That's where . . .' Pippo stopped himself, remembering Mario's warning about speaking out of turn.

Ernesto ignored him. 'It confirms our fears that the Republicans are unlikely to win now. And if the Fascists succeed there, they will become more powerful here.'

Pippo frowned. He didn't understand most of what Ernesto told him, but it sounded bad.

'That is not good for the Communists.'

The young man sucked his teeth in agreement as he turned the page and read on.

'Or us Italians?' the boy ventured.

'Little one,' said Ernesto, putting the letter down. 'The British may believe there will be "peace for our time", but there will be a war.'

'A war? Why? Where? Will Italy be in it?'

'Italy should not be in it – we can't afford it. But the vain monkey who leads us will probably want to be Hitler's partner. The chance to join forces with a powerful country like Germany will be too tempting for him to ignore.'

'Who is Hitler?' Mario had explained the state of Europe to Pippo a number of times, but he struggled to remember all the names and countries.

'He is the leader of a country called Germany – now our neighbour.'

'They weren't our neighbour before?'

'No. Our neighbour was Austria, but Hitler marched in and took it over. He said it was what the Austrians wanted.'

'Was it what they wanted?'

'They thought it was, but I think they'll regret it.'

'Why?'

'Because Hitler is a dictator – do you know what that means?'

Pippo shook his head. Ernesto was very clever, and Pippo knew he had such a lot to learn if he wanted to be a true Communist like Mario.

'It's someone who rules their country by force. They use the police – and even the army – to control the people. They never let anyone say anything against them and they use violence to stay in power.'

'But . . .' Pippo's eyebrows furrowed.

'Yes, yes,' nodded the young man, 'it sounds like Mussolini, you're right. But we Italians are not like other people. We'll go along with someone like him while things seem to be going well, but the moment we don't like it any more . . .' Ernesto ran a finger along his throat, making a squelching sound.

'We'll kill Il Duce?' The boy's eyes widened.

'Maybe, maybe not,' shrugged the man, 'but it will be the end of the Fascists, for sure.'

'And then what?'

'And then it will be our turn.' Ernesto laid down the letter and slapped both hands on the table. Standing up, he put his hand on the lapel of his worn jacket and spoke to Pippo as if he were a crowd of hundreds.

'All workers will have rights — in the fields and the factories. They will be treated as human beings with equal pay for all. No more will the rich and unjust benefit from the bent back of the worker . . . no more . . .' He paused and glanced down at Pippo, who was looking up at him in awe. 'No more for now,' he said with a smile.

'But I want more,' pleaded Pippo. 'I want to know what will happen when we win. I want to hear how the workers will be united, and free from poverty. I want to know—'

'Later, compagno, later,' chuckled Ernesto. 'I have to write a reply to Bruno. Can you tell the time?'

'Yes,' said the boy proudly. 'Mario taught me.'

'Very good. Go downstairs and ask the Signora if she will give you a drink. There is a clock in the kitchen. When it says two o' clock, come back and knock on the door.'

'Sì, compagno,' said Pippo with a small salute. He placed his cap back on his head and left the room, closing the door carefully. Running down the stairs two at a time, he wondered what the Signora would give him to drink.

Last time, she had made him fresh juice from a box of big sweet oranges that had just been delivered. He had never tasted anything like it.

But when he reached the kitchen, the Signora was not there. He waited for a while, peering into a large pot of bubbling ragù and opening the heavy icebox door, letting out a blast of freezing air. Shivering, he shut it quickly and looked up at the clock. The small hand was pointing to the one, and the big hand was pointing to the five. It was nearly half past one. So, he calculated, he still had quite a long time to wait for Ernesto to finish his letter.

Bored, Pippo left the kitchen and ambled into the restaurant. He could just see over the wood-topped bar to the small, busy trattoria. Pictures covered the walls – old photos of streets and people, paintings of food and views – and from the wooden beams on the ceiling were strung old raffia-covered bottles.

Signor Ferrari finished uncorking a similar-looking wine bottle and gave it to one of the waiters, who quickly whisked it away to a nearby table. The silver-haired man turned and saw Pippo.

'You're waiting for a reply?' he asked gruffly.

The boy nodded.

'Sit down.' The Signore gestured towards a stool on the other side of the bar.

Pippo followed his instruction and clambered up onto the tall stool. From there he could see the length of the bar, where there were rows and rows of liqueurs and spirits of all shapes and sizes. One day, the boy promised himself, he would try each and every one of them.

'What would you like?'

Pippo shrugged. He had been delivering messages to Ernesto for a few weeks now and more times than not, he had to wait for a reply. Each time he sat down with either the Signore or the Signora, he was given something delicious to drink or eat, so he decided to let the Signore decide.

'I know just the thing,' said the man with a smile. 'We have a half-finished . . .'

He looked around behind the bar for a moment before lifting up a green bottle with a pale blue label. Then he picked up a small glass and, with a flourish, poured the clear liquid into it. Pippo thought it was water, but the drink erupted into a million bubbles as soon as it hit the bottom of the glass. The boy grinned, itching to try this special drink.

'What is it?' he asked, peering into the glass to watch the bubbles rise and burst, rise and burst, making the water sparkle. 'It looks like magic.'

'It's water with gas,' said the Signore. 'Try it.'

'If I drink it, will it make the bubbles stop bubbling?'

'No. As you drink it, the bubbles will keep on popping — on your tongue, in your mouth and all the way down to your stomach.'

Pippo thought he was going to burst with excitement himself as he slowly lifted the glass and took a drink. Signor Ferrari was absolutely right. He felt a series of tiny explosions against his tongue, and kept the liquid in his mouth as long as he could before swallowing it. The sensation was so unusual, he instantly took another sip, and again held the water in his mouth, feeling the bubbles on his tongue and against his teeth.

Swallowing again, he grinned at the restaurant owner.

The Signore smiled back and leaned across the bar to ruffle Pippo's dark hair.

Suddenly, the doors of the bar were flung open and a group of men, all dressed in black clothes, their shirts buttoned high at their throats, marched in.

The customers gasped and one woman let out a small scream, but then they all fell silent, their forks still in their hands.

'Where is he?' demanded one man, a black hat set tightly on his greased hair.

Signor Ferrari looked blankly at the man for what seemed to Pippo like an impossibly long time before he shrugged. The boy realized that the white-faced Signore suddenly looked a great deal older than he had a few minutes before.

The men began to make their way amongst the tables, the diners cringing away from them. With an order of a single word, the men followed their leader through the bar hatch and into the kitchen, where the Signora had obviously reappeared because Pippo heard her shriek. She quickly dashed through into the bar and stood beside her husband, taking his hand and holding it tightly.

The boy looked around to see everyone's gaze follow the sound of the men in black stamping up the wooden stairs, and customers sinking in their seats as they heard the shouts and crash of doors overhead. Soon the chairs scuffed as some of the diners grabbed their coats and left the restaurant.

He turned a worried face to Signor Ferrari, who raised his hand and held it still — *stay where you are, boy*, the hand said. Pippo sat tight and waited, listening to the noises upstairs and twisting the red band round and round on his wrist. And finally he heard it, a shout of exclamation, stomping boots running and then some scuffling. The boots came down the stairs again and, from his high vantage point, the boy was the first to see the men in black shirts leading Ernesto through the kitchen.

Pippo gaped. The young man's face looked wrong. Apart from his missing glasses, his hair was dishevelled, and blood ran from his nose and a slash by his eye, where his glasses must have cut into his face.

Ernesto stumbled, his arms held roughly behind his back by one of the men. His mother let out a brief cry, but her husband held her, stopping her from rushing to her son.

The young man lifted his head and shook it at his mamma — *say nothing*. Then he glanced around the bar and briefly caught Pippo's eye. Thinking of Signor Ferrari's raised hand, the boy did nothing — he didn't even attempt a wink. Everyone in the trattoria silently watched the young man being led through the tables and out of the door.

As he reached the entrance, the leader of the men in black shirts turned on his heel and raised his arm in salute.

'Il Duce!' he said loudly.

Some of the people in the restaurant returned the salute. Pippo did not.

The man shut the door and a moment later there was a squeal of tyres outside.

Then it felt as though the whole room exhaled in one breath, and slowly the general noise of the restaurant returned.

Pippo turned to the Signore to ask what would happen to Ernesto, but he was holding the Signora as she quietly cried into his chest.

The boy took one last swig of the bubbling drink, which no longer had its magical effect on him, slid off the stool, and walked as normally as he could to the door. Opening it, he looked left and right to see if the men in black shirts were still there. But they were gone. Pulling his message-delivering cap onto his head, he yanked the door shut, turned left and ran.

CLARA

1940

The Blue-Eyed Woman

I sit up straight and stretch my neck, first to the right, then the left. I have been so engrossed in my reading, I have barely noticed the time pass.

Listening, I hear the comforting sound of Filomena cooking in the kitchen and, taking a deep breath, I recognize the smell of boiled meat and know instantly that she is cooking one of her specialities – pork stew, using almost every part of the pig.

Each day, there is something that reminds me of my mother, and this scent triggers today's memory. The traditional stew is one Mamma made too, although ours was usually ears, snout and tail, whereas Filomena has slabs of fatty leg and ribs to add.

I often think that Mamma's cooking would be similar to Filomena's if she could have afforded the ingredients. For a moment, I wonder if she is cooking for herself or someone else, and what she has to eat. It would make me happy to think that she was cooking for Pippo, but in my heart I know they are not together. I am also sure that, wherever he is, Pippo has charmed someone into feeding him all of his favourite dishes.

Squeezing the red fabric of my wristband between thumb and forefinger, I wish for the millionth time that I had never left that room. That I had stayed and waited until Pippo had woken; then, if Mamma hadn't returned, we would have gone looking for her together. We might not have found her, but I wouldn't have broken my promise to look after my brother.

While I know the Signore gave up looking for them months ago — if indeed he ever conducted a search as he said — I look for them every day. Every street that I walk down, every shop I enter, every cafe we drink coffee in, I look at people, scrutinizing each woman and boy I see.

Pippo will be nine years old now, and I have often considered how he would have grown. Perhaps his brown hair will have darkened; his eyes may not seem quite so large now. I hope he is plump from eating plenty.

Mamma, in my mind, is exactly the same as the last time I saw her. Willowy, with an elegant face, the sparkling light in her eyes that are as mine — her face appears in my mind easily. But to my silent distress, I have to admit that I have forgotten her voice.

I am sure it is soft and kind, and I often remember the times when her words and accent slipped into a language from a previous life. But as quickly as it appeared it was gone again, concealed from us, banished from what she called her 'now life'.

As I shift in my seat, the book in my lap snaps shut and I inspect its cover. The author's name and the title, *Tre operai*, sit sparsely on the white cover. Zia says this and the books like these are hers, that she thinks it's important to remember there is more to life than Fascism.

The Signore would never buy a book where the heroes are suffering workers in a laundry. Their lives are so desperate that I am sure this is fiction and not based on truth. While I am a little unsure about the films we watch of Il Duce, peeling off his vest to help bring in the harvest while crowds of farmers cheer him, I know he is doing good for the people. He is the man who saved industry with the Institute for Industrial Reconstruction – the Signore told me about it. And he's built roads and railways, schools and hospitals. Not only that, but, as the Signore says, he and everyone else can take a paid holiday every year. The Signore doesn't as his job is far too important, but he could if he wanted to, thanks to the generosity of Il Duce. No, this and many of the books I have read, curled in this seat or in my bed, would not be the choice of the Signore.

Reading is my favourite thing to do. When I come home from school where I have been quiet and polite, keen and diligent, I want to escape. Which is why I am working my way through every book on these shelves. I want to avoid thinking about the girls in my class, bullies quick to tease pitilessly any who are not like them. And I don't want to think about the boys either.

As soon as I began school, I noticed the boys looking at me. At first, it was the older ones as they crossed the schoolyard to their block, and later those my own age whose eyes followed me as we marched or exercised alongside each other.

But they hold no interest for me. All of those at school

are from what they call 'good families' — and yet from their unkind and selfish behaviour, I cannot see what good qualities these families possess. And the boys in the street who whistle and call frighten me with their sneering lips and dirty fingers clinging on to cigarettes. They remind me of the men who attacked my father — the ignorant, narrow-minded people who hate simply because they cannot accept. The men my mother spent so long trying to avoid.

No, boys hold no interest for me. After I began school, though, my reading improved quickly and I started asking Zia if I could look at the books in their library. Take these, she said, handing me a collection of women's magazines.

Flicking through stories of film stars and singers I didn't know, and endless words about dresses, shoes, jewellery and make-up, I graciously thanked Zia and handed them back. It was the books I wanted.

When I tentatively asked her if I would be permitted to read them, she paused for a moment, then nodded at me.

'Of course — that's why they are here.' And she bustled off to write a shopping list, or paint her nails, or however it is she manages to fill her days. I cannot think of a person less like my mother than the Signora, but she is kind and thoughtful, and capable of great sympathy.

After a month of living with them, it had become clear that Mamma and Pippo either could not or would not be found. We returned to the room where they had disappeared and spoke to the landlord again, all for nothing. The Signore insisted that the police had contacted the orphanages with my brother's details but that no one had been found of his description. It was no surprise to me.

At breakfast one morning, as both Salvadoris dunked their bread rolls in their caffè lattes, I quietly stated that I would be leaving.

The Signore looked at me and shrugged before returning to his newspaper. But the Signora turned fiercely to me.

'No!'

'This is not my home . . .' I began.

'No,' she stated again, glaring into my eyes and raising a finger at me, its nail painted beautifully in ruby red. I thought I'd seen the tiniest trace of fear in her face, but in a moment it was gone.

With a small voice, I explained that I would be fine on my own and that I was sure I could find work and accommodation quickly.

'If she doesn't want to be here . . .' the Signore agreed.

The Signora turned her glare to her husband.

'Clara,' she said without taking her gaze from the Signore, 'would you leave the room for a moment?'

I slid off my chair and crossed the room silently, heading towards the stairs and my room at the top of the house. As I started climbing, wondering if I'd be permitted to keep a few items of the nearly full wardrobe of clothes I'd acquired, I slowed my step, straining to hear what was being said.

'There are places for abandoned children like her,' the Signore said. 'Institutions . . .'

'How dare you,' I heard his wife growl.

'What?'

I stopped climbing the stairs.

'You are probably responsible for—' The scraping sound of the Signora's chair on the tiled floor covered her words. Then her heels clicked angrily towards the door, which she slammed.

I stood as still as I could, trying to listen to their conversation, but once the door was shut their voices were muffled, their words unclear. It was obvious that they were arguing about me and so, for the second time, I headed for the front door, picking up my coat and satchel as I passed them.

The door had just clicked behind me when I heard the Signora calling my name up the stairs. I didn't know what to do: go back inside or run before she realized I was gone. As I dithered, the Signora must have seen my figure through the frosted glass because she flung open the door before I'd taken a step.

For a moment, I thought she would shout at me too and I winced a little. Seeing the wrinkling around my eyes, the Signora stopped, took a deep breath, and bent down a little to look into my face.

'Clara,' she said calmly. 'The Signore and I would be honoured if you would live with us. We will continue to look for your mother and brother, but while we are searching, I would like to know that you are safe. And as long as you are with us, you will be completing your education.'

I didn't move, thinking about whether I wanted to stay in a house where at least one of its three inhabitants did not want me.

The Signora reached out her hand and gently took mine. As I looked into her green eyes, I saw tears fill them.

'Please, Clara,' she whispered. 'Please stay with me.'

I nodded, letting her take my bag and coat, hanging them on the hook again. She was wiping her eyes as she shepherded me back into the dining room, where the Signore was slurping the last of his coffee and pulling his jacket on over his shirt. He nodded his head to me, and I knew then that we'd both accepted the situation because of what we felt for the Signora; him, his love for his wife, and me a kind of friendship that I still find hard to understand.

After he left, the Signora poured me some more hot milk and said, 'Clara, if you'll be staying here a while longer, I think you should call me something other than Signora.'

We were both quiet for a moment.

'My name is Carolina . . .' she said, but I quickly shook my head.

'Zia?'

Slowly I nodded. Yes. Aunt. That made sense. Not a real aunt, but what I might call a friend of my mother's.

'Zia,' I agreed.

Suddenly, the memory is broken by the sound of a shout.

'Carolina! Carolina! Filomena! Anybody!'

At the sound of the Signore's voice, I dash towards the hall and stand by the door to the library, looking at his flushed face and broad smile as he waves a folded newspaper.

'Clara!' he bellows, more delighted to see me than ever before.

At that moment Filomena appears at the kitchen door.

'Signore?'

'Where is the Signora?' he asks excitedly.

'Out,' says Filomena flatly.

'Where? Oh, it doesn't matter. Glorious news, ladies – it has finally happened.' He clicks his heels together and pauses before announcing loudly, 'Il Duce has spoken. He has declared war on *Inghilterra* and *Francia*.'

I glance at Filomena. Her face is as stern as always, but I see her instinctively cross herself.

I look back at the Signore and see he is staring at me, wide-eyed with delight.

'Clara! Filomena! Is this not the best news?'

I do not know how to react, so I wait for Filomena, who asks, 'Can war ever be good news?' in a way that does not seem to be a question.

'We will not be at war for long.' The Signore waves his hand, batting away the idea. 'We are now aligned with the most powerful force the West has ever known. France is falling to the Germans as we speak. England will be next, and then a new Europe can emerge – with Hitler and Mussolini at its head.'

'Humph.' Filomena makes a noise that expresses her disapproval wordlessly.

'It seems you are not alone in your dislike of war,' says her employer. 'I witnessed some trouble at the square on my way home. But mark my words,' he adds with a firm nod of his head, 'this will be good for Italy.'

'Will you have to go and fight?' I ask quietly.

The question makes the Signore blink, his smile dropping momentarily. 'No, Clara, no.' He shakes his head. 'I perform a crucial role in the running of local government. My job is to ensure our homes are protected from any attack, and to mobilize our support for the leader. I cannot be sent to battle — I am Il Duce's own voice here in our city.'

'Ah,' I say with a smile. 'Well then, it is very good news. I am happy to hear it.'

Filomena turns and leaves, muttering under her breath as she goes.

The Signore watches her go and, for a moment, I feel sad for him. Since my arrival, he has slowly softened towards me. He is never as familiar as Zia, and I still call him Signore, but learning as I do about Italy and Il Duce at school, we often talk about our country and its ambitions. Zia is less interested in Fascism but I sometimes see her watching us together, and she seems pleased.

'Tell me how our lives will be different when the war has been won, Signore.'

'Well,' he says, rubbing his hands together and walking the length of the hallway, 'our beloved country will grow. Other countries that Germany and Italy have taken control of will be, what's the word' — he taps his temple — 'redistributed between us.'

'Like the Roman Empire?' I ask. This period of Italy's history is often taught at school, and now, perhaps, I understand why.

'Exactly!'

'And then?'

'Then, Clara, Italy will enjoy stability. The constancy of an economy that is run under a steady hand.'

He looks at me and tries to explain. 'The country will be run in the same way as the military. Businesses will be more efficient and everyone will work hard, so productivity will rise. We will not be dependent on other countries to produce things for us — we will do it all ourselves. And when the benefit is clear, we will continue to spread our doctrine to more countries. Understand?'

I nod my head. It makes sense. Thinking again of the three characters in my book, I cannot believe that their lives are so hard. Il Duce will help all of us.

The Signore leans against the wall, eyes to the ceiling, imagining this perfect world. I turn to go, but when he hears me, his eyes snap to mine.

'Where is she?' he asks.

'With her sister,' I reply, before returning to the library and my book.

I cut another small piece of dough and gently use the knife and my fingers to roll out the shape. But instead of a tiny shell-like dome, I've made a lopsided triangle. I try again but this one is worse — a flat disc with a hole in the middle.

'Like this,' says Filomena, patiently showing me again. I watch closely, but the way she moves the knife and her fingers seem to be exactly what I've just done.

'Keep trying,' she urges with a nod of the head. She returns to her rolled length of pasta dough, chopping and shaping, chopping and shaping, until she has a small mound of orecchiette, while I fumble over my next one.

'Not bad,' she says. 'That one actually looks like an ear.'

'I wouldn't want to have ears like this,' I say, picking up the misshapen pasta.

'More, more,' encourages Filomena, scattering hers across a large wire tray.

We both return to our rolls of dough.

'Make the most of the food while we have it,' says Filomena sharply.

'What do you mean?'

'War means hunger.'

'But the Signore says it will be over . . .'

'That is what they said the last time,' Filomena snorts. 'Italians do not want war. It is not our way. We are not Germany. And when the soldiers arrive in France, or wherever they are sent, and they ask what they are fighting for, what will Mussolini say?'

'The glory of Italy?' I suggest.

She snorts again.

'He won't say it, but he is sending our men out to fight for Hitler. That's the truth.' She shakes her head. 'So we can say we were on the winning side.'

'Will Hitler win?'

She shrugs her shoulders, flour showering from her apron. 'I can see no good coming from being friends with a bully. And two bullies together? It spells trouble.'

I am quiet. I want to believe the Signore and his optimistic outlook, but our country being at war has unsettled me. I have no concern for a lack of food. I have been hungry before. But I am sure that now the authorities will have no interest in searching for a missing woman and boy. My stomach lurches as I feel once again the fear that I will never see my family again.

The thought makes me sigh shakily and I sense Filomena cast a look at me. But I concentrate on my pasta curls, which are starting to look a little more like hers.

There is a quiet knock at the door, the one that leads out into the tiny courtyard and the steps up to the street.

Filomena skitters another handful of pasta across the mesh and stands, wiping her hands on her apron.

I put my knife down and watch her walk to the door and push it open. Her large body fills the space and, while I try to peer past, I cannot see who she is muttering with.

I watch her reach into her pocket and pull out a coin, thrusting it into an outstretched hand. She gently pulls the door shut and, as she turns, I see her push a small bunch of grey-green leaves into her apron.

'Is it ruta?' I ask, as she returns to the table.

She sniffs and nods. 'You know of these things, don't you.'

I remember my mother hanging a fresh sprig over the door at every new home. 'To protect us,' she'd say, whispering a few words under her breath.

'A little.'

She nods. 'Your people understand its powers.'

'My people?'

'I've always known. Your skin may not be dark, but those eyes . . .' She looks at me as if drawn into me.

'However,' she says quietly, not shifting her gaze from me, 'you are kind, and you care for the Signora and . . .' She pauses a moment. 'I trust you.'

These are serious words for her to utter and I appreciate their importance.

Filomena suddenly blinks and I see her make a decision. She turns and walks quickly to the door, throwing it open and calling up the steps.

Another hushed conversation follows, and then she moves aside, waiting for whoever it is to come into the kitchen.

I wait too, watching as a shadowy figure appears. Shrouded in a black scarf, a small, stooped woman slowly edges into the room. Filomena closes the door and indicates that she should follow.

I cannot take my eyes off the person who walks towards me. She has no stick, but walks with a painful shuffle, her tiny black shoes scuffing the ground. Her black dress is old and worn but clean, and I see a golden ring on the middle finger of one of her wrinkled hands.

Filomena pulls out a chair and the elderly woman slowly sinks into it, resting for a moment.

'A drink?' Filomena asks the visitor.

Yes, the scarfed head nods, and Filomena turns to the pantry to fetch a bottle of wine.

The way she treats this woman surprises me – she rarely shows the Signore so much respect. She returns with a small glass and pours some of the sweet white wine into it. The head nods appreciatively.

Unable to take my eyes off the figure, I gather the pasta shapes in front of me and throw them onto the wire mesh. Filomena collects the rest of the pasta and the knives, and takes the tray to the other side of the kitchen where it will dry.

'Clara,' she says, returning to the table and seating herself between the old woman and me. 'The Signora may be able to help you. She sees things that you and I cannot. What has been and what will be.'

I take my eyes off the woman and turn to Filomena.

'I thought,' she says gently, with a kindness in her voice that I have not heard before, 'you could ask about your mamma and brother.'

I stare. With her charms and whispered prayers, I have

always known Filomena is superstitious, but I had not expected this. My mind spins. What will I ask? Will I dare to enquire if Mamma and Pippo are alive? Do I want to know the answer? What if she says they are gone forever?

No. I stop the thoughts whirling. I know that they are both alive. I feel it. Deep inside my body, I know neither of them is dead.

'Clara?' whispers a thin voice.

I look at the woman and watch as her wrinkled hand grasps the scarf and pulls it down onto her shoulders. Her hair is white streaked with grey, giving it a silvery glint in the light. Despite the deep wrinkles, the skin on her face looks as soft and downy as a peach, and I have to stop myself from reaching out to stroke it. Her features are fine and her mouth turns up a little at the edge, giving her a slight smile that I believe must always be there.

As I observe her, she raises her eyes to look at me and I gasp. One of her eyes is a blue so bright that it sparkles like a jewel. The other is completely white. The black in the centre is gone, but as I stare, I see the faint green outline of colour where her iris lies almost hidden by its milky cover.

Now I understand why Filomena believes she can see what others cannot.

'Clara,' says the whispery voice again.

I nod.

With her shimmering blue eye, she takes in my face, reaching into my eyes to see my soul. I feel her white eye probing too, searching for secrets and truths.

The woman stares for a moment longer, unblinking, before saying to me, 'Give me your hands, child.'

Hesitantly, I offer both hands across the table, and

she gently dusts the flour off with the back of hers. Then she leans over and traces a finger over the lines and the shapes they create across my palms.

Filomena looks at me. I return my gaze to my hands, trying to read what she can see.

'You are . . .' she murmurs, then stops herself and looks at Filomena. In the briefest of moments, I notice her blue eye take in the large kitchen, my school uniform, the food on the counter waiting to be cooked for tonight's meal.

She adjusts herself a tiny amount, as if she is altering her prediction, then continues, 'You are alone.'

I nod.

'You came to this place with family. But now they are gone, and you are alone.'

I say nothing. I do not move. I simply listen.

With a tiny intake of breath, she says even more quietly, 'You ache for your mamma,' and gives my hand a small squeeze. 'She is gone. She is far from here. But . . .' She closes her eyes for a moment. 'But she is alive. And she knows that you are safe.'

A shaky noise escapes from my mouth.

'Where?' is all I can say.

She shakes her head. No. 'It is too far. It is somewhere I do not know. She does not want to be there. She wants to be with you. But she cannot.' She shakes her head, as if repeating Mamma's wishes. 'She cannot.'

'If it is so far, how can she know I am safe?'

'She knows,' is all the woman says.

We all sit as still as stones and the silence roars in my ears. I watch as my fingers begin to curl, closing the outstretched hands and hiding their secrets. The old woman reaches to the red band tied around my wrist and strokes it gently.

'Your brother,' she says. 'He is not with your mother. But you know that.'

I look up at her and stare into her glimmering blue eye. She nods and I can only agree with her. I do know he is not with her. I know that he is close.

'Listen for him,' she says in a voice like a sigh, 'and you will hear him.'

I remember a time when I thought I had heard him. Now, I know it wasn't my imagination. It wasn't my wishful mind playing tricks on me. It had been him, my Pippo. I had heard him. Next time, I promise my little brother, I will not give up so easily.

The old woman releases my wrist and reaches out for the glass of wine. She sips it, unspeaking, and I feel her serenity ebbing towards me in small waves. Even Filomena relaxes, her constantly busy hands finally resting in her lap.

We sit in a comfortable silence until the woman has finished her wine. Then she turns to Filomena, who blinks quickly, as if waking herself, and reaches into the pocket where she keeps her small store of coins.

No, the woman raises her hand. No. But she lets the cook help her out of her chair and, as she shuffles towards the door, Filomena grabs a small loaf of bread and pushes it into her accepting hand.

She is about to step over the doorway when she stops and turns towards me.

'You *will* see him, Clara,' she says, her low voice carrying through the kitchen. 'You will see your brother again.'

I close my eyes, letting relief wash over me like warmth. It is as comforting as the water in the baths that I have become so used to.

'Thank you,' I say earnestly. But the woman just nods sadly, turns to the right and steps out into the shadowy evening.

PIPPO

1940

The Circle

Pippo was never very good at reading.

'Why do I need books when I can talk to people?' he'd asked. And the boy was so good at talking that Mario had taken a moment to answer him.

'Perhaps,' he'd said thoughtfully, 'you won't always meet the right people to talk to.'

As the boy had sat on the steps of a church, sharing a cigarette with Botte and feeling far older than his nine years, he'd looked around his gang of friends. Allocco, who sat on the step above him, moon-faced with large eyes — what else could they call him but 'Owl'? The fact his nickname also meant 'Fool' was just a bonus. He couldn't read at all, but he had a knack for knowing where to get cigarettes and sweets and all the things that were being added to the rationed list each week.

Botte had been to school and was considered the cleverest of them all. It was how he'd got the nickname 'Barrel': while the rest of them raced around the city doing jobs and finding other ways to make money, Botte was most likely to be found sitting reading a discarded newspaper while munching on cheese or salami.

Glancing at the tall boy leaning on the church wall, Pippo felt a tiny pang of envy. They called Paolo 'Ceffo', which meant ugly, when he was in fact the best looking of them. The girls loved Ceffo. '*Bello* Paolo,' they'd call, and giggle as they passed. He'd just slick back his hair or pull at the collar of his shirt and give them a wink. Ceffo didn't read, or talk much for that matter, but he had a stash of magazines that needed no words, which he always shared with his friends.

It was no surprise to Pippo that they called him 'Boccalone': big mouth. He preferred the thought of being a chatty bird, but tucked that thought away with all the other memories of his mamma and sister. He talked about them less and less, even to Donna, but whenever he thought of them, there was an ache deep inside him that he found hard to bear.

In the time since he'd lost them, he'd found that talking or thinking about something else helped – often something about his new life and his new family. So when he heard Donna sing Gino to sleep, and remembered the gentle voice of his mother in his ear, he'd hum '*Bandiera Rossa*' quietly to himself. And when he saw a girl in the street with hair as dark as Clara's, he'd feel in his pocket for a coin, pull out a copper-coloured *centesimo* and weave it through his fingers, watching the King's head flash at him until he forgot the pain.

He'd tried to read the books Mario gave him, reminding himself how much he had wanted to learn from Ernesto. But the words would swim, and his mind would dart onto something other than the story or the subject, and the book would sit in his lap, pages unturned while he chatted to Mario and asked Donna endless questions.

Anyway, he'd think to himself, Ernesto had been caught, so maybe being well read didn't make you clever. Maybe it was here on the streets that you learned to be smart. What good were books when there was no work? What good were books if there was no food? He would never say that to Mario, though.

Sometimes he went with Mario and stood with a group of men at the street corner, waiting for a truck or a horse and cart to pull up. If it did, the driver would point at a few of the men and they would scramble into the back, and they'd be taken to wherever the day's work was.

Pippo had never been chosen, and often Mario would come home from a morning's pointless waiting and slump into a chair by the table.

'Maybe tomorrow, my love,' Donna would say, stroking his dark hair and leaving her hand to rest briefly on the back of his neck, before returning to her chores.

But the boy knew the reason Mario wasn't chosen was because he was a Communist. And although no one ever told the authorities, when there was a group of men to choose from, the ones who had no political opinions were picked first.

Pippo worked as hard as he could. Running messages and making deliveries, whether for local businesses or his underground comrades, earned him a little money which he passed on to Donna. Whenever his friends said he should pocket some — treat himself to that penknife he really wanted — he said he couldn't. He told them that Mario and Donna were not his parents. They didn't have to feed and clothe him, he'd say, they just did it. They treated him as one of their own, no different from Gino and now little Violetta. That was why he passed on all his money to them: he didn't need a knife as much as he needed a family.

'It says here,' read Botte, peering at the tiny newsprint, 'that olive oil will be the next thing to be rationed.'

'Olive oil?' said Pippo. 'Olive oil? How will we cook? Donna uses it all the time.'

'She'll just have to use less of it,' said Botte.

'Maybe not,' grinned Allocco.

'*Dai!*' shouted Pippo at the round-faced boy. 'How can you know where to get something that's not even on the black market yet?'

Owl shrugged his shoulders and continued to grin.

Pippo twisted the band on his wrist.

Botte was just about to read something else to the boys when they heard shouting from across the square. Pippo saw Ceffo squint, press off from the wall and start striding towards the noise.

'What is it?' asked Pippo, already on his feet and trotting after him. Ceffo didn't reply, but Allocco, who was suddenly by his side, shouted, 'The cafe – look – it must be the radio.'

They all began to run towards the small coffee shop on the corner of the piazza, where Italian state radio piped out all day.

'He's done it,' Pippo heard a woman shout. 'He's finally done it.'

'He's an idiot if he has,' replied a man in a hat.

'He's a leader,' a fat man said, his tummy jiggling as

he half walked, half ran towards the cafe. 'Leaders lead.'

'And fools follow,' said a woman's voice from behind them.

'What is it?' shouted Pippo at whoever was listening. 'What is happening?'

'War,' said the trilby man, briefly looking down. 'If what we've heard is true, Mussolini's taken us into war.'

Pippo and his friends gathered together as they reached the edge of the square and a crowd pushed them forwards. The announcer on the radio proclaimed in a tone both grave and triumphant that Italy had entered the war with Germany.

'We are fighting the plutocratic and reactionary Western democracies. We are now at war with France and England and' — here his voice swelled with pride — 'we will win. We will win!'

'*Vinceremo!*' shouted some of the men and women who surrounded Pippo, raising their arms in salute.

Others booed and jeered at them. 'What are we fighting for?' the trilby man asked. 'This isn't our war. It's Hitler's. Leave him to it.'

'You should watch what you say,' said a man Pippo couldn't see.

'The war's nearly over,' said the fat man. 'And Italy will be on the winning side.'

'The war in France is almost over,' replied the man in the hat, 'but what about the English?'

'Pah,' scoffed a man with a pig nose. 'They are running from France with their tail between their legs.'

'They've beaten Germany before.'

'Not without America. And America does not want to go to war.'

'And what about Russia?'

'What about them? They're with Hitler too.'

'But is Germany with *them*?'

'What do you know about it anyway?'

'I'm a schoolteacher. I teach history,' the man replied. 'Or at least I did,' he said quietly, more to himself.

Pippo looked up at the teacher and saw his face lined with worry. The sight of it made him think of Mario and, shouting to his friends, 'I've got to go. I'll see you tomorrow,' he ducked out of the crowd and started running.

He ran the length of the piazza before turning down the main road. He was going so fast that there wasn't time to stop when he saw a man coming out of a shop door. He crashed into the man's legs, almost knocking him over.

'Sorry, Signore,' he said quickly, putting his hands up in apology.

The man was not tall, but he took a moment to straighten himself to his full height and look down at Pippo. His suit was smart, his hat crisp, and on his lapel sat the Fascist Party pin — an axe emerging from a bundle of rods set over the Italian flag. The boy stood nervously still, knowing just how dangerous this man could be.

'*Scusi*,' he said again quickly. 'I was running home. The news . . .'

'Yes,' the man beamed, holding up a newspaper, 'glorious news, no?'

'*Sì, sì!*' nodded Pippo enthusiastically. Working with the underground movement had taught him that people were less suspicious of you if you agreed with them. 'I was going home to tell my family. They will want to celebrate, that's for sure.'

'Excellent!' said the man, a broad smile underneath his pencil moustache, the accident forgotten.

Just then, Pippo heard the sound of shouting rising from the square again, but this time it sounded angry. Police whistles pierced the air, and the boy noticed the man's eyebrows pull together in concern.

Although he was desperate to return to watch the unrest, Pippo knew he had to get home, so he dodged around the man and ran.

Donna let out a deep breath and sank into a chair. Mario shook his head without taking his eyes from Pippo.

'You're sure?' he asked.

'I'm sure!' gasped the boy breathlessly. 'I heard it on the radio and everyone in the piazza was talking about it. They were arguing, and when I came away, there was trouble, the police were there. And I talked to an official about it too. He was really happy.'

'He would be,' said Donna scornfully, 'because it wouldn't occur to him that we are on the wrong side.'

Pippo thought for a moment. 'The same side as Germany and Hitler. But also Russia. Don't we want to be like Russia? Our fellow Communists?'

Donna and Mario were quiet, thoughtful, and the only sound in the small house was Gino's slurping as he sucked soup from a small bowl, his large brown eyes set firmly on his parents.

Mario sighed. 'It's complicated, Pippo.'

'But they've invaded countries too. How is that different from what the Germans did?'

'They are spreading Communism,' said Mario.

'I don't understand.' Pippo shook his head. 'How is it different just because it's Communism, not Fascism?'

He tugged absent-mindedly at his wristband, but started when it suddenly came apart in his hand.

Donna saw the look of panic on his face and leaned towards him to tie it on again but, before she could take it from Pippo, Mario stepped forward.

'Let me have that a moment,' he said. 'Look.' He pulled the strip of fabric along the table into a straight line.

'This' — he pointed to the end of the red strip on the right — 'is Fascism. A dictator rules absolutely. Everyone must do as he says, and no opposition is allowed. *Capisci?*'

Pippo nodded.

'See this?' He pointed to the left end. 'This is Communism. Everybody works for the good of the people.'

'But doesn't Stalin make all the decisions?'

'He's a leader who wants what's best for everyone. Hitler is only thinking about his power.'

'What will he do with that power?'

'I imagine he will build businesses and cities — with all the profit going to him and his friends.'

'Won't that give more people jobs?'

'Well, yes,' said Mario, 'but the point is, in Communism the workers do their work for their fellow worker. No one is rich and no one is poor.'

'So,' said Pippo, thinking of Botte, 'if you are fat and lazy, you will have the same as someone who works very hard?'

'Who would be lazy when your neighbour needs your help?'

Pippo didn't believe Botte would think about anyone other than Botte. And he wasn't sure about Ceffo either.

Pippo nudged the red band, creating a dent in it. 'What if someone doesn't want to be a Communist?'

'What?'

Donna chuckled as she stood and went to the cooker to begin their meal.

'There are people who like Mussolini. If Italy changed to Communist, would they all change their minds?'

'Not at first,' agreed Mario. 'But over time, perhaps, with a little help . . .' He hesitated. 'Yes.'

'Hmmm,' said Pippo, moving the wristband with his other finger now. 'And—'

'*Basta*,' said Mario, standing, 'enough.'

'Just one more question, Mario?' pleaded the boy.

The man looked at him and nodded.

'Do you think Hitler and Stalin could ever be friends?'

Mario looked down at the table and saw that Pippo had twisted the strip of red fabric into a circle — its left and right ends meeting at the top.

'Impossible,' he said, turning and walking away.

The boy looked at the circle for a moment, before shrugging and picking up his bracelet for Donna to tie around his wrist again.

Pippo stopped running and looked up at the wooden sign that hung over the pavement just ahead. 'Trattoria Ferrari' it read in a swirl of yellow and red.

The boy ambled up to the restaurant's dusty windows and peered in. The chairs were perched upside down on top of bare tables. Outlines marked the walls where the pictures had hung. Only a few empty bottles stood lonely on the bar.

Pippo imagined he could still hear the chatter of diners inside, while old men sipped coffee, smoked and argued amiably at the tables outside. The smells would be different every time he entered the glass doors, depending on the day's special – the rich, salty garlic of spaghetti alle vongole, the deep, red wine tang of a rabbit ragù, and at celebrations, the smoke and pepper of grilled steak.

He remembered the last time he had seen the Ferraris. Mario had taken him and the two had sat at the bar, perched on stools so high the little boy's legs swung and he wondered if this was how the monkey in his picture book felt up in the trees.

Signor Ferrari had smiled at Pippo and ruffled his hair, but the smile stopped at his mouth, unable to reach past his sadness to his eyes. Mario had told Pippo that when Ernesto was taken away, the restaurant owner had asked Mario to help find him. Pippo thought what a kind man Signor Ferrari must be, because it soon became clear that each and every customer was a friend to the Ferraris, and they all did what they could to help.

One customer's brother worked in the prison service, and he had looked up their records, but Ernesto's name was not on the list. Another knew a woman whose son had been taken away too, but she couldn't find him either. Eventually, a tall gentleman in a smart suit had offered his services. He knew some people who knew some people who knew the mafia, and the mafia knew everything there was to know.

Signor and Signora Ferrari had accepted his offer, then waited, day after hand-wringing day, until finally word came back. Mario said he had seen him, the tall suit as he sat at the table, sipping a glass of wine, quietly explaining that their son had been taken to a concentration camp on an island. He was safe.

After that, the Ferraris relaxed a little. They wrapped up food parcels to be delivered to their son and sent them away with the tall man, a piece of meat or bottle of fine wine pushed into his hand as a thank you – Pippo had seen that for himself.

And then, one day, Mario had come home and sat heavily in a chair.

'What's happened? What is it, Mario?' the boy had chivvied, as he and Donna and Gino crowded towards him.

Sighing, Mario had rubbed his face.

'I've just come from Ferrari's. It's Ernesto. He's dead.'

Pippo gasped and looked from Mario to Donna, who was shaking her head in disbelief.

'Do they know how . . . ?' she'd asked.

Mario had shaken his head. 'He was a boy of books. He was not made for prison.'

'Their only child,' Donna had said, rubbing her pregnant stomach.

'Their hearts have been broken into a million pieces and scattered to the wind. They will never recover.'

Pippo, for once, only had two words.

'I'm sorry,' he'd said, putting his hand on Mario's slouched shoulder.

The man had looked up and tried to smile but, failing,

pulled Gino and Pippo to him and, as Donna leaned over him, he rested his head on her belly.

A few weeks later, Pippo had been called to a large house on the road out of town. All he knew was that he was to collect a parcel. When he'd reached the door with coloured glass windows, he rang the bell, hearing it tinkling deep inside the house. A maid in a white apron had opened the door and asked him to wait outside.

Pippo had tried to stand still, but was jigging impatiently when the tall man in a dark suit opened the door. Sucking on a cigarette, he had looked the boy up and down through the smoke, before reaching into his inside jacket pocket. Pippo saw a flash of blue – gleaming like a bird's wing – as the suit's silky lining was exposed.

'You know Ferrari's?' the man had asked, his voice deep and gruff as he'd pulled out a small paper-covered package.

Pippo nodded quickly. The questions he'd wanted to ask the man had built up like a line of traffic in his mouth, but by then he'd been experienced enough to know there were some people who should not be quizzed so he'd kept his lips pressed tightly together.

'Take this. Do not stop anywhere,' the man had said, slipping the parcel into his waiting hands.

Pippo had nodded, tucking the packet into his belt and pulling his shirt over to cover it, waiting to be dismissed. But the man had then reached over towards his head. Pippo had thought he was going to pat his hair, but instead the man had tugged slightly at Pippo's right ear, and when he turned his head to look, he saw a large silver coin resting in the man's palm. And the boy wasn't quite sure how the coin ended up in his own hand — between gasping at the magic, glancing at the man's smiling face and looking for the money, he'd discovered it was there. He'd quickly slipped it into his pocket in case it disappeared again.

The man had nodded his dismissal, and Pippo had run as fast as he could to the city centre and the trattoria. He'd been panting as he pushed open the doors and went through the hubbub to find the Signore.

He had been down in the storeroom, shifting crates of wine, and in the shadowy light, Pippo had suddenly realized that Signor Ferrari had become an old man. His hair had turned completely white and he'd grown thin, with shallow dips where his rounded cheeks had once been.

'Aha, Pippo,' he said when he'd noticed him. 'How's Mario?'

'Good, Signore. He's working today so that makes him happy. Do you need some help with your boxes?'

'No, thank you. I've nearly finished. Do you have something for me?'

Reaching under his shirt, Pippo had pulled out the packet and handed it over. Deliveries sometimes required a reply, so he had stepped back, waiting, unaware that his finger had begun running a line along the wall's bricks.

Signor Ferrari had carefully unwrapped the paper, and there in the folds were two small pink books. He'd looked up and noticed Pippo peering over to see. Gesturing him over, he'd sat down on a crate and opened the first book to show the boy. It had a picture of him, looking serious against a black background.

'What is this?' the boy had asked. 'A book about you?'

'It is.' He'd run a finger down the writing on the page opposite. 'It's called a passport. If you want to travel to another country, you have to have one.'

'You're going away? Where are you going? Why? When will you leave? When are you going to come back, Signor Ferrari?'

The old man had chuckled. 'I shall miss your questions, Pippo. The Signora and I are going to America.'

'America!' The word had come out of his mouth in an extended gasp.

'We have family there. It has been' – he searched for the word – 'unbearable,' he finally decided on, 'to stay here without . . .' His voice had broken a little. 'Without Ernesto. So we will leave. Start a new life somewhere else. Somewhere you can read whatever you want, write whatever you wish, and have whatever opinion you care to.'

'So,' Pippo's mind raced ahead, 'so you're going to America, and you're never coming back?'

'That's right.'

'But who will run the restaurant? Where will everyone eat? What will we do without you?'

'Pippo,' the Signore had said, resting the books in his lap and looking at him. 'We cannot bear it here without him. It is killing us staying. To live, we must begin new lives. Look,' he'd said, lifting his hand.

He opened the other book and this time, a faded picture of the Signora sat on the page. 'This beautiful woman is now called Signora Toscani. We will become new people when we land in New York.'

'Why? Why have you changed your names? What is wrong with Ferrari?'

'We cannot risk the authorities making a connection between our son — a criminal in their eyes — and us. So, when we leave, we will leave everything. Even our names. Do you understand?'

Pippo had thought for a moment, remembering the men in black who had taken Ernesto away. They had seemed like the sort of men who liked to destroy things — businesses, families, lives. He could understand wanting to get away from them.

'When are you going?' the boy had asked sadly.

'When you least expect it,' the old man had said quietly.

And he was right. One morning a few weeks later, Donna came into the house early with some fresh milk.

'The Ferraris,' she'd called through to Mario, who was in the other room, 'they've gone. No one knows where they are.'

Pippo was about to say, 'I do,' when he stopped himself. He thought of the Ferraris leaning over the railing of a huge ship, like the one he'd seen in Botte's newspaper, looking to the horizon and a new life. He knew they would not look back at Italy, the country that had killed their son.

People keep disappearing, thought Pippo, as he stepped back from the dusty windows of the empty restaurant. As he pulled his message-delivering cap down snugly on his head and turned left to start running again, a thought flitted through his mind. Who would be next?

CLARA

The Librarian

Up and through. Over and stitch. I feel my eyebrows stuck in stern concentration as my fingers grip the needles tightly.

'Relax,' says Zia gently, her own needles moving so quickly they are just a blur of wood. She doesn't even need to look at what she's knitting, the intricate movement is so instinctive to her.

I realize I have forgotten to breathe, so I stretch my back and inhale deeply. The dark blue scarf will take months to finish at my current speed. But as I edge closer to the fire to warm my feet, I think of the young man who may need my poor offering and I try my best to knit a little faster. Yarn back, then up and through.

Everyone is knitting, encouraged by schools and other organizations to help our brave military men who are facing a difficult winter. There are few details in the newspapers that I have taken to reading, but the Signore says he has heard that the army is occupying a part of the Alps in France, and the navy is fighting in both the Mediterranean and the Atlantic.

'Your scarves and jumpers could be helping a soldier in the mountains avoid frostbite, or a member of our excellent Regia Marina stay warm in deep seas. A pair of socks you knit may even make it onto one of our submarines,' he'll say proudly.

I have seen Zia knit socks. She uses four needles and, given my trouble with two, I think our men would do better to rely on her knitting than mine.

Even Filomena has taken up the needles to 'help the poor boys', as she says. Her speciality is balaclavas which she lines with soft cotton. On the grey lining she stitches messages like *Coraggio* and *Vinceremo*. *Be brave*, she urges them. *We will win*, she writes, hoping to give them the strength she believes they need.

Although she still thinks Italy should not have entered the war, she says she wants to do something. She often admits she'd rather send the men a duffel bag filled with *cantucci*, her deliciously crunchy biscuits. But as she isn't permitted to send food, perhaps the next best thing would be to keep them warm.

'How is school, Clara?' Zia asks as we knit.

Her question pulls an image of Emilia's pinched face up in front of my eyes, and I drop a stitch. I huff, and make a fuss of picking it up again.

'Mmmm?' she asks wordlessly again.

'I like history and writing, and I'm getting better marks in mathematics,' I say, avoiding what I know her question to be.

'Very good,' she nods. 'And have you any friends you would like to invite over?'

'No one special,' I say, frowning at my needles. I am hoping with all my being that she does not ask exactly who it is that I visit after school. He would not be what she wishes for.

My new friend is Signor Leone. He is sixty-five years old and bald with a frizzy white beard. Since we met two weeks ago, we have spent hours together and, thanks to him, I have discovered more about our history than I have in two years at school.

We first met when I decided to walk home past the university after school one day. The buildings are all constructed of faded orange brick, old and resolute, the students and professors nestled deep inside their walls like rabbits in warrens.

Looking up at the elegant frontage, I wondered how students are chosen. Can anyone apply? What does it cost? How many students are girls? I know women are permitted to study, and that there are women who lecture classes, but from the posters I see and the lessons I learn at school, I know Mussolini would rather we girls stay at home and have babies. I understand it is our noble work to repopulate our country – to create tomorrow's heroes. We must also be physically strong and love to be outdoors, dressed in plimsolls and sporting a charming glow. Perhaps Il Duce thinks we don't have the time to be educated before we put our healthy bodies to good use.

Although I have never questioned it, I find this contradiction baffling. Emilia and her friends, however, seem to understand what Il Duce requires of them. Emilia in particular, her long pale brown hair always beautifully curled, softening her angular features, cannot wait to leave school and marry whichever officer her father, an army general, chooses for her.

'Since the war began, there have been far fewer social events,' she often complains to her adoring companions, 'but Mother will no doubt organize something, and of course I shall have a new dress.'

Would I like new clothes, to wear to elegant parties, I wondered on my walk home. Perhaps.

But as I looked at the beautiful building in front of me, filled with learning, I spotted a small doorway with the word *Biblioteca* carved in the stone lintel above it. Crossing to it, I was standing outside, wondering if a child would be allowed in, when the door swung open and a serious young man carrying two large books under his arm stepped out. Pausing for a moment as he blinked in the sunshine, he noticed me. Raising questioning eyebrows, he held the door open for me.

'*Grazie,*' I nodded and, with a confidence that surprised me, I stepped into the cool entrance. Once inside I stopped and the door swung shut, leaving me lost in a temporary darkness while my eyes adjusted to the low light. Breathing in, I squeezed the red bracelet in between my fingers as I smelled cold stone, dust and musty books. It was a scent I would come to love.

As the library appeared before my eyes, I saw that it lay completely beneath the building above. Ancient steps carved from stone led down from where I stood to an open area with a single large desk in the centre. Aisles of books spread so far they disappeared into darkness.

Simple electric lights hung from the ceiling, casting an orange hue across the space. I tentatively stepped downwards, running my hand along the smooth amber stones that lined the walls. Looking down at the desk, I saw it was empty, but a clicking sound caught my attention. An elderly man was walking towards the desk holding an enormous leather-bound book under his arm. Sensing me, he stopped and looked up, and I stood still, unsure whether to carry on down the steps or turn and leave.

The old man seemed to understand my uncertainty, lifting his arm and waving me down. Yes, he smiled, you are welcome.

When I reached the bottom of the stairs, I crossed quietly to the desk, where he now sat.

'Can I help you?' the man asked. His half-spectacles sat on the bridge at the top of his large nose and he peered over them at me.

'I, I . . .' I stumbled, then fell quiet.

'This is your first time in the library,' he spoke for me.

I nodded.

'You are not a student . . .'

I shook my head.

'. . . yet,' he finished.

Shyly, I nodded.

'But you would like to explore the library. Perhaps spend some time reading here?'

I followed his eyes, which were directed behind me to the space under the stairs I'd just descended, where a short row of empty desks stood, each furnished with a small lamp.

'Yes please,' I said quietly.

'And is there anything in particular you're looking for?'

I pondered for a moment, becoming more comfortable in his company.

'History books?'

'Aha! A historian.' He stood and stepped towards the corridors of books. 'Which period? The Age of Napoleon? The Crusades? The Iron Age?'

His words meant nothing to me; I just looked at the long line of books, from ground to ceiling, overwhelmed.

'Why don't we start,' his voice dropped to a whisper, 'with the Empire?'

I nodded, confident I knew some of the subject – it was taught at school. He walked me to an aisle and chose three books off the shelves. Crossing back to the desk, he explained why these particular books were a good introduction to a broad knowledge of the period. He sat with me for a while, showing me the chapters he thought particularly worthwhile, before returning to his desk to leave me to read.

Turning the pages, I was amazed. This was not what I had learned. There was achievement and glory, but there was also civil war, assassinations, crises. It was fascinating, and when I happened to look at the clock on the wall and realized I'd been reading for over an hour, I scrambled the books together and took them back to his desk, murmuring my thanks.

'Come back whenever you wish,' he smiled at me.

I nodded, knowing I would return as soon as I could. It was a few days before I told my first lie to Zia, so desperate was I to visit the library again. I had been invited to a friend's house to study after school, I told her, and I felt nothing but guilt when I saw the delighted look on her face.

I didn't have it in my heart to tell her that I have

no friends. Emilia and her cronies sneer at me, while others in my class have their own friends and do not seem to need more. And I didn't think the Signore would approve of me visiting a university library. 'University,' I've heard him say, 'is a breeding ground for undesirable political opinions.' Libraries, I thought, were probably deemed equally dangerous.

So I invented friends to study with, social events to attend, and increased my number of after-school activities, just so that I could go to the library and enjoy its cool, calm peacefulness.

The librarian's name was Signor Leone, although he asked me to call him Saba, just as his grandchildren did. I knew that by telling me they called him this, he was warning me that he was Jewish. I had heard people, even teachers at school, speak rudely of Jews, but he was kind and friendly and I liked him. I could see no reason not to spend time with him and, with his guidance, I discovered the difference between a library and school. While teachers talk of how wars extended the Roman Empire's reach across the continent, books have taught me of Pax Romana, two centuries of peace and prosperity, society and law, architecture and art.

At school we learn of Mussolini and Hitler, Fascism and power, but I found the library filled with pictures and words of great peace and beauty. The Renaissance, with its flourish of art and science, made me wonder why a true leader of Italy would want to align us with the harsh words and straight lines of the German creed.

History books showed me that ours was a country of elegance and ideas. I followed Saba's bony finger as it traced the outline of a flying machine designed by

Leonardo da Vinci, and peered at pictures of the pointed striped dome of the cathedral at Florence. I read of how ballet was first performed in Venice, and dreamed of one day going to see a performance for myself.

'When you have understood what it is to be Italian,' Saba Leone said, 'then we'll turn to the rest of the world. I have a feeling you are going to like Shakespeare . . .'

I had no idea what Shakespeare was, but I adored it anyway.

Up and through. Over and stitch. I feel Zia's eyes on me, but I concentrate on the dark blue yarn.

It takes another week of intense evenings knitting before Zia shows me how to finish the scarf, by sewing some short woollen tassels on each end. Both she and Filomena admire it, and even the Signore tries it on for size and approves it for use by our soldiers.

Over breakfast, Filomena produces a small cotton bag containing three black balaclavas. Zia fetches two pairs of grey socks she has made and I add my blue scarf, carefully rolling it and putting it into the bag.

While Filomena tidies away our breakfast dishes, Zia kisses the top of my head as she always does, and wishes me a good day. I swing my satchel over my shoulder and pick up the bag of knitted accessories as I call out my goodbyes and leave for school.

As I walk along the pavement, I realize I feel almost happy. Yet whenever I notice a slight spring in my step, a lighter sense to my core, I think of Pippo and Mamma, and a stab of guilt punctures my good spirits. A tinge of blue falls over my thoughts, however pleasant, and sadness settles again in my stomach.

I think of Pippo every day; the old woman's words still echo in my head: 'You *will* see him, Clara.' I try not to think of the fact that she did not say I would see my mother — only that she was alive.

Every trip I take out of the house, I flick an imaginary switch, opening my mental airways to Pippo. Like Zia tuning the large wooden radio that sits by her armchair, there is constant subdued static, but instinctively I search for the sound of him.

I know that, like last time, when he is near I will feel rather than hear him, that his personal electricity will make my skin tingle and my heart flutter. The static will suddenly clear and I will hear his laugh, his voice, his sound.

But until I am reunited with either him or my mother, I turn my mind to a simple daydream. If I feel lonely, or when time seems to drag, I imagine a place where I am completely content. Over time, the dream has developed, tweaked and perfected until I cannot improve it. And now, as I walk along the busy pavement, I take myself there.

In my mind, I am an adult. I am alone, but I know my mother and brother are near. I sit in a comfortable chair by a window. Outside, dazzling red and orange flowers sway in the garden below, and beyond a small wall lies a field of wheat which the wind sweeps through, creating gentle golden waves.

And all I have to do, each and every day, is read books. Today, in my mind, an ancient reference book lies in front of me and I carefully turn each thin page, learning something new, gasping at a fact or marvelling at an invention.

I am still dreaming of my peaceful, learning existence when I arrive at school. A sense of dread falls over me as I walk through the tall grey gates. Children dash and shout, play and sing, but I make my way to the main entrance and wait for the first bell to ring.

I pass a group of girls and notice they all have bags of knitting too. Today is one of the days the military support officers will come to collect whatever has been made for the men. Suddenly, from behind me a sneering voice says, 'Let's see what Cacca Clara has made for our gallant boys,' and my bag is plucked from my hand.

The nickname has stuck with me since my first day, when the teacher asked my name. Suddenly struck as I occasionally am by a stammer, I struggled to say my name. Since then, the more vicious girls in my class have copied me, putting their emphasis on the vulgar *cacca*.

I turn to see Emilia yank open my bag and begin pulling out the knitted items.

'Stop!' I say, although not loudly, as I see her fling Zia's socks over her head. Her followers laugh in mean snorts as she digs in the bag and tugs out one of Filomena's balaclavas.

'Not bad,' she says, before noticing the embroidered word. '*Coraggio?*' she asks. 'Any boy would certainly need that before getting too close to you, eh?'

'*Mangi cadaveri*,' one of her cronies throws at me, to squeals of laughter from the others.

I don't know how any of them know if I have bad breath — from eating dead bodies, as the slang goes — none of them has ever been close enough to me to smell my breath.

'Of course, some of us have people to do menial work like this,' Emilia says with a jeer. 'Mother and I certainly wouldn't knit things. Anyway, Papa says the soldiers have more than they need and that they dine like the King every night. Not that urchins like her' — she juts her sharp chin in my direction — 'would know anything about it.'

Pressing the red wristband between my thumb and fingers hard, I wait for the teasing to end so I can gather my things and escape until the school doors open. But Emilia is not finished yet.

'Ah . . .' she says with glee. 'This, I believe, is what you've made.' Pinching it distastefully with her thumb and forefinger, she drags the blue woollen scarf out of the bag and my heart sinks. Misshapen and uneven, for the first time I see it as a soldier would see it. She is entitled to torment me for the ugly creation.

But then I remember the pride in Zia's eyes as I knitted the final row, and I feel an anger rise in me — not for the hours of work I have put into the scarf, but for the kind woman who has done nothing but care for me and support me, ever patient with my unskilled knitting. While I do not, she deserves better.

'Give that to me,' I say, quietly but with a menace that surprises even me.

Emilia stops waving the scarf above her head and looks me in the eye.

'What did you say, Cacca Clara?'

'Give that to me,' I repeat slowly, holding out my hand. I feel heat rise from my throat to my face and I focus my ire as I stare into her eyes. For the tiniest moment, I see fear flash across her face, and I wonder what it is that frightens her.

'Catch,' she says, and throws the scarf onto the high railings that border the school. Just at that moment, a bell rings and the girls turn and run to the main entrance, leaving me to gather my knitted pieces and, standing on tiptoes, unhook the scarf from the top of the pointed metal post.

By the time I reach my classroom, I am a few minutes late, but I manage to sneak to my seat without our teacher noticing. She is admiring a khaki green jumper that Emilia is holding out to her. 'Yes, Signora, it was all my own work,' she smiles serenely.

'I hope you have all made items of such high quality for our brave soldiers,' the teacher says to the class. 'Now, everyone, put them in your bags and leave them on the hooks outside. A member of the services will be coming later to collect them.'

We file outside to hang bags and sacks on our named hooks with our hats, then return to the classroom and our seats.

The warm day seems to drag, with one lesson after another filled with facts and information that I either know already or question its validity. Since I have spent time with Saba Leone, I am beginning to wonder if our textbooks have been written with truth in mind, or propaganda. It is not a question I can ask at home: the Signore will countenance nothing other than devotion for Il Duce.

I am wondering if this is a query I can put to my new friend, as we whisper our conversations in the gloomy light of the library, when the teacher claps briskly and we all stand.

Two officers, smart in their uniforms, enter the room. One of them carries a large box which he places on the table and opens. It is empty.

'Children,' says our teacher, 'these gentlemen are here to collect all that we have produced for our brave fighters. Go and get your contributions and bring them here.'

We follow her instruction silently, and form a long line along the edge of the classroom. As each student places their knitted handiwork into the large box, they send a prayer of good luck to the serviceman who will wear it. I decide I will pray that my scarf reaches someone who can see past how it looks and at least find a little warmth in it.

Suddenly, there is a wail from the front of the room. I know before I lift up my head that the noise comes from Emilia.

'It's gone, Signora,' she cries, pulling her bag inside out to demonstrate.

'The sweater?' asks the teacher.

'Yes. It was in here, you saw it.'

'Does anyone know where it is?'

No one answers. The soldiers look on, disinterested in the drama.

'Has anyone seen Emilia's green sweater?' asks the teacher again.

'Signora,' Giorgia raises her hand. She is one of Emilia's most loyal supporters. 'I saw Clara with the sweater.'

'Really?' The Signora looks at where I stand further back in the queue.

No, I shake my head, unable to speak.

'Clara did tell me that she wished she had made it, Signora,' says Emilia. Her voice has a sickly sweetness to it. 'I said I was sure her knitting was very good as well, but she said she was too embarrassed to send what she had done to the soldiers.'

'Is this true?' our teacher demands.

No. I shake my head again, confused by the lies.

'Come here, Clara,' says the Signora, and I approach her desk.

Emilia stands just behind our teacher and the smirk on her face makes my stomach tighten.

'Empty your bag,' instructs the Signora.

I put my bag on the table next to the box and pull out the balaclavas. Next are the socks, and there at the bottom is a khaki green sweater. Gently, I lift it up and hear a roomful of students gasp.

'Signora, I—'

Our teacher raises her hand to stop me from talking and, looking at me with narrow eyes, she points to the door.

I carefully place the balaclavas and socks in the soldiers' box, then hand the sweater to Emilia, who takes it graciously, before heading to the door to stand outside. I know, when the soldiers have left and my fellow students are at work, the Signora will come outside to discuss my punishment.

As I stand, fearful of what the teacher will say, horrified at the thought of Zia being called to school, I think of my scarf. It was not in the bag. I know I put it there; I remember rolling it carefully and tucking it down the side after rescuing it from the railings.

Blinking, I turn right to the hooks where our hats and school bags hang. Taking a step towards it, I see my leather satchel hanging open. Another step closer and I see a small length of blue wool. The tassels of my scarf, I think, relieved that I can still donate it to the military.

But when I reach into my satchel to take the scarf out, my fingers wrap around yarn. Lifting my hand, I see it is nothing but a length of dark blue wool, the kinks where knitted stitches once were still visible.

PIPPO

1940

A Message from Churchill

Far away in the distance was a black shape. Pippo squinted and turned his head, trying to see what it was. It moved, and he knew instantly it was a person; a tall, lean figure dressed in dark clothes.

But he couldn't see who it was. He had the feeling he should know, so he kept peering at it. People buzzed around noisily, trying to distract him, but he kept his focus on the shadowy silhouette.

As he watched, he saw the person walking — walking very slowly, but yes, he thought, they were definitely walking towards him. The crowds became louder, shouting and waving their arms, obscuring his view. '*Va vai!*' shouted Pippo to the throng that nudged and pushed him. 'Get lost!' But it seemed the bodies just jostled him more. He shifted this way and that, standing on his tiptoes to see the figure and, when he finally did, he saw it was closer, much closer, still walking slowly but steadily.

A light shone down on the figure to reveal long black hair and eyes that glowed like amber, and instantly he knew who it was.

'Mamma,' he breathed. Then: 'Mamma, Mamma, MAMMA!' he shouted as he starting to run towards her, feeling his heart tight in his chest. But with every step he took, the mass of people pushed him back. He tried to grab them and shove them away, but it felt as though his arms just flailed through the air, never touching them.

'Mamma!' he shouted over and over. He knew that she was walking towards him, but so painfully slowly he thought she might never reach him. He could see her clearly now, her long, glossy hair, her golden eyes soft and warm, her lips set in a smile meant for him alone.

She was walking towards him but he could get no closer to her. He called to her but she couldn't hear him. Time and again he reached for her, tried to shout for her, run to her, but to no avail. His breath quickened in panic. He wanted to fall into her arms, hold her, kiss her, to never let her go – if only he could reach her.

Then, he saw her open her mouth and speak. He thought he wouldn't be able to hear her – he couldn't even hear himself shouting – but there, there it was, her voice speaking quietly, as if she were whispering into his ear.

'Wait for me.'

A sense of calmness flooded over him, instantly releasing the frustration and fear. Blackness invaded his sight and, with a long deep breath, he opened his eyes.

A small face peered anxiously at him. Gino, with his mother's gentle features, sat at the end of the bed and looked at him, concerned.

'You did shouting,' he said quietly. 'Mamma. Mamma. And waving your arms . . .'

'Forget it,' said Pippo, sitting up and turning his back to the boy.

Gino sat very still, trying not to shiver in the cold draught as he watched the older boy run his hands through his cropped hair and rub his eyes, pulling himself into wakefulness.

Wait for me.

Pippo could still hear the words. It was just a dream, he told himself. It meant nothing. But the words stayed with him. As he pulled on his clothes and helped the younger boy get dressed, he heard them again and again, his mother whispering them quietly in his ear. And he let them stay, let the feeling of calm they created soothe him as he followed Gino out of the bedroom, let his mother's intent lie in his heart. Because whether it was a dream, or if she had found some way to speak to him, he knew that if she could find a way to do it, she would make her way back to him. All he had to do was wait.

Gino climbed onto a chair at the table while Pippo poured some milk into a pan, adding some water as Donna had told him to. He watched as the small boy pulled a wooden board towards himself and carefully picked up a knife. Slowly, he sawed an uneven slice of bread from the flat loaf, and then another.

Pippo nodded to Gino when he turned to him, poured the warm watery milk into a small cup and passed it to the little boy. Then he tipped what was left into another chipped cup for himself and sat down at the table.

The two ate and drank silently, Pippo listening for the now fading words in his ears, Gino watching the bigger boy intently. When they had finished their break-fast, Pippo rinsed their cups in a bucket of water, and was just running his hands over his hair to dampen it down when he saw a piece of paper wedged behind a glass on the shelf beside him.

Gently pulling it down, he unfolded it and looked at the formal script. His reading was slow, but he knew enough to recognize the words.

The door banged open and Donna bustled in, carrying Violetta with one arm and a small bag of food with the other.

'Every day the money buys less,' she said to the boys, putting the bag on the table and pulling her woollen shawl from around her shoulders. 'And every day there is less to buy. The shops are bare, I don't . . .' She stopped when she saw the letter in Pippo's hands.

'It's come,' he said simply.

'Yes,' she said with a sigh. 'We knew it would.'

'What is it, Mamma?' asked Gino.

'Nothing to worry about, Mouse,' she said, stroking his hair.

'Where is Mario?' Pippo wanted to know. Perhaps he had left already. Many of his friends' fathers and uncles had received their conscription papers, and some had been given less than a week to report for duty.

'He's gone to see . . .' Her eyes darted to Gino, who watched her intently, 'Someone. About that letter.'

'Bruno? Was it Bruno? Or Mattia? Or, or . . .'

Donna shook her head, but said nothing. She didn't want to talk about it in front of Gino. She dropped the baby gently into Gino's lap and started putting the meagre shopping in the cupboard.

'Can he get out of it?' asked Pippo, dropping his voice as he watched the little boy play with the baby.

Again, Donna shook her head. 'Not without paying. We barely have enough to feed ourselves, so that kind of money . . . it's impossible.'

'Could we borrow it?' said Pippo, his mind racing through the secret comrades in the party. 'We could talk to—'

'No,' Donna interrupted sharply. 'That's not our way.'

Pippo knew it. Mario and Donna believed in doing what you could for others, but asking nothing in return. If someone needed their help, they helped. They did it for love and for humanity, not out of expectation.

At times, it frustrated him. He'd watch his friends and their families collect favours like sweets in a jar, to be called in when their need arose. It's just our way, he heard regularly, but it was not his adopted family's way.

'So, what then?' he asked. 'We must do something. He can't . . . we can't . . .'

Donna straightened her back and put her hands on her hips. 'We wait. We see what happens. We carry on living, hoping that things will get better.'

Pippo looked at her face. He could see a shadow behind her bold stance. Was it fear? She was a strong woman, but her chosen path meant she had always needed to be so. She had married Mario against her father's wishes. She had moved to a new city with her husband just months before he left to fight in Spain. She had gone to meetings with him, read books about politics, even hidden comrades in her home — all for the love of her man and their shared principles.

Pippo thought of what she had done for him. He wondered how many people would have stopped to help a small boy. And, when his family couldn't be found, would have made him a home, given him a family.

For a moment, Pippo wanted to tell Donna of his dream. The words were on the tip of his tongue — *She told me to wait for her. My mamma is coming for me.* And he knew that this woman who had been his substitute mother for years would want it to be true. She always insisted he call her Donna, corrected people when they assumed she was his mother — not because she didn't want to be, but to let everyone know that he had his own mamma. She was just doing the job until Pippo's mother could do it herself.

Chirpy whistling filled the air, and Gino and Violetta lifted their heads from a game they were playing with a small box of buttons.

'Papa!' shouted Gino before Mario had even opened the door.

Donna and Pippo turned to watch the smiling man with the black beard walk into the room.

'Treats!' he grinned to everyone, lifting a small paper bag.

'Me, me, me!' called Gino, jumping up and reaching for the surprise. Mario leaned over him and held the bag in front of him.

'We believe in common ownership, Gino,' he stated sternly. When his son looked up at him with a perplexed look on his face, he said gently, 'Share, Mouse, share. They're for everyone.'

The boy nodded seriously and, taking the bag from his father, peered into it.

'Nuts!' he squealed with delight, sticking a hand in and pulling out a small fistful.

'Here, Mamma,' he said, dropping a few into Donna's open hand.

'Pippo.' He turned and dropped a few more into the older boy's hand.

'Papa,' he said proudly, releasing a few more of the precious nuts.

'Violetta . . .'

'Not for this little one,' said Donna, whisking the baby girl into her arms. With one hand she pulled the shell off a nut and bit into the small green kernel inside. Taking a piece from her lips, she popped it into the child's mouth and laughed as Violetta gummed it ferociously.

'What are they?' asked Pippo, turning a shelled nut in his fingers. The green colour looked both unnatural and familiar.

'Pistachios,' said Mario happily.

'Like the *gelato*,' said Pippo, wondering how long it had been since they'd had ice cream.

'Pistachios,' said Donna, chewing hers thoughtfully. 'From Sicily?'

Pippo saw Mario look at his wife, and sensed a moment between them as he slowly nodded to her.

The men and women huddled closer, both to fend off the cold of the stone-walled cellar and to try to read the papers Bruno held.

Pippo hopped from leg to leg, trying to get a peek of the worn pages, but even though he squirmed in beside Mario, he couldn't see.

'What does it say, Mario?' he pleaded. 'Tell me, please?'

'Shhh,' hushed the man, 'I'm reading.'

'He's right,' said Bruno, tapping a finger at the paper. 'We've always been friends with them.'

'With who? Friends with who, Bruno?'

The man ignored the boy.

'No lust for war,' said a woman, finishing one page and passing it on. 'That's true. This man knows us better than our own leader.'

'Who? Who knows us?'

Mario turned to Pippo. 'This,' he told him, pointing to the papers, 'is a speech. It was made by the prime minister of *Inghilterra*.'

'He speaks Italian?' said Pippo, surprised.

'No. It's been translated.'

'What does he say?'

'He is talking to us, the Italian people. He's saying that we've always been friends — the Italians and the British. In the last war, we fought on the same side — against the Germans.'

'Did we?'

'Yes. And many *Inglese* joined our struggle in Spain. I trained with one; a good man. But now, Churchill says, we are at war with each other. He says his armies will destroy ours.'

'But they won't,' Pippo stated. 'Will they?'

'They might,' Bruno said.

'Does he want to gloat? Does he want to defeat us with his words? He won't do it. He—'

'No, Pippo,' said Mario gently. 'He's blaming Mussolini. He's saying he knows that we, the people of

Italy, do not want this war. We don't want to be on Germany's side. Mussolini does, but we, the people, don't. Here, at the end' — Mario pointed at the last page — 'he says only we can do something about it.'

'Like what?'

'That's what we're talking about.'

'So what *are* we going to do?' asked the boy.

'I think the first thing to do is to find a way of contacting the English. Perhaps they have a plan.'

'But they're the enemy.'

'That depends whose side you are on,' said Bruno, collecting the papers and folding them carefully. 'Time to go, everyone,' he told the group.

Pippo looked around. The Communist meetings had changed since he first came. The numbers had dwindled as the authorities had cracked down on anyone suspected of opposition. Some party members had been arrested; others had disappeared, leaving friends and family wondering if they'd been taken by the Blackshirts or had escaped into the night to find a new life elsewhere. He trusted Mario and Bruno to keep him safe, but he knew others came despite their fear.

The number of men in the group had fallen since conscription had begun in earnest, too. And there were fewer women; struggles with less money and food meant there was little time for ideology.

The location for the meetings also moved regularly. Tonight they had gathered in the cellar of an empty shop. Wooden boxes lay broken and rotting around them and a single bare bulb hung from the ceiling.

Shaking hands and kissing, the men and women

wished each other good luck as they took their turn to climb the stone steps into the dark shop above and sneak out through the back door, keenly watching for police lurking in the shadows.

As they waited their turn, Pippo strained to listen to Mario's whispered conversation with Bruno.

'When are you leaving?' the curly haired man asked Mario.

'Soon. It's all arranged.'

'They've helped you?'

'A little. Contacts mainly.'

Pippo knew they were talking about Mario's departure. He and Donna had sat down with Pippo the previous evening to explain. Mario had been told to report to the Regio Esercito offices two days after Christmas. With his known political history, he would be sent to the most dangerous war zones – Russia, most likely.

'I cannot do it,' Mario had said, shaking his head. 'I cannot fight for something I do not believe. And I cannot endanger the lives of my fellow soldiers by acting stupidly. Donna and I both believe the right thing for me to do is to leave.'

'Go where? And when? And how—'

'One question at a time, sparrow,' Donna had laughed. Pippo could see the worry on her face, but he knew she would do all she could to make Mario's leaving easier for the children.

'It's better if no one knows where I am going,' Mario had said.

'Not even Donna?'

'Not even Donna. It's too dangerous. And I will be going soon.'

'Will you say goodbye?' Pippo had felt his voice waver and tears start to rise. Annoyed, he'd ground his teeth and fiddled with his red wristband.

Mario had put his large hand on the boy's shoulder. He'd understood more than Pippo did how much his mother's disappearance still affected him. 'I will say goodbye,' he'd said earnestly.

Since then, the boy had begun to piece together the secret of Mario's departure. The pistachios were from Don Orlando, the man in the suit who lived at the expensive house. Everyone knew, but no one ever mentioned, that he was connected to the mafia. The green nuts came from Sicily, the home of the mafia, and he always seemed to have plenty to share with those he granted favours for. But he was no Communist. In fact, he was seen meeting government officials more than anyone else. There was certainly no question of that man going into the army – he was too busy making the city run smoothly.

Pippo realized that although Mario didn't want to ask for help, Don Orlando had offered it. And if anyone could help a man disappear, it was him.

Listening now to the conversation with Bruno, he understood what Mario was saying. Don Orlando had connected him with people who would help him become someone else. Just as the Ferraris had been given new papers with new names, so too would Mario. Someone who couldn't be called up to fight. But also someone who couldn't return to his old home. As long as the war continued, he would have to remain disappeared.

'However you do it, it's desertion, Mario.'

'I know. I understand. But hell, Bruno, we could be

shot for meeting here. I'm going. And maybe it will be me who connects with the *Inglesi*. Maybe I'll be a spy for them. Maybe I'll help them destroy that lunatic – before he destroys our country.'

'*Buona fortuna*, Mario,' said Bruno, gripping his friend's left arm and pulling him into his body for an embrace.

'At the end of this madness, we'll meet again, Bruno,' said Mario gruffly, 'I know it. I will come back, wait and see.'

His words brought a memory back to Pippo. The memory of a dream, lost now, but words that had stayed with him.

Wait for me.

CLARA

1942

The Bus Journey

The gift is wrapped in white tissue tied with a fine green ribbon. It is small and light, long and cylindrical. I look at Zia quizzically and she grins in reply.

Gently, I slide the ribbon down and unroll the tissue, revealing a gold tube. For a sickening moment, I think it is a bullet. But as I turn it in my hand, I realize it is a lipstick. Easing the lid off, I turn the base and the lipstick appears, a soft pink, the colour of a pale rose.

'Mine?' I ask her quietly.

'Of course,' she smiles. 'I thought fourteen was the perfect age for your first lipstick. Now,' she says, gently turning me to the right, towards the mirror hanging on the wall beside us, 'let's see it on.'

I bring the lipstick to my mouth and ever so slowly start to apply it, copying what I have seen Zia do countless times.

'That's right,' she nods, pursing her lips in unison with me, 'and then rub them together like so.'

I gaze at my image in the mirror and see how the pink brings out the blush of my cheeks.

'I thought as much!' exclaims Zia, an expression of delight on her face. 'Rose is your colour. With this beautiful dark hair,' she twists a curl in her finger, 'and such stunning eyes, anything stronger would look wrong. And red,' she puckers her own scarlet lips, 'is far too adult.'

'Thank you,' I say, reaching to give her cheek a kiss, but stopping just shy as I have seen her do, to avoid leaving a mark of colour.

'My pleasure,' she says, stroking my face lightly.

I smile. Zia gives me her big, open-mouthed grin in return, and I know she is pleased with her gift.

I look at my face in the mirror again. My forehead is high, framed by curtains of dark hair which I wear tucked behind my ears. My nose is long and straight – Roman, the Signore calls it. And my eyes, which Filomena says are the colour of golden syrup, full of silken light, are large and round.

Perhaps it's my age, or perhaps because I want to please Zia, I have begun to pay more attention to my looks than I have before. Instead of letting my hair curl as it wishes, I wrap it in rags overnight to give myself perfect ringlets. Instead of biting my nails, I let Zia shape them with her nail file, and on occasion have even let her paint them with a clear varnish. I find myself interested when Zia points to a photo of an American movie star in her magazine and explains how her dress would suit my colouring.

Or maybe, like so many others, I am looking for a distraction. Something, anything, that will help me escape the war and the suffering that surrounds us. We, and the people we know, have been lucky – certainly until recently. From listening to Filomena, food has been harder to find, even if your pocket is full of money as hers is.

The less fortunate are truly struggling. On my way to school, I often see women, babies crying on their hip, queuing outside bakeries. The butchers have had empty windows for months now, and the fruit and vegetable carts carry a pittance. A poster that hangs on a street corner on my way to school shows a photo of soldiers beside a large gun and asks, 'Butter or cannons?' Yesterday morning I saw that someone had painted the word *Burro!* over the top. Who wouldn't prefer butter, I thought. In the afternoon the poster was gone, quickly removed by the authorities.

Filomena grows what she can – as well as her herbs, now tomatoes, spinach and courgettes flourish in pots outside the kitchen. These days she substitutes pasta with rice, meat with tinned fish, and creates new dishes from oats, beans and stale bread. She tuts at the articles I show her that explain how to make mayonnaise without oil and omelettes without eggs. I know that she misses good olive oil as the children miss sweets.

'Now,' says Zia, opening my bedroom door, 'let's go downstairs. Filomena has a special surprise for your breakfast.'

I carefully place the precious lipstick on my dressing table, seeing a fleeting image of my mother's meagre possessions packed into a small bag. I haven't had a memory like this of my mother or Pippo for a while, and it makes me stop for a moment, feeling both the pain of missing them and the guilt of forgetting them.

Taking a deep breath, I turn my pink lips into what

I hope is a serene smile, and dash down the two flights to the kitchen. There, Filomena has placed herself proudly in front of the table. Zia stands beside her, hands clasped in anticipation of my reaction. With a fleeting glance between them, Filomena moves her large body to one side to reveal a plate. On it, carefully placed, are two pieces of toasted bread, butter scraped thinly across it. Nestled safely between them lies a small, brown, perfectly smooth egg.

'An egg?' I ask. 'For me?'

Filomena nods proudly, as if she herself has laid it.

'Yes, beautiful,' says Zia. 'Last night, after you had gone to bed, the Signore came home with a chicken. We're going to keep it in the yard. We didn't know if it would lay, but this morning Filomena found this in its cage.' She points at the egg.

'Our own eggs,' I marvel, before a frown crosses my brow. 'For breakfast?'

Zia laughs. 'I saw it in a magazine once – in America, this is what they have all the time.'

I pull out the chair and sit down in front of the plate of food – the most marvellous start to the day I can imagine. The Signore, I note, is not here; presumably he left for work early, as he does often these days.

'We'll share it,' I say, picking up the knife to tap the shell.

'No,' they reply in unison, shaking their heads.

'There will be more eggs,' says Filomena, sitting down to watch me eat.

Self-consciously, I begin peeling the brown shell off the egg until the white is half uncovered. Unable to wait longer, I pick it up and bite the top end of the egg, but to my surprise, the yolk is still runny and it bursts into my mouth, a sticky line dribbling down my chin.

Laughing at my shocked face, Zia says, 'It's how they eat it in America! Look here, you take your bread and soak up the yolk.' She picks up the toast and presses into the bright orange centre of the egg I hold. With my other hand, I accept the bread when she offers it and sink my teeth into the crunchy toast, partly soaked in the yolk.

Regardless of how they eat on the other side of the world, I think this must be the most delicious egg I have ever tasted. I close my eyes and savour the smooth, rich flavour. The chicken outside the back door must be a very happy animal to have produced such a wonderful egg.

I can still taste the sticky yolk on my tongue as I bounce uncomfortably on the speeding bus. Despite my silence on the matter, Zia discovered that school was becoming more and more difficult for me.

At first it was just Emilia and her friends, rude words and small acts of unkindness directed at me. While I had never made friends with any of the other children, they had at least treated me with civility initially — as an outsider but a benign creature. When the war began in earnest, though, there was a fear of all things different. And I was definitely seen as different. Gradually, too, Emilia's influence spread and boys began to call me vulgar names; girls would bump into me, causing me to drop my books. One day, I sat at my desk to see the word *Stronzo* scratched into the wood. Turd. I tried to cover it with my books, but the teacher saw it. She looked at me with surprise, but said nothing.

Two days later, Zia accompanied me to school. She and I sat in the administrator's office, listening to a woman with permanently pursed lips explain why the establishment believed I was not a suitable student.

'But her marks,' interrupted Zia.

'Satisfactory,' came the curt reply.

'Then what? I don't—'

'It is a matter of character. The other students do not like or respect her. They, along with her teachers, believe she does not truly follow the doctrine of this school.'

I turned to Zia, wanting to explain that the woman sitting opposite with a face as starched as her white shirt was right. I did not fit in. In my first years, I had listened to the Fascist teachings, believing every word and supporting our hero leader. But as I'd read with Saba Leone, I'd come to realize that it was not what I thought. Fascism was as cruel and unkind as the girls in my class. It bullied and frightened. It made people follow out of fear — not admiration.

And I wanted to say that the more I came to know him, the more I could see that the Signore was no longer the devotee of Il Duce he had once been. I saw the fear in his eyes. Fear of losing his job. Fear of being denounced. Fear of his fear being discovered.

I felt above my fellow students, safe in my belief that I was better educated than them simply because I had read more widely. But in dangerous times, I had decided the only thing I could do was to try to become invisible. No matter how I kept to myself, though, Emilia and the others wouldn't leave me alone.

Presented with evidence of my difference, Zia's face became etched with confusion and distress. The Signore would be angry – this was one of his conditions for me continuing to live with them, and to be expelled would look bad for him.

As the two women discussed me, my mind raced. I should leave. Leave the house so the Signore would not be disgraced. If he didn't ask me to go first. Would he? Over the past few years we had become, if not friends, then comfortable acquaintances, finding common ground whenever we could for the sake of the woman we both loved. Where would I go if he asked me to leave? I realized I'd become accustomed to the comfort. The young child who had tried to sneak out on the day I'd arrived at the house would probably have fared better on the streets than the young girl used to a soft bed in a safe home.

But as I watched her, Zia's beautifully shaped eyebrows dropped, then narrowed.

'I believe you're right,' she said, an edge of steel in her voice. 'Your establishment does not suit Clara. She is intelligent and resolute, and those, I think you'll find, are true Fascist traits. "Better to live one day as a lion than a hundred years as a sheep" – that's what the sign outside says. Well, this girl has the heart of a lion. She has seen more and experienced more than any of the children in this school. And she has learned more reading the books on our shelves than she ever did in your classrooms. You are not creating lions here, you are churning out sheep. Sheep who will do nothing but follow the sheep at the front.'

The woman pursed her lips even tighter and sucked in air, clearly about to berate Zia. But Zia continued before there was time.

'I shall be reporting you and this school to my husband. He is responsible for the funding of key establishments in this city, and I am sure he will be interested in the way a clever student such as Clara has been treated.'

The woman's pinched face contorted with surprise. 'Signora,' she stammered, 'I'm sure—'

'Come on, Clara,' Zia said, standing, 'we'll find a school that understands what true Fascism means.'

I stood and together we left the woman's office.

Outside, Zia pulled me into an embrace. 'I'm sorry,' she whispered into my hair.

'But the Signore . . .'

'Don't worry about him,' she said, stroking my hair.

Within days a new school had been found and I was enrolled. It was further — a bus journey away — but I instantly felt more comfortable there. My teacher, a woman with a kind face, pointed to a girl with short curly hair and a gap in her front teeth, and told me to sit next to her.

'Hello,' the girl said quietly, and I noticed she had a bit of a lisp. 'What beautiful eyes you have.'

Touched by her warm words, I turned to her and gave her a smile.

'I'm Clara,' I said, not a trace of a stammer to be heard.

Now, as the bus bumps along, I think about the lipstick and wonder when I will be able to wear it. There are few parties these days. No one seems to want to celebrate, not while news of bombings across the country shouts from our radios and newspapers. And no one would be able to provide enough food for a party. Although, I think, with our new chicken, perhaps Filomena would be able to make some sort of cake. But where would she find the sugar and butter . . .

Suddenly, I hear him. Far away, I hear laughter that jingles through the air. The sound disappears as quickly as it arrived, but a tingle flutters in my chest and spreads through my body, and I know I am close to my brother.

I feel more sensitive to sounds and scents, and my eyes seem sharper as I scan the bus. I am sure he cannot be on board, but he feels so close I have to check.

My scrutiny turns to the window and I look out at the bustling street. The pavement is filled with people rushing to work and school, but I examine as many faces as I can while we rumble past. I know he won't be the little boy I last saw four years ago. He will now be older than I was then. Surely I will know my own flesh and blood when I see him, though. Could that be him? No, too fair. And that? No, those are not his eyes. I keep searching, squeezing the red band on my wrist with anxiety.

The tingling intensifies and my fists involuntarily clench.

And there he is.

A boy. Bigger, of course, hair cropped short, his face dirty, his clothes ragged, but something jumps in my chest and all my body tells me it is Pippo.

'Stop!' I shout with all my might. But the bus is full and everyone is chatting loudly. I pick my satchel up and pull it onto my shoulder as I clamber over the person sitting next to me, heading for the door. Pippo was running fast in the other direction, and if

I don't get off the bus soon, I won't be able to catch him up.

'Stop!' I shout again, pushing past some more people. A man beside me notices and calls out to the driver, but he still doesn't hear and the bus lumbers on. A wave of anguish washes over me as I feel the distance between Pippo and me grow impossibly far.

Then I hear a woman shout, 'Stop – someone has to get off.'

And then a man closer to the front calls, 'Driver! Stop!'

I hear brakes hum and the bus lurches, then slows. With renewed energy, I squeeze through the people beside me, muttering, '*Scusi . . . Permesso . . . Scusi.*'

Lifting my head, I see the other passengers pulling themselves apart to create a path for me. I dash through the gap and call my thanks to them and the driver as I stumble down the steps onto the pavement. Immediately, I begin to run. The street is busy and I weave around the people as best I can, trying to catch up with my brother before he is lost.

Pippo, I think. It's Pippo. Over and over his name repeats in my head. My leg scratches against someone's bag, my lungs begin to feel tight, but I keep on running as fast as I can.

Pippo. My little brother, Pippo. I see a gap in a group of people ahead and duck through it, finding myself on the edge of the road as a car rips past at speed. I skitter along the gutter, leaning away from the next car as it passes, gasping for breath as I do.

As I search for a way back onto the pavement, a break in the walking people, I try to sense the tingling in my chest — perhaps it will tell me if I am close, or if I should give up. I can feel nothing but my heart racing, can hear nothing but my own panting. I look up, close to despair. And there he is. The back of his head. I see his bristly brown hair as he runs along the edge of the pavement some distance ahead of me, a large parcel wrapped in brown paper under his arm.

He turns his head to check the traffic, and I know it is him. It is my brother. My beautiful brother. As he dashes across the road, weaving between cars, I turn to follow him — if I am fast I can catch him. I draw breath to shout his name, but instead all that comes out of my mouth is air. Confused, I wonder why I have stopped running, why the road has changed angle, why I see a bicycle wheel. Then there is a flash of blue sky before I hear a deep thud that presses out the light.

The pain appears first. A metal rod of heat pushing from the back through the centre of my head. I keep my eyes tightly shut until it starts to abate. As it fades to nearly bearable, I squint my eyes open, but the bright white light seems to hurt almost as much as my head and I snap them shut again.

'Can you open your eyes?' a gentle voice asks, quiet over the hubbub that suddenly seems to surround me.

I try to do as the voice suggests. I attempt my right eye first. The light doesn't seem quite so intense with just one eye, but my vision is hazy and blurred. I open my left eye, in the hope that it will help to clarify things. Slowly, the white seems to regress and other colours come to the fore — greys and blues and browns.

'She's awake,' I hear someone say. An old woman is

speaking. It is not the gentle voice I heard before. I want to see who spoke first and peer, moving only my eyes, around me.

The coloured shapes begin to morph into people, and I see that they are leaning over me as I lie on the ground. A thought occurs to me — modesty urges me to check my skirt has not ridden up and I reach a hand down. The movement sends a sharp stab into the centre of my head again, but the relief that I am not exposed is almost worth it.

Suddenly, I remember my brother. 'Pip . . .' I gasp, but as I sit bolt upright my vision swims and I feel my body fall from under me.

'Whoa,' says the gentle voice, and firm hands grasp my shoulders and lower them slowly to the ground. 'Take your time,' it says, 'you hit your head on the pavement.'

I obey the voice, knowing I would be unable to run after Pippo in this condition.

As I open my eyes again, I see a young man leaning over me, concern lined around his eyes. Is he a man or a boy? Perhaps he is in fact closer to my age, but his face gives the impression of someone who has seen more of life than I have. However old he is, it is a handsome face. His hair is swept back, as though his fingers have just been run through it, and his dark eyes twinkle despite the bright sunshine.

'What happened?' I ask, ignoring the others who lean over me.

'You were about to run in front of a car. I grabbed you to stop you, but then a bicycle ran into the two of us.'

He lifts his arm and turns his elbow towards me, where spots of blood lie on a wide, red graze.

'I'm sorry,' I mumble, 'and thank you.'

The boy-man shakes his head and smiles. 'It's nothing,' he says, before worry clouds his face again. 'How is your head? You fell against the pavement.'

Lifting my head, I reach my hand to where the pain is worst and gently stroke a swelling. Wincing, I pull my hand away and inspect it.

'It's not bleeding,' confirms the young man, as I notice the small crowd I have drawn drifting away.

I try to move slowly and he helps me sit up. When the dizziness starts to fade, I look at him and attempt a smile. It hurts so I let it drop. And as I do I think of Pippo — long gone by now. The old woman with the blue eye said he was near and she was right. But did she know if I would ever be with him again? I force myself not to think of my brother now, of how close I was to him; if I do, I fear the tears will overwhelm me and I may never recover.

'Do you want me to take you home?'

Distracted, I turn to my rescuer. 'No, thank you,' I say, but when I see his face fall a little, I suggest he could help me to the bus stop.

As we walk, I let him hold my arm, offering support that I need more than I'd like to admit. He asks where I was going in such a rush that I was nearly killed. I can't bring myself to speak of Pippo, so I tell him that I thought I saw someone I knew. He asks my name and, hesitantly, I tell him. He may have saved me from a terrible fate, but I am reluctant to open myself too much to him.

The more we talk, the more I realize that he is used to talking to women. He is not chatty, not — my heart stabs with pain briefly — as Pippo is. But he speaks gently and has a quiet charm which most boys who approach me do not. He tells me his name is Paolo, but that his friends call him Ceffo. I giggle at the nickname — we both know he is not ugly in any way.

As we wait for the bus together, he asks if I live nearby. No, I say, this is my route to school. He admits that he is not from this part of the city either, that he is just here . . . on business, he concludes.

Although I am wary, I have to accept that I am comfortable with Paolo. The buses are infrequent — the war has affected fuel deliveries, and fuel bought on the black market can sometimes be full of impurities, causing the buses to break down. But while we wait, we talk, and I am surprised to find myself releasing small pieces of information to him. In return, I learn that he is the only man in the family, that there is little money so he works to help them. He is vague about what employment he has, but I understand that these days: everyone takes work where they can.

Finally, we see my bus rattling towards us, and I lift my satchel gingerly over my head and shoulder.

'Paolo,' I say, 'I thank you again, a million times.' I reach out my hand to shake his, but instead of this formal goodbye, he grasps my hand and looks directly at me.

'Clara,' he says earnestly, 'Clara, will you meet me one day? For coffee.'

'Coffee?' I chuckle, shaking my head and making it hurt as I do. 'Where can anyone get coffee these days?'

He shrugs. '*Gelato* then.'

I look at him quizzically.

'Clara, will you meet me for a piece of dry bread and a glass of water?'

I smile at him and he beams in reply. As the bus stops beside me and opens its door, I am about to repeat the words I always use, 'Thank you, but no thank you.' Then I look at Paolo — his confident stance wavering the smallest amount as he senses my rejection.

'Yes . . . I will,' I say, surprised at myself.

'*Signorina!*' shouts the bad-tempered driver. 'Are you getting on or not?'

Embarrassed, I step onto the bus, but turn to lean out of the door.

'When? Where?' I ask.

'Here!' grins Paolo. 'On Saturday.'

I nod, about to reply when the driver simultaneously starts driving and pushes the lever to shut the door. The vehicle lurches, and I grab a railing to steady myself. As the bus pulls away, I rush to the nearest empty seat on the right to see Paolo the Ugly trotting beside us.

'At four!' he shouts, and I nod emphatically.

I realize as I sink into my seat, resting my throbbing head on its back, that I have, for a short time, forgotten about Pippo.

PIPPO

1942

The Woman in Green

The little girl's cough sent shivers through him. With every wheeze, every thick, wet rasp, Pippo felt more useless. He wanted to do something. He wanted to help Violetta however he could, but he just didn't know how.

He knew that Donna felt as powerless as he did. With Mario gone, there was no insurance, and while there was free healthcare for the needy, a local government official had announced an exclusion for the families of men who had evaded conscription. They'd been to the hospital, but had been turned away by a hard-nosed woman with a clipboard. There was not enough medicine for everyone as it was, she'd said – 'find your own doctor' had been her advice.

But doctors cost money, and there was little paid work and nothing left to sell. And so they sat, Donna holding in her arms the thin, listless girl, rocking her gently and singing her favourite song, Gino perched on a chair at her side and Pippo at the table watching, wishing he could cover his ears to stop the noise of that cough.

Suddenly, he jumped out of his chair, startling Donna, who looked up at him with an unbearable sadness in her eyes.

'I'll go and talk to Bruno,' he told her.

She shook her head, her hair falling across her forehead, lank and unbrushed. 'I've already spoken to him, he has nothing.'

'I'll try again. Tell him her breathing is worse now.'

'He has nothing to give, Pippo,' said Donna quietly.

When his funds from the Russian Communist Party had dried up, Bruno had taken a job as a street cleaner. Pippo knew Mario's friend had used a heart condition he'd had from birth to evade conscription. Instead, he swept the streets, where the boy realized he was hiding in plain sight. Now Bruno could stop and exchange a few words with passers-by, or check bins for secret messages left there. But he had little money to share.

'I have to do something,' the boy told Donna. 'I can't sit and watch.'

The woman looked at him and nodded.

'Go,' she said, and glanced at Gino, whose worried face was fixed on hers. She reached over to take the small boy's hand and gripped it reassuringly, and Pippo saw his face relax a little. But then Violetta coughed again, a deep, racking cough that shook her whole body, and Donna returned her attention to her daughter, hushing and shushing her until the attack passed and the child was left wheezing with exhaustion.

Not one of the small family looked up as Pippo left the warm, humid room. He took a deep breath as he stepped out into the street, pulling the door softly shut behind him, before setting off at a slow run to find Bruno.

He wondered where he should look first. There were no meetings of the Communist Party now but, as it was early, he thought Mario's old friend might be cleaning the square and so he headed left, towards the centre of the city, where queues had already formed in front of shops with nothing to sell. Children played at their mothers' feet, occasionally stopping to complain they were hungry, only to be told they would have to wait. Pippo himself had become used to the hunger — there had been less and less each month since Mario left. The last few days, his fear for Violetta had made him forget the constant growl in his stomach.

He ran past the cinema, where before the war he and Botte had slipped into the dark room and marvelled at the stories on the big screen. His friend joked that it was the longest Pippo had gone without talking, but the boy had been entranced by the experience. The flickering picture, the characters who were good or bad, beautiful or evil, music that turned the tale from romance to tragedy — he had adored every moment.

They had tried to sneak in again, but the cinema owner had put his staff on watch for youngsters such as them, and they hadn't made it in. These days fewer people went to the cinema, and Botte told him the films were just propaganda for Mussolini — the last thing Pippo wanted to watch.

When he reached the square, he spotted Bruno straight away. He was leaning on his broom, smoking a cigarette and reading a newspaper. He looked up as Pippo approached and gave the boy a smile.

'*Buongiorno*, little man,' he said, folding the paper and sliding it into his pocket.

'Bruno,' panted Pippo, surprised that he was out of breath after such a short distance. 'Can you help? Violetta is very ill, she needs a doctor . . .'

'Hush,' said the man, raising his hands, '*calmati*. I've already spoken to your mother.'

Pippo bristled slightly at the man calling Donna his mother, but didn't bother to correct him. 'She's much worse now – she won't stop coughing. And she won't eat. She just lies in Donna's arms. We're so frightened for her. She's only tiny, Bruno. You must help, you must!' Pippo heard his voice rise with emotion, stopped and took a breath before adding quietly, 'Mario would have done something if it were you.'

Bruno looked anxiously at the boy and put a reassuring hand on his shoulder. 'My pockets are empty, Pippo, but let me think. All the doctors I know have been called up. But . . . there is someone. I haven't seen him for a long time, but my name may still have some value with him.'

Pippo blinked quickly, dispelling the tears that threatened.

The curly haired man glanced around them before leaning towards him and whispering, 'Visit Don Orlando, you know the one I mean – the tall gentleman who used to eat at Ferrari's. Do you remember where he lives?'

Pippo nodded.

'Go there,' continued Bruno, 'and tell him I sent

you. Tell him I owe a debt to your father. Then tell him what you need. If anyone can help, it's him. Now,' he patted the boy's back, 'go now — he'll be home at this time.'

Pippo didn't wait to thank him. He turned on his heel and ran. It was a long way to Don Orlando's house, but he kept a steady pace through the busy streets until he reached the road that led out of town. Houses that had seemed so grand and elegant now seemed jaded and worn, and Pippo briefly wondered if their inhabitants were as hungry as he was.

When he reached the house with the coloured glass windows in the door, he stopped. Breathing heavily, he leaned forward, resting his hands on his knees as a dizziness swam around his head. Suddenly, he heard a noise from the side of the house and, not ready to face Don Orlando, he dashed behind a large bush and ducked down.

Peering through the leaves, he saw a side door open and a woman step out. Dressed in a smart green suit and hat with ruby red lipstick, she finished tucking an envelope into her handbag and clipped the clasp shut, before reaching out her hand. Just inside the doorway, the boy could see the gentleman, as elegant as ever, a serene smile at his lips as he shook the woman's hand.

This, Pippo knew, was business not romance. There was no kiss of the woman's hand, no flirtatious smile in return. Instead, the woman nodded and turned, heading up the path to the road, her heels tapping quickly. In no time she was gone, turning the corner to another road, another life.

The door clicked shut and the boy sat back on his

heels, feeling his tired muscles stretch. He spent a few moments composing what he would say before looking around, slipping out from behind the bush, and walking up to the main entrance of the house.

He rang the bell as he had done before, and heard the same tinkle deep in the house. He was wondering if it had been one or two years since he had last been to the house, when the door in front of him opened. The same maid stood looking at him suspiciously.

'Message for the Signore,' he said, trying to sound convincing.

'Wait here,' she said, indicating with her eyes the space just inside the doorway. She closed the door gently before leaving to fetch her employer. Pippo turned his red band round his wrist distractedly, pulling an image of little Violetta lying in her mother's arms to the fore of his mind.

When Don Orlando appeared, he frowned at the boy. 'You have a message?' he asked.

'Bruno told me to come,' the boy said, a nervous crack in his voice.

'Bruno,' repeated the man, raising an eyebrow. He looked at Pippo, and the boy realized how ragged he must look. Despite Donna's efforts to keep his clothes clean and darned, there were holes in his trousers and shirt, and his shoes were ill-fitting and worn.

'This way,' said the man kindly, and the boy followed him through the high-ceilinged hallway dressed with polished furniture. Don Orlando stepped into a room with a large table in the centre, a place set for one. A basket of breads and pastries lay untouched, and Pippo's stomach growled loudly when he saw it.

Embarrassed, he gripped his tummy, but the gentleman picked up the basket and offered him one. Pausing only for a moment, he chose a piece of bread and took a large bite, trying not to eat it too quickly. While he ate, the man sat at the table and poured a cup of coffee for himself, leaving it black and strong.

'Would you like some?' he asked, when he saw Pippo watching him. 'It's chicory — even I can't get real coffee,' he smiled.

No, the boy shook his head. He had indulged too much already. He finished eating and cleared his throat.

'How may I be of assistance?' the soft voice purred.

'Sir,' began Pippo. 'My sister is very ill.' On his journey to the house, he had decided, to avoid any unnecessary confusion, to claim the family as his own. 'We have done everything we can, Don Orlando, but she needs a doctor before it is too late.'

'Your father?'

'He is away,' said Pippo, his eyes on the woven rug he stood on.

'He is a . . .' The man paused. 'A friend of Bruno's?'

The boy nodded without looking up. 'Bruno said to say he owes my father a favour.'

The man shifted in his seat and, peering through his eyelashes, Pippo watched him take a fold of money from his trouser pocket. He was pulling out a note when he stopped, and the boy held his breath.

'Have you been here before?' he asked quietly.

Pippo felt his shoulders sag. Would this affect the man's decision? He nodded.

'I thought I recognized you. You knew the Ferraris.

And your father's name is . . .' He thought for a moment. 'Mario?'

Pippo looked up at him and nodded.

'I thought so.' Don Orlando patted his own knee in self-congratulation. 'I never forget a face.'

Pippo relaxed a little as the man returned to his money, but, as he put two notes on the table, more money than the boy had seen in a long time, he stopped again.

'Mario,' he said thoughtfully. 'I helped him once. If I remember correctly, Mario would not have wanted you to come to ask for help. Am I right?'

The boy dropped his chin to his chest.

Don Orlando rolled the two notes around his finger, thinking. Pippo peeked at him, unsure what to do. He was about to ask if he should leave, when the tall man suddenly stood up.

'This,' he said, folding the banknotes in half and handing them to the boy, 'is a loan. There is no interest, but I expect you to pay it back when you can.'

Pippo accepted the money and slipped it quickly into his pocket. 'Thank you, Don Orlando. I will pay it back as soon as I can.'

'No rush,' he replied. 'I have a great deal of respect for your . . .' He stopped thoughtfully for a moment and looked at the boy. 'For Mario,' he corrected. 'I think he would approve of this transaction. Now, go. Take care of his family. Family comes first. Always.'

'Sì, Don Orlando,' nodded Pippo, his legs twitching to run to the doctor. But before he could, the gentleman picked up a tiny bell and rang it. Instantly, the maid was at the door.

'Please wrap these rolls and pastries,' the man said, waving his hand over the basket. 'They are a gift to this boy's family.'

The girl quickly took the basket and soon returned with a full paper bag, its end carefully rolled closed. She handed it to Pippo, who took it from her gratefully and tucked it under his arm.

'Don Orlando . . .' He felt that words of greater appreciation were required but, as he searched for them, the tall man shooed him away. Without waiting, Pippo turned and dashed to the door, letting himself out of the main entrance and sprinting onto the road. He could feel the warmth of the fresh baked goods resting beneath his arm, and he tried not to crush them.

The boy ran, not allowing himself to think of the meeting with Don Orlando, only focusing on the fastest route to the doctor's house. He hoped and hoped that he was not too late, that there would be some medicine the doctor could give little Violetta that would rid her of that terrible illness.

Once or twice, Pippo stopped running, his heart pounding in his ears, his chest heaving and his legs quivering. But as soon as he'd regained his breath, he was off again.

As he ran along a busy main street, his head down as he barged past people, he heard his name being shouted. He looked up and saw Ceffo. He raised his left hand and waved briefly at his friend, then pointed in the direction of home without slowing, and Ceffo nodded his understanding and watched him go.

A moment later, he became aware of a tingling that

started at his neck and travelled down his back. He slowed for a moment, but decided it was only tiredness and, as an old bus trundled past noisily, pushed his body back into the rhythm of running.

He had to get to the doctor before it was too late.

CLARA

1942

In the Pantry

The old man furrows his brows at me.

'An egg?' he says in quiet astonishment, 'for breakfast?'

I nod, my eyebrows raised in similar bewilderment.

'And was it delicious?'

I nod again. 'The best egg I have ever tasted.'

'Do you think you could become accustomed to eggs for breakfast?'

I nod once more, thoughtfully. 'But I'm not sure Mussolini would approve.'

'Ah,' says Saba, 'it is the food of the enemy.'

'It's how the Americans eat it.'

'And the English.'

'Really?'

'And the French.'

'Is it only Italians who do not eat boiled eggs for breakfast?'

'Oh, the others don't just boil them.'

'No?'

'The English fry them with sausages, and pancetta, and mushrooms.'

'Sausages?' I say, surprised.

'And the French eat them scrambled — as light and fluffy as a cloud.'

'Have you tasted French eggs?' I ask. I have never considered that Saba Leone might have been anywhere other than in this library.

'Yes — I've seen a little of Paris,' he says modestly.

'Why were you there?' His coyness has raised my interest.

'My work.'

'You were a librarian in France?'

'No,' he chuckles. 'I have not always worked in a library. I was an academic — a professor.'

'Of what?'

'Languages. I often travelled around Europe, researching ancient dialects.'

'Where else did you go?' I ask, pushing aside the book of the Vatican's history that we have been reading together. I can't believe I have known Saba for years and this is the first time I've heard of his life before the library. We have spoken of his family and his work at the library, but mostly we have talked of history and literature, art and geography.

'To Madrid — before the war there — Lisbon, London and,' he smiles, 'to some small islands off the coast of Scotland.'

'Scotland?' I try to imagine the map of Europe I have studied so many times. I can picture *Gran Bretagna*, a long island lying in a diagonal line from Italy. Scotland, I remember, covers the top third, a land of mountains and valleys and wild weather.

'Beautiful,' says the old man, a wistful look on his

face. 'I went to meet people who spoke Gaelic — which is in the same family of languages as ours. But Clara, did you know,' he says, sitting upright, a twinkle appearing in his eyes, 'I could speak a dozen languages, understood the origins and development of numerous dialects, have translated more scripts than I can count, but at first I could barely understand a word they spoke! It didn't matter. They are a proud people; toughened by a hard life, softened by their love of their own stunning landscapes.'

He pauses and I watch him take a journey into his memory, returning gradually with a hint of a smile on his lips. 'I was a stranger, but they made me welcome. There is no place that I am gladder to have been.'

I let his words hang in the cool air of the underground library.

'Saba?' I say, pulling him back to our conversation.

'Hmm?'

'If you are a professor of languages, why are you working in the library?'

The old man looks at me sadly, unconsciously rubbing his swollen knuckles.

'The Racial Laws of 1938,' he replies simply.

'I don't know . . .' I hesitate, embarrassed. I have learned a great deal about Fascism over the years, but these days I understand I have only learned what the Fascists want me to know.

'They were Mussolini's series of laws — anti-Jewish,' he glances at me, 'anti-Roma, anti-everyone-different legislation. Part of it was to remove all Jewish teachers from their positions. Because of my faith, I could no longer work at the university.'

'Why do Fascists hate the Jews?' I ask. I understand the fear that being different raises in ordinary people, but I wonder why so much venom is directed at the people of an ancient religion.

Saba sighs and rubs his hairless head. 'I don't know, Clara. There are places where the Jews have been persecuted for centuries.'

'But why?' I repeat. I have seen cruel cartoons, heard callous jokes, I've even caught the Signore saying rude things about the Jews, but Zia always hushes him, saying that is Hitler's opinion, not the Italians'. Pictures in the newspapers and on posters usually depict an avaricious old man, but I wonder where this perception of a people began.

'Some simply say we killed Jesus. Others believe us to be greedy and sly based on a centuries-old reputation for being misanthropic.' The old man shrugs wearily, as if he has spent a lifetime trying to understand it. 'Here in Italy, our people settled and were accepted. They say my family has lived here since the 1400s.'

I open my mouth to speak but I don't know how to explain. To say that since the death of my father, I have truly understood persecution. That I have moved home more times than I can count. That even though I have felt the security of community, I have never felt the solidity of a true home. Instead I have always felt like a moth, fluttering from here to there, only landing for a brief time before lifting off for another aimless journey. Even now, while I live in a loving and wealthy home, I know I am only a temporary resident. As soon as I find my brother and Mamma returns, I will leave.

I close my mouth.

'And yet, Mussolini believes the Jews are not part of the Italian race,' continues Saba. 'And so they labelled us Jews on our documents, then began to remove us from Italian life. We are banned from jobs and our children from schools, marriage with non-Jews is forbidden — we are even barred from tennis courts.'

I feel a deep frown sink my forehead. Saba Leone is the only Jew I know. It dawns on me that he is the only one I have met in this city because the others have been excluded from my day-to-day life.

'But surely you are still working for the university — even if you are not teaching,' I say.

'The Rector is a kind man. In fact, I taught him. When the laws came into being, we agreed that I would volunteer at the library, so that I may continue to work. He has arranged a personal monthly "donation" that more than covers my expenses. I am able to be with the books I love and, occasionally, I find a willing student.' He nudges me gently with his elbow. 'Not only that, this position affords me some safety. While other universities and schools promote attacks on the Jews, the Rector has made it clear that this school is a place of tolerance.'

I consider the elderly man's life. He cannot share his incredible teaching with young people — at the moment it is only I who can benefit from his vast knowledge. He must hide in the shadowy depths of this library. He cannot eat, drink or socialize as others do, and even his worship has been curtailed. After such an unsettled start to my life, I can understand the need to stay in one place, especially when your family roots run deep into this earth. But I can hear my mother's voice say that there are times when you find yourself no longer welcome.

'Why will you not go somewhere else, Saba?' I ask quietly. 'Somewhere you can be a Jew without fear or restriction?'

He pushes his glasses up his nose and slowly nods. 'It must seem strange – to stay where you are not wanted. My wife passed some years ago. Our children are adults now, and they all left before the war. That was one area where the government was helpful – emigration!' He snorts before continuing. 'I may be a Jew, but I am an Italian too. I have travelled far, but I have always come home. To Italy. I do not want to leave.

'Now,' Saba says, pulling at his white beard as if to draw a close to the conversation, 'let us see why Pope Pius IX was better known as the prisoner of the Vatican.'

I nod, feeling I have learned more than in my usual visits to the library, and pull the book towards us.

Walking home from the library in the evening dusk, I swing my satchel casually by my legs. I know I should be thinking about what I have learned at the library today – both the fascinating story of the papal palace and the life of Saba. But instead I think of Pippo.

How close I was to him. As he ran past the bus, he must only have been a few feet away. I try to make firm the image of him, but it is blurry now. Of course, I returned to the same spot every day this week, waiting and watching in case he ran past again. But no – he was not there. No tingling in my being told me he was near again. I will go back, I decide. Perhaps not every day, but when I can.

My mind meanders from Pippo to Paolo. Tomorrow is Saturday and I will be meeting him. Now I have a reason to wear my lipstick. We may not be going to a dance, but I would like to look nice to meet this boy. The thought of Paolo pulling his fingers through his hair makes a hundred tiny birds flap their wings inside my stomach.

Ridiculous, I think to myself, before returning to my daydream and enjoying the strange sensation. Will he kiss my cheeks when we meet? Will he hold my hand as we walk to wherever we're going? And if we sit on a bench to talk, will he slip his arm around my shoulders?

One day when we were going to the newsstand to pick up one of Zia's magazines, I remember watching the man and woman in front of us. He was walking beside her, talking constantly — for a moment he reminded me of my brother. From what I could hear, the man seemed to be showering her with compliments. She was as beautiful as a summer flower, her hair tumbled like a fountain of chocolate down her back, and her eyes were as delicious as caramel. The woman laughed, amused, and the man was emboldened to slip his arm around her waist. At first the woman tried to politely wriggle out of his clutches, but he grabbed her with his other hand, pulled her to him and planted a kiss on her cheek. Shocked, the woman slapped his cheek and he let go, laughing. As she walked away, he stopped and watched her go before kissing his fingers and dramatically blowing it to her. I saw the woman give herself a little smile.

I myself have received the attention of boys — and even men. Embarrassed, I have always walked away, my head dropped, hoping that they will lose interest and ignore me. Seeing this woman revel in the admiration, react against it and then smile at it again, made no sense. Did she like it or not?

Confused, I turned to Zia, who had seen me watch the scene. She smiled and shrugged. She couldn't explain it — this was just how love in Italy was.

She and the Signore are affectionate with each other at home, although more restrained when in public. At times they have rows with raised voices, arms and hands delivering gestures as hurtful as their words. I came to realize quickly that Zia thinks the Signore reveres the Fascists too much, and that he believes she wastes her time on frippery and nonsense. But she clearly loves him, and he worships her.

I understand nothing, except that there is a lot to learn about men and love. And now, with Paolo, I am prepared for my first lesson.

As I drift closer to home, I hear a strange noise. It is a slow, mechanical wail and, as I look around for its source, my mind races to place the sound. Looking up, I see the speaker attached to the bell tower above the church, and it comes to me. It is a warning siren — bombers are coming.

I have heard this whine before, false alarms when we practised running to the shelters. But I was at home and the sound was distant. Now, as I stand beneath the speaker, it is so loud I can hear nothing else.

Suddenly, a man rushes past me, knocking my arm and waking me from my daze. I must get to a shelter. Quickly thinking about where I am, I decide that although it is a few minutes further away, I will head home.

As I turn to my right and begin running, I wonder if I have made the best choice, as everyone else on the street is heading to the public shelter behind me and I am swimming against the tide. I push and stumble, holding my arm up above my face to protect myself, but the panicked people have soon passed and, although I continue to run, I notice others are walking casually, obviously deciding this is nothing more than another drill.

The noise of the siren has stopped now, but that, I know, is a brief pause. It will begin again imminently. In its absence, I hear the sound of my boots hitting the paving, my satchel filled with books knocking my hip, my quick, panting breaths. And then I hear another sound. A low buzzing – like a giant bee travelling through the sky.

I look up, but there is nothing to see save a few wispy clouds settled against a bold blue background. An uneasy feeling fizzes in my stomach and, deciding that I do not trust the clear skies, I quicken my pace. Seeing the end of our street up ahead, I relax a little. I know that at this time of day, Zia and Filomena will be in the house, preparing the home and our evening meal for the return of the Signore.

As I pass quickly through the empty street, the siren begins again, a mournful start that builds in volume but only partially masks the buzzing, which has grown into a rumble. Aeroplanes. Now I am sure.

Sprinting up the step, I open the door and call for Zia. She does not reply, but Filomena shouts to me from the kitchen. I drop my bag by the door and run to her. She hovers by the pantry. We do not have a basement, but the Signore has decided this windowless storage room is the safest place to hide in the event of an attack.

'Where is Zia?' I ask breathlessly.

'I don't know,' says Filomena, pulling open the door of the pantry.

'But—' I come to an abrupt stop. She must be here. She is always here at this time of day.

'She said she had to run an errand,' replies the cook, distractedly pushing her greying hair under her scarf. 'Come on, get in here. Where have you been? You should—'

Her words catch as we hear the blast of an explosion.

'Quickly,' she says, bundling me into the pantry. I press myself against the back shelves and watch her pull the door shut.

Together we stand quietly in the cool, musty room. I realize I am squeezing the red band on my wrist. It is quiet and, for a moment, I wonder if we have mistaken the noise. Perhaps it was a car backfiring, or—

Another heavy boom resounds – this time closer – and the explosion rocks the house under our feet, rattling the nearly empty jars and bottles on the shelves beside us.

I look at Filomena and see the fear in her face. This strong woman who I thought to be courageous in all situations has shown me she has a limit, and this bombing has pushed her to it.

Reaching out, I take hold of her large, square hand. She looks at me, surprised. Then, as we hear the sound of aeroplanes overhead, she pulls me to her. As I rest my head on her pillow-like bosom, I think of Pippo somewhere in this city, and hope that he is safe. And Zia too, wherever she is. The Signore will be at his office shelter and Saba, I decide, will be safe in his basement library. For a moment, I clench my right hand and wonder where Paolo will be taking cover, but then the rumbling intensifies and is followed by a whistle that grows louder and louder. Together, we shiver and hold our breaths, waiting for the next explosion.

PIPPO

1942

The Crater

The first time the bombs fell on the city, Pippo felt a mixture of fear and excitement. As he huddled with Donna, Gino and Violetta in Signora Romano's basement, he wished he could see the planes flying overhead. It was likely to be a British attack, so maybe he'd be able to spot a Lancaster, or even a Halifax.

He and Botte had studied pictures of all the aircraft – Allied and Regia Aeronautica – in the newspapers they found. Botte pointed out there was little chance they'd see the large Italian bombers; they were more likely to spot an enemy aircraft on a mission. They peered at the bulbous nose of the Lancaster, at where the bomb aimer would lie, looking out of the clear dome, choosing the perfect time to drop the aircraft's huge load, and where two guns could be used against Italian or German attackers. His friend read to him about the four Rolls-Royce engines – the same designer as for the motor car – and they'd both longed to hear the sound of the aeroplane.

But as the noise drew closer to his home, Pippo knew it was a wish they had not really wanted to come true.

He understood the danger it brought with it. Perhaps more than Donna, he and his friend knew the weight of the bombs these aircraft carried towards them.

'They won't come here,' she had said in hopeful denial, when he had spoken about the aeroplanes. But Botte had told him of the factories on the edge of town that might be targets. His own brother had worked at one before he was called up, he'd reminded Pippo, helping to make helmets for soldiers.

As they sat, the women talked in raised voices, telling the children to be quiet, although Pippo didn't know why – the pilot couldn't hear the man next to him in the cockpit, so couldn't possibly hear the noise of childish chatter in a building far beneath them. Unconsciously, the boy turned his red band round and round his wrist.

The basement smelled terrible. Despite the fresh, cool breeze of the October evening outside, the damp space was filled with the stink of too many people. Three families shared the space; ten children, and all the youngest seemed to have done their *cacca* at the same time. A little girl had been sick from fear and, although her mother had cleaned it up, hushing and scolding her at the same time, there was nowhere to put the stinking cloth, so it sat with all the other soiled garments in the corner of the stone room.

As the drone of aircraft grew closer and the explosions began, shaking the ground and rattling Pippo's teeth, the children became quiet, hugging their mothers' skirts. Signora Romano began to pray loudly in a tremulous voice, calling on all the saints she could think of to protect her and her little ones.

Donna held Violetta in her arms, the child's eyes wide in her gaunt face. The medicine the doctor had given her was beginning to work, the cough abating and the colour returning to her cheeks. But he had warned that the recovery would be slow, and Donna must try to get dairy foods — eggs, milk, cheese — wherever she could. Pippo had promised to help, deciding to find his old friend Allocco to see if his knowledge of the black market was as good as it had once been.

Gino snuggled into his mother's black skirt, hiding his face from everything and everyone. If he could not see it, maybe it would not hurt him. But when a bomb landed nearby, rocking all of them and the house above, he looked up, his face distorted by fear.

Pippo stepped towards him and placed his hand on the boy's back, as he remembered Mario had done to him when he was anxious. Donna smiled weakly at the older boy and pulled him towards her. The family of four stood together, swaying and rocking when bombs landed nearby, coughing and wiping off the dust that fell from the ceiling when there was a lull.

When finally the explosions stopped and the aircrafts' drone became more distant, they turned around to check on the others in the basement. Signora Romano was on her knees, crouched over her children, giving her thanks to Santa Maria for delivering them through the terror. The other family sat together, holding hands and quietly whispering to each other.

Donna handed Violetta to Pippo, who tickled the little girl under her chin to raise a weak smile, while her mother spoke briefly to Signora Romano. Then, they gathered the few things they had brought with them to the basement, and made their way up the stairs and towards the main door of the house.

Blinking at the acrid smoke that hit them when they stepped outside, they stood together, looking out at the street. Pippo could hear the noise of the siren announcing the bombing was over, but it was just one section of an ugly symphony of sounds. Here, the creaking and crashing of large stone bricks falling from the destroyed building at the end of the street. There, the crackling and hissing of fire as it reached skyward from the roof of a house on the next street. And everywhere, the shouts of men directing help, and the screams of those realizing what, and whom, they had lost.

Making their way slowly, stepping over clothes scattered by a collapsed washing line, they walked along a street that had suddenly become unfamiliar. Smoke and dust blocked the late evening light, making everything grey. When they reached their door, Donna pushed it open and peered inside, as though some effect of the bombing that couldn't be seen from outside might be hiding. But the small, gloomy home was the same as ever, and Pippo felt grateful for that.

Pushing the door shut behind them, the boy watched as Donna bent to put Violetta on the floor, instructing Gino to take her and wash the dust from their faces. As soon as the younger children turned away, Pippo saw Donna's knees buckle and she crumpled into a chair.

'What's wrong?' he asked, stepping towards her. 'Are you hurt? Is there something . . .'

Donna looked at him, pushing a dark curl away from her face, leaving streaks of dust on her skin and hair.

She shook her head and sat in silence.

Pippo waited.

Eventually, she said, 'It's so hard, Pippo. To do all this on my own. Without Mario.' She sighed. 'No money, no food — I could bear it all if I had him by my side. It always felt . . .' She looked at the boy and tried to smile. 'It felt that we could do anything together. But now . . .' She breathed out slowly, turning her hands in her lap and looking at her palms. 'Now, I feel that I cannot keep us safe, cannot take care of us all, cannot hold us together.'

She linked her fingers and sat, gazing at the empty bowl her hands made.

Pippo stood still, trying to block out the clattering bells of a fire truck passing on a road nearby. Then, turning his back on Donna, he crossed to the kitchen and picked up the box of matches on the table. He lit the two candles held in simple candlesticks and, leaving one in the kitchen, returned to place the other on the stool beside the woman.

The two small children hovered in the doorway, unsure what to do. Gently, Pippo told Gino to take his sister and get ready for bed, and when the little boy whined that he was hungry, he told them he would make them something to eat.

Lighting the cooker, he put water on to boil and quickly washed his hands and face. Glancing behind him, he saw Donna, unmoving, still looking at her hands. He found the end of an onion and clove of garlic in a bowl, chopped them up, and slid them into a pan. Adding a tiny drizzle of oil, he left them to fry as he poked around the empty cupboards. He found a handful of rice and threw it into the pan. Then, he tipped in some hot water and stirred it.

While he waited for it to simmer, he poured some warm water into a cup. Donna took it without looking up at him, cradling it in her hands. Pippo laid bowls and spoons on the table as the children climbed onto their chairs, and carved uneven slices of stale bread.

'Put the bread into your soup,' he told them, as he spooned the watery rice into their bowls. Gino helped Violetta, first pulling her bread into small pieces and dropping them into the broth, then spooning small mouthfuls to her. She pulled a face but said nothing, accepting the food. When she had finished, she sat quietly, watching her motionless mother, while Gino and Pippo noisily slurped their thin meal.

'Tomorrow I will get more food,' Pippo said, to himself as much as the other children. 'Now, time for bed.'

Both children padded over to their mother and stood beside her. Gino laid a caressingly soft kiss on her cheek, while the little girl took one of her hands and held it gently in her own.

Slowly, Donna looked up at them. Then she pulled them both to her, gripping them tightly and kissing their heads. Pippo watched and waited, feeling for the first time in a long time that he was not a true member of this little family.

When their mother had hugged and kissed them enough to last them until morning, they headed to the bedroom door, where Pippo waited. Pulling the sheet and threadbare blanket over them, he told them a story. From somewhere in his imagination, he conjured a white horse with a beautiful long mane that flew across the country, pulling a cart full of apples and cherries into town and taking lucky children for rides on her bare back.

Gino fell asleep the instant his head touched the mattress, but little Violetta listened to the story intently, her eyes wide at the thought of such a magical beast. Finally, when her tired eyes could no longer bear the weight of her lids, she drifted to sleep, curling instinctively against her brother.

Pippo snuffed out the candle and turned to see Donna standing in the light of the doorway, watching him.

'You are a born storyteller,' she said, as he followed her to the kitchen. 'It is an art.'

'I am a born talker,' he said. 'I just say what comes into my head.'

'Thank you, Pippo,' said Donna, putting a hand on his shoulder. 'I am sorry I . . .' She stumbled over her words.

'No,' said the boy. 'I should do more to help you. Mario is not here, and I am not a child any longer.'

Donna smiled. 'You are eleven. You cannot fill the shoes of a grown man.'

'No. But I am old enough to work. Old enough to help. Let me do more for you.'

The mother nodded her head as she pulled an edge off the stale loaf and sopped up some broth.

'All right, Pippo. I will ask for your help more – and together we will get to the end of this war, whatever it brings.'

Pippo smiled, pleased at the thought of being treated as an adult now.

'I think,' she continued earnestly, 'we should start with learning to cook.'

The next day, when he had finished helping to clean the dust and debris from the front of the house, he ran to see the damage and check on his friends. He was amazed to find people going about their business, as if it were any other day. Men in dusty suits stepped over the rubble of collapsed buildings to get to their place of work.

He stopped to watch a woman picking through the wreckage of a place that the day before had been her home. As he looked on, he saw her pick up a china cup from between two fallen bricks. She inspected it, turning it over in her hands and lifting it to the light, but it was unmarked. Carefully, she wrapped it in her handkerchief and tucked it into her apron pocket, before resuming her slow, methodical search.

Pippo turned and carried on towards the square, hoping the cafe might have its radio on today. He wanted to hear if there was news of his city, and if other places nearby had been bombed. But when he reached the piazza, the cafe was closed, its windows shattered and awning hanging askew. On the street outside, a familiar figure swept broken glass into a pile.

'Bruno,' called the boy across the square, waving his hand when the man looked up.

'It finally happened,' said Mario's friend when Pippo reached him. 'I have been expecting this for weeks.'

'Who was it?'

'The British. They say it is the beginning of a bombing campaign, here and across Italy.'

'Are many people . . .' Pippo looked down at the broken glass.

'Yes,' nodded Bruno sadly. 'Are your family safe?'

'Donna and the children are fine,' he replied.

'Pippo,' said the curly haired main quietly, looking around and steering him from the cafe by the elbow, 'I have news for you and Donna.'

'Mario?' asked the boy in an excited whisper, gripping the man's arm.

'Let go. Be calm. We may be watched. No,' said Bruno as Pippo turned his head, 'do not look around.'

The boy plunged his hands into his pockets in a poor attempt at looking uninterested.

'Here,' said Bruno, handing him the broom, 'you sweep and I'll collect the glass.' From his trolley handle, he took a shovel and scooped up a mound of broken glass, pouring it into his metal bin.

Working together, they shuffled along the pavement as passers-by walked around them. When they had fallen into a rhythm, Bruno said, 'I have indeed heard from Mario. It seems he is leading a team of resistance fighters.'

'Resistance?' said Pippo, standing and forgetting his job. 'What do you mean? Resisting the British? The Americans? Or the Germans? I don't understand, Bruno.'

'Keep working,' said the man. 'He and the others in the movement are working for the Allies. They are passing information on to the British. They are sabotaging the movement of troops and munitions.'

'They are fighting Italy?' hissed Pippo, brushing a clean piece of pavement vigorously.

'I would say they are battling against Mussolini. They do not want us to be involved in this war any longer than we need to be.'

'But look what happened here last night,' said Pippo, holding a hand out to the smoke-filled sky. 'After this, do you still think it's right to fight Italy and not the British?'

'Now more than ever, Pippo,' said Bruno, pushing his cleaning trolley along the road. 'If they can destroy Mussolini and his government, then we could quit this war — side with the Allies. The bombing would stop overnight. And we would no longer be in bed with the real enemy — Hitler.'

Pippo shook his head. 'I don't understand it. I know Mario didn't want Italy to join the war. I know Il Duce,' he dropped his voice, 'I know he and the Fascists are against everything we stand for, but to fight — Italian against Italian? No, I don't understand it.'

'Well,' said Bruno, taking the broom from his hands, 'maybe you will soon. Tell Donna what I have told you, and see what she says. Her reaction may surprise you.'

The boy turned and walked away, dragging his worn boots on the pavement. It didn't make sense. He adored Mario with all his heart, but he could not see how he could possibly make things better in this resistance movement.

Suddenly, he heard his name being called. Looking around, he spotted Botte waving to him from the other side of the square. Breaking into a sprint, he headed to the corner where his friend stood.

Botte no longer had a reason to be called Barrel, since the war had stripped him of his flabby stomach. These days he was nearly as lean as Pippo, and he ran easily, unlike the heavy-footed tramp of his younger years.

Pippo dashed towards him, skirting people and fallen masonry, but just as he reached him, he tripped over an electric wire and stumbled. Botte grabbed his arm, supporting him until he regained his footing.

'Thanks,' he grinned, pleased to see an old friend.

'Have you seen any of the others?' asked Botte.

'No — you're the first.'

'Me neither. Let's check they're all right.'

'Good idea,' Pippo nodded. 'You check Allocco and I'll go to Ceffo's.'

'I'll meet you back here in an hour,' agreed his friend, and they both turned and set off at a slow run.

Pippo ran through streets where the smell of smoke and dust hung in the air. He had chosen Ceffo as he hadn't seen him since he'd bumped into him in the other day. He wanted to explain why he hadn't stopped, about getting medicine for Violetta. He knew his friend would understand.

Up ahead, where two streets joined, a small crowd had gathered to look at something around the corner. He slowed as he reached the people, an invisible barrier stopping them from moving too close to what they were viewing.

Panting a little, he pushed forwards. 'What is it?' he asked the crowd in general.

No one answered. There was no need. In front of him lay a huge crater where a large house had stood.

'It's gone,' said Pippo, his jaw dropping. 'It's all gone.'

'Direct hit,' a woman beside him said.

'But . . .' Pippo's eyes rose to the edges of the buildings still standing, looking for the names of the streets just to check. 'But this is where . . .' His words disappeared as if falling into the cavernous hole in front of him.

'Did you know someone from here?' the woman, young with a tired face, asked without looking at him.

'Yes,' he replied in a whisper, 'it's where my friend Paolo lives.'

'Lived,' the woman replied, her voice flat. 'I know him. I'm friends with his mother.'

'Is everyone dead?' he asked quietly.

'Yes,' the woman said without emotion. 'I spoke to the police. He said the bomb killed everyone.'

'How do they know? Maybe Paolo wasn't in the house. Maybe he was out somewhere? With a girl . . .'

The woman shook her head, staring again at the smouldering ruin. 'They found parts.'

'Parts?'

'Body parts. A woman, a little girl, and a young man.'

'Paolo.'

'Yes. And his mother, and his little sister.'

Pippo breathed out slowly and turned his head to the left. All of a sudden, he felt completely exhausted.

CLARA

1942

Zia's Secret

I lean against the bus stop and sigh. This is the fifth
Saturday I have stood here, waiting. Each week I arrive
at 3.30 and wait until 4.30. The first time, the day of
our original planned meeting, I waited until 6.30. But
Paolo never came.

I didn't want to wait so long. I told myself to give him
ten minutes, no longer. But as the minutes ticked by
on the clock that hung from the corner of the street
beside the bank, I made excuses for him. He had been
delayed, his mother needed him to run an errand, he
was Italian. But as the early evening drew in, I knew he
wasn't coming.

Briefly, I thought of trying to find him. But, of course,
I knew nothing about him other than his first name. And
when I remembered all the times I had tried to find my
own brother – asking shopkeepers and policemen,
scouring every group of schoolchildren I'd seen – I knew
I would be unsuccessful, and probably feel foolish as well.
All I could think to do was return each Saturday, and
hope that just once he would do the same.

This week, however, I notice that the clock is broken. Its face is cracked and its hands are stuck at twenty past twelve, and it occurs to me that the bomb would have struck a little after midnight — the bombings always happen at night.

The building that once stood opposite the bank is now just a shell, and part of it lies in a neat pile in front of its entrance. I have watched the trucks and tractors working their way around the city, pushing bricks and rubble out of the way of pedestrians. I wonder if this building, old and once elegant, will be rebuilt, or knocked down and another built in its place. While the war continues, some find it impossible to think of these things, but it reassures me to imagine a time when the bombing is over, when there is food in the shops and there is no fear.

For now, I take another look at the broken clock and decide that whatever time it is, I have been here long enough. I turn and begin to walk. I have no need to be anywhere, and Zia believes me to be at a friend's house so will not expect me home.

Taking a side street, I kick a piece of rubble with my boot. I hear the Signore complaining about the dust on his boots and his clothes, see him brushing his shoes when he comes home, as if cleaning the city's debris from his mind. Filomena too grumbles about the dirt in and around the house, mumbling to herself about the extra work, but I know, like all of us, she has adapted to a new life.

The bombings have been irregular, but deadly when they come. Every morning we emerge from our homes, not knowing if the house next door will still be standing.

So far, I am relatively unaffected. My school, our home, the library are all unscathed by bombs. My bus takes a different route these days after a bomb left a large crater in one road, and now we pass a church whose domed tower has been destroyed, leaving a circular hole in its roof. Every day, I join the other bus passengers as we all turn our heads to look at that church when we rumble past it.

The time when I am most conscious of the war is when we stand for roll-call at school. We all hold our breath, and will a response for every name called. A few times, the name has been met with silence. The teacher waits for a moment, then calls the name again, more gently this time. If there is still no answer, she marks her book and shakes her head sadly.

Meandering down the street, I think of Pippo, trying to remember the shape of his face, the look of his eyes, even his build, but it is hard to recall the running figure easily. So, once more, I allow myself to think briefly of Paolo. He could, heaven forbid, have been killed or hurt by a bomb. Or someone close to him: he mentioned a younger sister when we spoke. Or his home could have been destroyed – perhaps he and his family have gone to live with someone else. Or perhaps, and I fear this alternative is more likely, he simply decided not to come.

Why should he want to meet me? In my mind I list the qualities of my character that most disappoint me. I am distant – in my attempt to keep out of trouble I am seen as a loner. I am serious. Unlike other girls, I am unable to chat easily about any subject that pops into my head. I prefer to listen and learn, forming my opinions slowly. I am different. I don't look like other girls my age. My hair is black; my eyes are pale brown with a tinge of orange, sometimes yellow; the structure of my face appears different from theirs. Even when I wear exactly the same uniform as them, I feel different. And although I constantly try to sound the same, every now and then I say a word with an accent. At such times, I sound like Mamma – and I am reluctant to correct myself.

So, why would a good-looking boy like Paolo want to spend time with me? But then, I remind myself how he seemed to enjoy our conversation. For the first time, I felt I could talk easily to a boy. His relaxed manner rubbed off on me and I found myself comfortable. He seemed interested in what I had to say, looking directly at me as though the words I spoke were important to him. I run through the conversation in my head again and again, looking for clues that he might have just been pretending to like me, insincere in his attention. There are none but, as I often remind myself, I know little of boys.

With another sigh, I look up and realize I have been wandering, paying no attention to where I am going. I have reached a dead end, the road ahead made impass-able by another collapsed building. Turning to go back the way I came, I see that two streets have converged at this point. I think I must have come down the road to my right but, unsure, I look at the one to my left again. Neither seems familiar, so I turn to the right, hoping it will take me back to the main road, where a bus will take me home.

Ahead, a woman kneels in front of her doorstep, scrubbing at it as if to erase much more than dirt. It is clean, and yet she brushes at it, leaning into her work and murmuring quietly to herself. I walk past her, knowing that she will never be able to dispel the filth she sees.

This, I think, is how the bombing has affected us. If buildings are destroyed, we move to another – extended family take in their own, teachers hold classes in empty offices, horses are stabled in gardeners' sheds. But even if the bombs do not injure or scar our bodies, our minds cannot escape. We cannot unsee what we have seen, unhear what we have heard. We all act the same, but think differently.

Zia, for her part, has become busier. She no longer fills her day reading magazines and rearranging furnishings. Now she volunteers at a shelter for people affected by the bombing. The Signore complains every time he sees her leave the house with a basket filled with blankets or towels, but she tells him that our house has more furnishings than she knows what to do with.

He also moans that she leaves the house at strange hours, but she reminds him that emergencies can happen at any time. That was what she said on the night of the first bombing, when she didn't return until very late in the evening, by which time the Signore had come back from work and was distraught that she was not at home.

He tried to call the police to ask for help, but the line was down. I cannot believe the police weren't busy doing a thousand other things that night, but they might have found someone to help an important civil servant like him.

Filomena made us all warm, watery milk to drink while we waited, but as she and I sat in the kitchen, sipping from our cups, the Signore paced the length of the hallway back and forth. Eventually, the door opened and Zia entered, covered in white dust and black soot. As soon as he saw her, her husband pulled her into his arms, guiding her into the nearest chair. She looked dazed, her eyes blinking but somehow blank.

The Signore fussed about her, checking she had not been hurt, showering her with questions and barking instructions to Filomena — get a cloth to clean her face, get her something to eat, prepare her bed. Filomena ignored him, crossing to the drinks cabinet and returning with a small glass of clear liquid.

'What is that?' the Signore asked, and the large woman replied simply, 'Grappa.'

'No,' he scoffed, waving his hand. 'Take that farmer's brew away. Go and fetch . . .'

Zia reached out, took the glass, and drank the liquor down. She pushed the empty glass back at Filomena and, without looking up, gave it a small shake, indicating she wanted more.

While her glass was being refilled, the Signore squatted beside his wife and, cupping her chin with his hand, turned her face to look at him. For an instant I felt uncomfortable, even though they shared nothing more than a look.

'Where were you?' I heard the Signore whisper.

'I . . . I . . .' His wife struggled to speak.

'Why weren't you here?'

'I went to run some errands,' she replied finally.

'What errands?' he pressed.

Zia seemed lost for words, her gaze dropping to the floor as if the answer were there.

'I asked the Signora to get some tomatoes for me,' Filomena said, passing the refilled glass to Zia.

'Tomatoes?' the Signore spluttered.

'I heard there was someone selling black market vegetables – a fresh delivery from the country. The Signora is protecting me. She knows you would not approve.'

The Signore turned to Zia, who quickly nodded in agreement at Filomena's confession.

'You are right, Filomena, I do not approve. There are systems for feeding a nation in wartime and we must follow them . . .'

Zia coughed, a dry, dusty cough, and the Signore turned back to her, concerned.

'Clara,' Filomena said quietly to me, 'go and run a bath for the Signora. Put some lavender oil in it. We'll be up shortly.'

As I dashed up the stairs, I saw Filomena take the glass from Zia's hand and give it to the Signore, then gently lift her to her feet. The Signore, watching with furrowed brows, said nothing.

In the bathroom, I set the taps running and found the old perfume bottle on the shelf. Filomena would crush lavender buds and mix them with olive oil and, after particularly tiring days, Zia liked to add a few drops to her bath.

'The Signora believes that the scent relaxes her,' Filomena had told me, 'but lavender has many medicinal benefits. No wonder we Italians have used it since the time of the Romans.'

I'd nodded when she'd told me, instantly remembering the scent and how our mother would rub it onto our bumps and bruises. Tipping the bottle, I let a few drops fall into the rushing water before replacing the lid. As I watched the bath fill, wafting the familiar smell of lavender through the bathroom, I wondered why Filomena had lied for Zia. I knew there had been no tomatoes to buy, no evening errands to run.

I believed, and still do, that Filomena did not know where her Signora had gone that night. But I think she might have an idea. I hope with all my being that she was not with another man. I adore Zia and care greatly for the Signore — now I can see through his bluster to the man who lives his life afraid of so much, especially the thought of disappointing his wife. I see what they are to each other, and I would not want that love broken. Enough has been destroyed by this war.

I stop walking with a gasp. I am at a junction. My mind has been ambling again, and so have my feet. I look around and know that I am completely lost. I turn, looking for the way I have come, but I feel as though I have never seen these streets before. There is no one about to ask, so I close my eyes and take a deep breath.

'Which way?' I whisper to myself, and open my eyes. As I glance along the road ahead of me, I am amazed to see a familiar figure. Crossing the road with strides as long as her heels will allow is Zia.

I call to her, but a car passing at the same moment drowns out my voice. She is walking quickly so I start to run after her, dashing across the road to follow her path. She turns down another street and I run a little faster still to catch up, hoping I won't lose her.

Reaching the corner where she turned, I am relieved to see the street ahead open out into a small piazza. She is crossing it, and I am just about to call to her again when I see her open her handbag and pull out a large envelope. As she reaches a bin, she drops the packet in it, without even breaking her step.

I start running again, and am grateful when I see her stop to talk to the road sweeper. They are discussing the weather when I reach her, tapping her shoulder and saying, 'Zia, thank goodness I've found you.'

As she turns to me, I see the expression on her face is one of shock and — it takes me a moment to recognize it — guilt.

'Signora,' says the cleaner, tipping his hat further over his curly hair and brushing his way away from us.

Zia ignores him and stares at me. 'What are you doing here? Have you been following me?'

'No!' I laugh. 'I am lost. I . . .' And now I am the one to feel guilty. I have not spoken a word to Zia about Paolo, although I know she would have been delighted to share gossipy chats about boys with me. 'I got off the bus at the wrong stop,' I finish feebly.

I am surprised that she does not pick up on my weak excuse — surely she can see I am lying. But she is distracted, her eyes darting from me to something behind me, and back again.

Turning to what she is looking at, I see nothing. There is no one in the piazza at all, no cars, no movement. Only the street cleaner, humming tunelessly to himself as he reaches into the bin, and begins pulling out rubbish and putting it into his metal trolley.

I look back at Zia and realize she is watching him, and I feel my mouth drop open as it dawns on me what is happening.

The trolley rumbles as the cleaner pushes it away from

us, his humming turning to whistling as he goes, but I do not take my eyes off Zia.

Finally, she looks at me. An emotion passes over her face, and I wonder if it is relief when she finally says, 'I think we both have secrets, Clara. If you will tell me yours, I will tell you mine.'

I think about her offer. There is little value in my secret. A boy I met briefly never appeared for our date. Apart from some embarrassment that he had perhaps never intended to meet me again, there is little to discuss.

On her part, though, I fear there is much to confess. And I wonder if I am the best person to hear these revelations. I look at her face and see her give a worried smile, an eager shake of the head, and I know that she wants to tell me.

Slowly I nod. She offers her arm and I take it as she turns, and we walk back the way we have come.

'You first,' she says.

'It was nothing,' I say, believing my words more than ever. 'I met a boy.'

'Ooohh,' squeaks Zia with glee. 'At last, I'm so happy. Tell me everything. He is *bello*, isn't he?'

I can see her delight is genuine, but I also wonder if she is stalling to avoid revealing her secrets a little longer.

'I thought he was,' I shrug. 'There is not much to tell, Zia. We talked for a while, and he asked me to meet him again. I waited, but he did not come.'

'Oh.' Her face drops. 'I'm sorry, Clara. Truly, I am. It would make me very happy for you to find love, especially during such dark times.'

We walk on in silence, and I wonder how to ask her

about her secret. I cannot think of a way to form the question other than, *Are you a spy, Zia?* So I say nothing.

Eventually, she says, 'I think, judging by your reaction, that you saw what I was doing back there. I think you saw me drop an envelope into the bin. And then you saw that envelope being retrieved by the cleaner.'

She looks at me and I nod.

Zia sniffs a deep breath and lowers her voice. 'I am trusting you to say nothing of this, Clara. Not to your friends, not even Filomena. She has an idea of what is happening, but I have confided in nobody. If I tell you, you must promise not to speak of it. The consequences for all of us are . . .' She closes her eyes for a moment. 'Unthinkable.'

'You can trust me,' I say with complete honesty.

She gives me a stern look before relaxing a little. Again, I feel she is relieved to be sharing her secret with someone. Keeping her shoulders back, her neck straight, she looks ahead as she says, 'I have never approved of Fascism. The Signore used to work in administration for a building company, but it was an unreliable job. When times are bad, as they were back then, there are no new buildings. He applied for jobs in government offices for the security. We were trying for a family and he wanted to provide.'

Zia glances at me and gives a small cough. 'The fastest way to be approved for a position was to join the Fascist Party, so he joined. At first, we used to laugh about it – like the time Mussolini pretended to queue for his ticket for the football World Cup, when his seat was waiting for him in the royal box. But slowly, my husband began to agree with some of the policies.

'He thought it was right that Italy should produce everything it needs and not have to buy from other countries. And Il Duce made great efforts to improve the health of the nation, to tackle malaria — who wouldn't want that? But as time went by, and he spent more and more time with other Fascists, he gradually stopped pretending to be one of them and became one.

'And that was when the promotions began. He rose from administration jobs to managing people and making decisions that affected a great many people in the city.'

'And what about you, Zia? What did you think?'

Zia sighs, her head dropping slightly. 'I was thinking about myself in those years. I lost baby after baby, Clara. Perhaps that's why he turned to the party — it was a distraction from the heartbreak, from my sadness.'

I squeeze her arm, linked with mine as we walk.

'When I began to come out of my bubble of grief, I could see he had changed. His allegiance had shifted from me to Mussolini. If I made a comment teasing Il Duce, he would scold me — gently, of course, but he would not laugh.

'Ah, Clara,' Zia sighs again, 'I should have done something then. I could have tried to pull him back, to persuade him to get a new job, to find new interests. But I am ashamed to say I didn't. My life was comfortable. For the first time we had money, and I had the time to enjoy it. I was selfish and self-indulgent.'

'No,' I say gently, shaking my head.

'Yes,' she nods. 'There were times, like the time I first met you, when I felt in my heart that I should do something. If not change his opinion, then use his position to make a difference. But if I objected, I did so quietly. And Fascism is about who speaks loudest.'

We walk in silence for a while, Zia's face a cloud of trouble as she mentally sifts through the opportunities where she may have made a difference.

'What made you change your mind?'

'The war,' she says simply. 'It was wrong. Of course it was. Knitting socks wasn't enough for me, but I didn't know what to do.

'Then, one evening, the Signore brought some work home. There was nothing unusual about that as you know, but I happened to read one of the pages on his desk. It was a briefing on the planned movement of munitions and supplies in our region – the military was updating the administration so they could clear roads and railways. While he was sleeping, I copied out the key information. I knew it would be useful to someone.'

'The enemy,' I say quietly.

'Who is our enemy, Clara?' asks Zia sharply. I see by the spark in her eyes that I have touched a nerve.

'Are the Allied countries not the enemy of Italy?' I ask, not quite as confused as I intended to sound.

'They are Mussolini's enemy. Great Britain has always been our friend. Germany is no friend; anyone can see that Hitler is just using us.'

If I had received no other education than that of my school, I would have believed her words traitorous. But thanks to my time at the library with Saba Leone, I understand.

'What did you do with the information?' I ask.

Zia stops walking and, glancing around to ensure no one can hear us, turns to face me.

'I have told you too much already, Clara. You must know that I am putting you, me and everyone involved in danger. You have had no experience other than Fascism . . .'

'I am not a Fascist,' I say through tight lips. 'Have you forgotten that I have not always lived in your house?'

She stares at me for a moment. 'You're right, I'm sorry,' she says. 'But your school . . .'

'I have been reading, Zia. Reading and learning. I know more than you think I do.'

'Perhaps you do,' she nods. 'But that doesn't mean I should share much information with you — or anyone.'

I glance to the right but there is no one near us. 'I understand, Zia,' I say. 'But if you want someone to talk to, you can trust me. I won't tell anyone.' I lift my wrist and, when she looks down at the red band, I pinch it between my thumb and forefinger. 'I swear,' I say.

Zia knows that I believe the red band I always wear connects me to my brother, my mother and even my dead father. She knows it is the most important thing I have, and by swearing on it, I am swearing on the lives of my family.

'Come on,' she says eventually, 'it's safer walking.'

We fall into step with each other as we carry on along the street. There is a busy road at the junction up ahead and, when she begins speaking, Zia talks quickly — she must tell me before we might be overheard.

'There are people everyone knows as . . . helpers. An intermediary between the likes of us and . . . important people.'

'Mafia?' I whisper.

She tilts her head. 'Through a friend, I made contact

with a gentleman. A man of quiet power. I explained that I had information that may be of value to others. Information that may help end the war sooner. He took that scribbled note and, sometime later, I heard that he wanted to meet me again. He said the details I had supplied had been gratefully received and asked if I could get any more. Since then, I have been . . .' She pauses, dropping her voice. 'Sharing information. They say—'

'Who is "they"?' I ask.

She ignores me. '—that a resistance group has been established. That they are working with the British. That the information is going . . .' She stops suddenly as two men turn down our street and walk past us.

'Enough,' she says quietly. 'I have told you enough. All that I ask, Clara,' she says, taking hold of my right hand and squeezing it, 'is that you tell no one. The truth is, the Signore is my husband. He is a good man, but he is guilty of losing himself in the moment, being seduced by power, letting others lead him down the wrong path. I am confident that when the war ends, he will come back to me. I only pray it is not too late.'

PIPPO

1943

The Return

'*Attenzione. Attenzione.*'

The familiar voice of the official announcer crackled over the radio and Pippo held his breath. Bruno had knocked on the door as he, Donna, Gino and Violetta had been eating their meagre supper, and told them to go to the cafe and listen. They had been waiting for nearly an hour, the children playing in a thin jet of water that was spraying from a cracked pipe, casting rainbows across the slowly darkening square. Donna sat on the shaded pavement next to Pippo, occasionally wiping her face with her scarf. Despite the clock chiming half past ten, it was still and warm.

A few more people had begun to arrive, looking expectantly at the radio that sat on the table by the cafe's open doors. When he saw them gather, the bar's owner turned the volume up high and whispered to his wife. Pippo knew that if the announcement they were waiting for proved unpopular, there might be trouble, and the couple would quickly carry the chairs inside and lock the doors.

Standing up, Donna called for the young children to stand beside her and, as they shuffled closer to the radio, she put a protective arm around them. When the music stopped abruptly and there was a moment of hissing silence, she and Pippo glanced at each other.

'Attention. Attention. His Majesty the King and Emperor has accepted the resignation, from the post of head of the government, prime minister and secretary of state, of His Excellency the Knight Benito Mussolini,' said the voice. For a moment, there was quiet, just a few small gasps of surprise.

Then, as shouts sounded, Pippo squinted at the radio in an attempt to hear the voice as it continued, 'And appointed as head of the government, prime minister and secretary of state, His Excellency the Knight, Marshal of Italy Pietro Badoglio.'

'Pippo,' breathed Donna, 'it has happened. It is finally over.' She looked at the boy with tears in her eyes.

'Fascism is dead!' he heard someone in the crowd shout and, slowly, the noise of the crowd began to grow. Women and men began to laugh and cheer. Some broke off from the throng and ran the length of the streets, shouting the news. Lights clicked on and windows opened as word spread.

Pippo reached his arm around Donna's waist and squeezed. Mussolini had been leader since before he could remember; he knew nothing else. Since he had first listened to Mario speak of the Communist Party, he had joined the fight against Il Duce, but it had taken the British and Americans landing in Sicily, the bombings and the turning tide of opinion to herald his end.

As Mussolini had faded from view, so had the fear of him. And now he was gone.

The boy had no idea what his departure would mean for the family or for Italy – but he let her sense of relief flood over him.

'What will happen now, Donna?' he shouted over the noise.

'Armistice,' she said, smiling and pulling her small children closer.

'What's that?'

'It means the end of the war, boy,' a man beside them crowed. 'Mussolini is gone, so we can surrender. And we can tell Hitler to get lost.'

'The Germans!' A woman spat on the floor. 'The sooner we break from them the better.'

The crowd around mumbled their approval of this, but a man in a white shirt hushed them. 'He just said the war continues,' he said, and groans spread through the growing crowd.

'I've heard enough, Pippo,' said Donna, turning and taking the hands of her children. The family walked down the street, Gino and Violetta staring wide-eyed as people fell out of their homes and into the road, singing and cheering. Shouts of 'Down with Fascism!' and 'Death to Mussolini!' rang out as the news spread.

An elderly man with tears in his eyes embraced Donna and Pippo, before swooping Violetta up in his arms and swinging her around. Giggling, she wobbled as he plonked her back down on her feet, and Pippo realized how rarely he heard the sound of her laughter.

He saw true joy on the faces of the strangers around him, and it seemed as if the collective melancholy of hunger and want, the feeling that despair was closer than anyone cared to admit, had, for the moment, been swept aside.

They stumbled home, the clamour from the streets getting louder as more and more people heard the news. As he helped Donna prepare the children for bed, the shouting and cheering continued. And as he laid his head on his pillow, he heard a group of people singing some distance away. Closing his eyes, he strained to hear the words of the familiar tune. That melody – he knew it, but he couldn't remember how. Then the words became clear and he realized why he hadn't heard the song for what seemed like the longest time.

'Bandiera Rossa la trionferà
Bandiera Rossa la trionferà
Evviva il socialismo e la libertà!'

Pippo went to sleep with the words spinning round in his head. The Red Flag will triumph, cheer Socialism and freedom. Freedom.

The next few days were jubilant but confusing. Il Duce was missing and everyone had heard different stories about his disappearance. Mussolini had been arrested. Mussolini was dead. Mussolini was in Germany. Pippo decided that no one really knew except those closest to him, but it didn't really matter because he had gone.

Now there was a general – Badoglio – in charge. Together with the King, he had decreed the country would fight on. The elation faded slowly as these words sank in. What were they fighting for? Hadn't they only been in the war because Il Duce wanted it?

Pippo remembered how people had argued it was a

good thing to go to war, that Italy would fight nobly and be proud to support Germany in a glorious victory. But over the years, those voices had become quieter as the war revealed that the Italian military had not the arms, the supplies or the passion needed to fight the enemy.

Hunger and poverty became as real to friends and neighbours as the terror of what might fall from the skies. Pippo understood that no one had the energy to do anything other than make it to the end of each day. Perhaps tomorrow would be better, but most likely it would be worse. No one spoke about how noble the Italian military were now. No one talked of the pride of the nation.

But since the announcement, people had become animated again — they felt free to talk once more. They met in the streets and spoke of how the war must end soon. How could it carry on? Surely Hitler would accept defeat as Mussolini had? Bruno carried on his job as a cleaner but told anyone who would stop to listen that the anti-Fascist parties would rise and, as soon as the war ended, they would take power.

When Pippo spoke to him one day, the curly haired man told him that there were huge strikes in the north. People were demonstrating against the war — and protesting for more food.

'Where will the food come from?' the boy had asked.

'Everything will be as it was before, Pippo,' the man had stated cheerily. 'And when Socialists and Communists take power, the wealth of the nation will be shared equally.'

'But the soldiers will come home. We will have to feed them, and we don't have enough food for ourselves.'

'Who do you think has been sending them food all

through the war? I'm sure Mussolini was feeding them well – a man cannot fight on an empty stomach. And there will be more men to work the fields, to drive the lorries to bring the food to the cities, to work in the factories to make pasta . . .'

Pippo had looked at Bruno, unconvinced.

'Don't worry, comrade,' the man had smiled. 'All will be well. I feel it in my bones.'

Everyone seemed to share Bruno's optimism. Even Donna. There had been a few times when Pippo had heard her singing as she worked, and now she found the time to play a little with Gino and Violetta, delighting in their stories and games. But Pippo still felt unsettled, an unease in his stomach.

Perhaps it was because the dream had returned. The dream where his mother walked slowly towards him had both haunted and reassured him for such a long time – but now it was different, somehow.

When he'd dreamt of his mother on that very first occasion, it had convinced him her arrival was imminent. 'Wait for me,' she had told him night after night. But she hadn't come. And for a while the dream had disappeared. When it returned, it no longer occurred nightly, but it still comforted the boy: she *would* come; all he had to do was wait.

Sometimes Pippo's mother walked impossibly slowly towards him. Other times she stroked his cheeks, running the end of her finger in a circle around his face and, when he woke, he could still feel the butterfly-soft lines she ran over his forehead, down his cheek, along his chin and up the other side. He'd lie still, not wanting to disturb the moment.

His memory had by then given up the image of her face and he could no longer recall the sound of her voice, so the vision of her in his dream was all he had. He clung to it, squeezing his eyes shut, but it always drifted away, like a ship sinking into black waters.

Since the day Mussolini had gone, though, the dream had once more appeared to him every night. On the surface, it was the same. Her face was clear, her voice strong. She told him to wait for her, again and again. And he trusted her. Alongside the hunger that had settled like an immovable brick in his stomach, though, was a quiver, a shudder, a sense of unease. As if her return brought something dark with it.

One morning, as his mother was still making her snail-slow journey towards him, a scream crashed into his dream. Pushing himself to a sitting position and shaking his head to wake up, he looked around. Gino's wide eyes stared at him.

'It's Mamma,' he whimpered.

Pippo jumped out of bed, Gino scrambling to follow, and the two boys dashed to the door. Yanking it open, for a moment Pippo thought a wild man had broken into the house and was attacking Donna.

But then he saw her face, collapsed into a muddle of emotions — relief, joy and love. As she laughed in disbelief, she stared at the man who held her in his arms.

'Papa,' Pippo heard Gino whisper.

'Mario!' shouted Pippo, his feet finally released from the spot on the floor they had seemed stuck to.

The man quickly turned his head towards the boys, his face thin, his dark hair long and bushy, his beard thick and wiry. The two boys hurtled into him, Gino clinging to his legs, Pippo throwing an arm around his waist.

'Look at you both!' Mario exclaimed, pulling them both to him without easing his grip on Donna. 'Pippo – you're nearly a man,' he said, his breath sour, his clothes fusty and stale.

'And you, Gino!' He looked down at the boy who stared up at him silently. 'You are not the baby I remember.'

Gino shook his head seriously. Pippo noticed he was about to open his mouth to speak when Mario looked around. 'Where is my Violetta?' he asked.

'She's still sleeping,' answered Donna. 'She sleeps through the bombs, that girl,' she laughed. 'I'll wake her . . .'

'No,' Mario shook his head. 'Let her sleep. It's early.' He smiled at Donna, and Pippo knew that there was nothing else in his mind but the woman in front of him. And when he looked at her face, he saw the anxiety and fear and worry that had caused tense creases to line her skin fall away. Light returned to her eyes with a twinkle.

'You must be hungry,' she said and, with an energy he hadn't seen for a while, Pippo watched her pour water into pans and wipe her chopping knife. 'You wash while I cook you something. There's not much but I'll . . .'

She stopped talking when she saw Mario reach into his bag and pull out a small shoulder of pork.

'It's only a piglet,' Mario apologized with a shrug. 'A farmer I stayed with yesterday gave it to me when I told him where I had been.'

Pippo desperately wanted to ask where he had been, but he waited. This time was for Mario and Donna. And he couldn't remember seeing so much meat in years – he and Gino simply stood and stared.

'Oh, Mario,' Donna said, taking the joint as carefully as if it were a baby. 'This will feed us all for weeks! What a breakfast we'll have, boys.'

Mario looked at Pippo. 'Has the war stolen your tongue, comrade?'

Embarrassed, the boy smiled and looked at his bare feet. 'No,' he said quietly.

'It's true,' Donna said, as she sliced a piece of meat off the joint. 'Now I think of it, you used to be such a chatterbox. Didn't your friends call you "Boccalone"?'

'Have you run out of questions?' Mario asked, pouring water into a bowl and rolling up his sleeves.

Pippo didn't know. He still wanted answers – but perhaps now he was nearly thirteen, he only asked the important questions: where could he find food, what was happening in the war, when would things get better.

'Mamma?' said a small voice.

They all turned to see a little girl standing in the doorway, holding a shabby grey cloth rabbit.

'Violetta,' whispered Mario, in wonder at the baby who had become a child.

'Who is he, Mamma?' asked the girl, pointing at her father.

Donna bent down and took her daughter's hand. 'This is your papa,' she said with a laugh. 'Go and say hello.' Gently she pushed the child towards her father's open arms, but the girls stood her ground.

'No,' she said in a determined voice.

'It is,' said Gino, taking hold of his father's hand and letting the man pull him into a hug. 'It is Papa,' he said with a giggle, as Mario tickled him.

Violetta shook her head angrily and grabbed hold of her mother's skirt, following her around the kitchen as she returned to her cooking.

'Give her some time, Mario,' said Donna. 'She doesn't know you yet.'

Pippo saw the hurt in the man's face as he nodded and, giving Gino another hug, asked the boy to fetch a towel to wipe his face.

'How long will you be here?' Pippo asked, as Mario splashed water on his face.

Donna stopped in her tracks. Pippo realized that she had thought he was back home now and would stay. The war was nearly over and there could be no fear of him being conscripted.

Mario dried his face and wiped his ears with the towel. He looked around at the family waiting for his reply.

'Not long,' he said, and Donna released a quiet moan. 'But I am here now, so let's enjoy our time together. Gino,' he said, and the boy stood to attention. 'Bring me my bag — there are presents for you all.'

That evening, when the excited children had finally gone to bed, Mario, Donna and Pippo sat at the candlelit table. Mario sucked on a cigarette, then rolled it between his fingers as he slowly blew smoke towards the ceiling.

'We need you,' he said. 'Both of you.'

'Who is "we"?' asked Pippo.

'The resistance.'

'The enemy?'

Mario shrugged. 'An armistice is being negotiated right now,' he said. 'General Badoglio is talking to the British and Americans, trying to get us out of the war. But they want assurances that he may not be able to deliver.'

'Why not?'

'Because of the Germans.'

'If they get the armistice they want, what will happen to Italy?' asked Donna.

'The British and Americans will bring their forces in to clear out any Germans who are still here.'

'The Nazis will leave?' Pippo said.

'They are retreating in Russia. In Germany, they are being bombed relentlessly. But here, in Italy . . .' Mario sighed. 'There are rumours that the Nazis are infiltrating the north. That they will make a stand against the Allies.'

'*Dio mio*,' said Donna quietly.

'Could Italy fight on the side of the British?' Pippo asked.

Mario nodded. 'Or we could stick with the Germans.'

'How . . .' Donna began, then stopped. 'How could that lead to anything but civil war?'

'Civil war,' Pippo repeated, a chill running through him.

'It's possible,' admitted Mario. 'It's the last thing anyone wants, but we have to plan for every possibility. Whatever happens, we need people in every town and city who are willing to help.'

'How?' asked Donna.

'Information.' Mario tapped ash from his cigarette. 'We need runners.' He looked at Pippo, whose back straightened immediately. 'And eyes and ears,' he said to Donna.

'You are asking me to be a spy,' said Donna, shaking her head.

'More than that. I am asking you to become a partisan,' replied Mario gravely.

'But the children . . .' Donna began.

'I wouldn't ask, my love, but whatever you thought Mussolini was capable of, Hitler is ten times worse. There are risks in fighting the Germans, yes, but the true danger lies in letting them win.'

Donna sighed. Her husband leaned towards her and took her hand, rubbing her skin gently. 'I have asked you to be brave before, but now I do not ask for my political beliefs. This is for our children's future, possibly their very existence.'

'Are you not a Communist any more?' asked Pippo.

'Of course!' grinned Mario. 'But,' he said, his broad smile slipping a little, 'this is not like the Spanish war. There we fought for ideas and ideals. Here, we are fighting for humanity.'

Mario looked at Donna. 'I never understood how men joined up and went to foreign lands, sent by our leaders to fight for gain and greed. But now I believe we should fight; for the sake of our children.'

His wife looked wryly at him. 'You know I will do whatever you ask, but you cannot be suggesting the Nazis are baby eaters. Not even Hitler could be guilty of killing innocent children.'

Mario's head fell, his unruly hair tumbling forward. 'You have no idea of the things I have seen. And worse, stories I have heard from soldiers who have survived massacres, escaped from places of such evil I cannot tell you.'

Pippo's throat was dry. He gave a small cough before speaking.

'I am with you,' he said, but his words made all three of them stop. As he had spoken, his voice had dropped, surprising them with its deep and heavy resonance.

Mario thumped his left shoulder with a grin. 'With those words, Filippo, you become a man.'

CLARA

1943

Lost in the Smoke

I wake to the sound of rumbling. Is it an earthquake? No, I decide, as I notice that my bed is not moving and the glass in the windows is not rattling. As I become more alert, I hear other noises — stamping and shouting. Quickly, I pull on my dressing gown and dash to push open the shutters.

Although the house sits on a side street, from my window I can see the main road. There, I spot a squat, heavy vehicle slowly drive by, its tyres reverberating on the cobblestones. Then, after it passes, rows of soldiers follow, guns resting on their shoulders, boots stomping on the ground. An officer walks alongside them, barking orders.

Germans.

The Signore warned us this might happen. From the day Mussolini was arrested, he has returned home with concerns and warnings. I had noticed his National Fascist Party pin had disappeared on the same day as Il Duce. When the fall of the Fascists was greeted with such joy, he said he wanted to avoid any trouble. Zia urged him to leave his job, find another where he wouldn't be associated with the government, but he insisted he'd stay.

'I am only a civil servant,' he said quietly. 'All I have ever done is what I am told to do.'

From Zia's reaction, I wondered just what his superiors had told him to do, and how readily he had acted on his orders. In the past year, I have seen the Signore's enthusiasm for Mussolini wane with the fortunes of our forces. His bravado has faltered, his confidence faded and his ambition disintegrated. When a more senior colleague was killed in an air strike, he waited anxiously to hear who the replacement would be. Zia threw her arms around him with relief when he returned home with the news that another had been chosen. Instead of rising through the ranks of the Fascist government, I could see that he wanted to become as quiet and small as a mouse, unnoticed as he went about his business.

But as the little mouse worked, he read every paper and document that passed across his desk, and some that did not. He absorbed every piece of information about the war, the state of the country and its leader and, in the evenings, he and Zia discussed at length the impact it might have on us. 'If the Germans come,' the Signore warned, 'everyone will have to be careful.'

I would sit in the corner, listening, and worrying for Zia. Now, as I watch the Nazis march into our city, I hope with all my being that she will see the danger and stop carrying messages.

Gently pulling the shutters closed, I tie my dressing gown cord around my waist and quickly head downstairs to the kitchen, where Filomena is clattering pans angrily.

Zia is already there, dressed in a pink satin dressing gown.

'Do you have to make such a noise?' Zia asks Filomena, sipping her coffee and wincing as another pan slams on the cooker.

'Germans!' spits the cook. 'Nazis, here in our city. How can this be possible, Signora?'

Zia shrugs an elegant shoulder.

'Have we been invaded?' I ask.

'I think' – Zia pulls a chair out from under the table for me – 'they call it occupation.'

'Occupation!' shrieks Filomena. 'Occupied by the Nazis. We've just got rid of our own Fascists and more arrive to take their place.'

I see that she is not actually cooking anything, just moving pans from place to place, so I reach for a small loaf sitting on a board and start cutting a slice for myself.

'Where is the Signore?' I ask, opening a jar of jam. I know it is one of the last of Filomena's cherry jams, so I spread the thinnest amount on my bread.

'He left early,' says Zia, pulling a pack of cigarettes out of her pocket. She lights one as I take a bite and chew, wondering what he will find at work.

'No school today,' Zia says, as she slides the pack back in her dressing gown pocket.

I make a 'mmm' sound through my breakfast as I nod.

'I wouldn't be surprised if the Signore finds his office closed down too,' says Filomena, stomping across the kitchen as heavy-footed as a soldier. 'There will be even less food now they're here, as well.' She shakes her finger at us. 'You will see. They are evil through and through, those Germans.'

'Perhaps it won't be too bad,' suggests Zia, with an optimism I know belies her sharp mind.

'Won't be too bad?' repeats Filomena. 'It will be one hundred times worse. The British will bomb the city even more, trying to hit them, and we will be killed along with them. We, the people who never wanted to hold hands with Hitler, never wanted to go to war. We will be killed.'

'None of us is going to be killed, Filomena,' Zia says softly. 'Now, please stop banging those pans. Are there any eggs?'

'No eggs,' replies the cook with a large sigh. 'Even the chicken knows today is a very bad day.'

It is late in the evening when the Signore eventually comes home. Zia and I are playing cards and, for once, I am winning.

'Darling,' she says, rising to meet him and kissing his sallow cheek. 'What happened?'

'They are as efficient and as ruthless as their reputation suggests,' he says, as he sinks into an armchair.

We sit and wait for him to explain.

'They have taken over everything,' he says. 'Every letter, every document must be seen by them. Our office is managed by a captain who speaks passable Italian. They do not share information that we do not need to know. So I have no idea which roads are open or where troops will be stationed. Instead of managing the movement of supplies and people through our city, my job now is solely to organize the maintenance of shelters and the clearing of roads after bombings.'

'But that's a good thing,' says Zia, perching on the

arm of his chair and stroking his hair. 'Now no one can accuse you of collusion.'

He ignores her, shaking his head. 'Their power is driven by fear — and judging by their attitude to violence, there is much to be afraid of. And there's more. They are planning arrests — anyone they suspect of dissidence. The Jews, too — they're rounding them up and taking them away. My colleagues are involved in arranging the trains.'

'Not all of them?' I say in disbelief.

'Every single one they can find.'

'Where are they taking them?'

'Camps. They say they are being taken away to work. But I do not like it. There is a way that they speak of the Jews, as if they are not human beings.'

'But darling,' says Zia quietly, 'we have been here before. The Racial Laws, remember? When you arranged—'

'Shh!' says the Signore suddenly, and I see Zia's eyes flutter as they both glance at me briefly. 'It is one thing to say a group of people are not true Italians. It is another to class them as animals. We moved people for their own safety then. It was not done with cruelty as this is,' he says.

I am only half listening. My mind is filled with worry for Saba.

Bang, bang, bang.

My knuckles hurt as I hit the old wooden door. I have been knocking for ten minutes now, my stomach tied in a thick knot. The Nazis' curfew meant I had to wait until morning but I woke early, dressed and slipped out of the house, running as fast as I could to the library. I hoped I was not too late.

Saba Leone has been sleeping at the library since his home was bombed. Again, the Rector came to his aid, allowing him to keep a mattress, some bedding and clothes at the library. He sleeps, the old man told me, in the Romance section. He likes to be surrounded by love as he dreams.

The street is quiet, apart from my knocking. As I stop for a moment to listen for movement from the other side of the door, I hear stamping. I turn and see six German soldiers led by an officer in black. They are heading towards me.

I step away from the door, hoping that they will pass. Perhaps they are going into the university. But as I watch the tall soldiers, their eyes shaded by their helmets, holding their guns on their chests, I can see they are making for the library.

Taking another step away from the door, I switch from wishing Saba would open the door to hoping that he is not there, that he is somewhere far away and safe.

But at that moment, I hear a click and a squeak, and the door slowly opens. The old gentleman stands blinking in the sunlight. His clothes are dishevelled and his hair is crumpled.

'Clara,' he says, peering blearily at me. 'Why are you here so early?' He drags his hand over his hair to smooth it down.

'I came to warn you,' I hiss, casting my eyes towards the approaching men. 'They are taking Jews away.'

Saba turns his head and, for a fraction of a second, I sense he is going to slam the door shut and lock it.

But then his chin lifts and he straightens his back, ready to face the soldiers.

The marching stops when they reach the library, and the officer in black steps towards the elderly man.

'Leone?' he asks, his voice sharp and loud in the quiet morning.

'Sì,' nods Saba.

'*Du wirst mit uns kommen,*' the officer says.

To his surprise, the old man replies in German. I cannot understand what he says, but the officer only answers curtly.

Saba points with his thumb over his shoulder and asks something else, perhaps if he can get some of his things, but the man in black shouts, '*Jetzt!*'

The elderly man jumps at the sound, but pulls the door shut, turning its handle before slowly releasing it, as if he is saying goodbye to the library.

On the officer's command, the soldiers turn on their heel, creating a space for the old Jew. He slips into it and they begin marching.

'Sab— Signor Leone,' I call, as I skitter alongside them. I am frightened of these soldiers, but more afraid that I will never see my friend again.

'Clara,' he replies, as he hurries to keep up with his guards, all of whom are a full head taller than him. 'Please tell the Rector what has happened. Ask him to contact my family – he has their addresses.'

'Where are they taking you?'

'They won't tell me.'

'But—'

'Don't worry, Clara, all will be well. I speak German – it will help me.'

'I can't . . .' Before I can tell him all the things I want to, how he has helped me, how I feel more complete since I began reading with him, how I owe him more thanks than he'll ever know, the officer in black pushes me roughly away. I stumble and trip on the edge of the pavement, and fall to my knees. I feel the scrape of gravel on bare skin, but ignore it as I raise my head to watch the six sturdy men in helmets march away a small, worn old man. It is only now that I notice he is wearing slippers.

The Signore runs his fingers through his hair as we all lean over the document lying on the table. It is a list of names and addresses, carefully typed onto official government paper.

'I shouldn't have brought it home,' he says, shaking his head. 'It will only bring us danger. I'll take it back tomorrow and tell them the truth – that it was given to me accidentally.'

'They'll ask why you didn't hand it back immediately,' whispers Zia, as if we may be overheard.

The Signore sighs and nods, unable to take his eyes off the list.

'Perhaps we should do something . . .' says Zia thoughtfully.

'There is nothing we can do,' her husband replies quickly.

I shake my head too, knowing what she plans to do.

'Look at some of these names, *Amore*.' Zia points at a few of them. 'Anna Jilani, Maria Toscani, Donna Pinto – they are wives, mothers, sisters.'

The Signore is silent.

Zia continues, 'Don't you think, *Amore*, as fellow Italians, we should warn them that the Germans have this information on them?'

Biting my lip, I hold my breath for what I know is coming.

'I . . .' Zia pauses before continuing, 'I might know someone who would find this information helpful.'

Her husband stares at her, his eyes softening before he eventually says, 'I know you do.'

'What do you mean?' she replies, startled.

'Did you really think it was a coincidence that I happened to bring home so much' — he searches for the word — 'useful information?'

I cannot remember a time when I have seen Zia lost for words.

'I have known for a long time that you were reading the documents in my case. I talked to you about things I should have kept quiet,' he continues. 'And when news of attacks or sabotage arrived, I knew the details were being disclosed.'

'I wasn't betraying you, *Amore*,' said Zia gently, placing a hand on his.

The Signore looks at her hand before taking it in his and linking their fingers. 'I know,' he says. 'I know that it was your way of trying to make a difference. You chose the right side, my darling. And I knew it. That's when I started putting documents in my bag that I knew would be helpful to whoever was receiving them.'

Zia's lips tremble as she smiles. Tears come to her eyes.

'You have been helping too,' she says. Her relief is tangible. 'You came back.'

The Signore looks into her eyes and nods.

'So, I can take this . . .' Wiping her eyes, Zia turns back to the list on the table.

'No,' he shakes his head gravely. 'It is different now. It is too dangerous. The Nazis are—'

She interrupts him. 'They may have people watching you, but they are unlikely to be interested in me. I can—'

'I can't let you,' repeats the Signore.

'*Amore*.' She takes his hand and holds it, looking into his eyes. 'I want to do this. For these people, for all our people, for Italy.'

The Signore looks at her.

'We are all Italians,' she says softly. 'Whether we are as strong and loud as a lion, or as quiet as a fawn in the woods.' She glances at me. 'Fascist, Communist, Catholic, Jew, Roma – whoever we are and however we live, now is the time to just be Italian. I want to be an Italian who helps other Italians. Not because of politics, not to be courageous, but because it is the right thing to do.'

The Signore looks at his hands, which lie motionless in his lap.

Zia continues, 'And I think you want the same. Why else would you bring this document home, show it to me – when you knew what I've been doing?'

The Signore is silent. Then, with a long sigh, he says, 'You're right,' in a voice so quiet I can barely hear him.

Zia grabs his two hands in hers and lifts them to her red lips, kissing them as she looks into his eyes.

'You must let me know where you will be; I will follow at a distance.'

'No,' she says forcefully. 'You must have nothing to

do with this. It is madness for anyone else to be involved.'
With these words, she turns her gaze to me.

Zia strides along the pavement. I hang back, ready to
slide into a doorway if she looks behind her.

I knew that it would be today from her unease at
breakfast. The Signore left early as usual, and she had
nothing but cigarettes, one after another, while I ate
my single slice of bread. I chatted with Filomena as I
normally would, and pretended not to notice the shaking
of Zia's hand as she lit another.

Later, I kissed her goodbye and left for school, but
instead I hid behind a low wall further down our street.
Now I see her leaving the house. She has scraped the
last of her ruby red lipstick out of its tube to paint her
lips, and put up her hair as elegantly as she can before
pulling her favourite green pillbox hat onto her head.
She looks stylish and unaffected by the war around us.

Luckily, she walks to the meeting point – I wouldn't
have been able to follow her on a bus. It's an upmarket
part of the city where once we shopped and drank coffee.
Now, many of the shops are closed, with either no wares
to sell or no customers to sell to. Some of the coffee
shops are still open, selling expensive drinks to those
who have money – German officers.

I watch as Zia walks confidently, clutching her leather
handbag tightly in her hand. As I scan the street, I see
the cleaner she delivered papers to before. He brushes
the pavement outside a cafe filled with black-uniformed
Nazis. They stand in the cramped shop, smoking and
drinking, chatting and laughing, and I wonder if they
think our occupation is a holiday.

Zia sees the officers too and her step falters. Surely this can't be right — she cannot drop off the carefully copied list of names into the cleaner's bin while it sits outside a cafe filled with Germans.

She is blocked from my view by a man walking towards me. I step out of his way, but as he passes, he whispers, '*Scappa!*'

Run.

The word takes a moment to sink in. And then I look at the scene in front of me again. The trolley bin sits directly outside the coffee shop. The cleaner sweeps his way away from it. The street is almost empty, except for a few people scuttling into side streets. Then I notice the owner of the shop next to the cafe quietly close its shutters.

At that moment, the cleaner turns his head and sees Zia. From the look in his eyes, it is clear there has been a mistake. She is not supposed to be here. He stops sweeping for a moment, an action that catches the attention of an officer sitting by the cafe's window.

The Nazi follows the cleaner's gaze to Zia, who has stopped walking and stands looking confused. Time moves slowly as I watch his eyes return to the cleaner, and then to the trolley bin in front of him.

His shout speeds time up again.

The cleaner drops his broom and dashes towards Zia, grabbing her hand and tugging her. She pivots, a shocked look on her face, and when she sees me behind her, she stumbles. I rush to her and together, the cleaner and I pull her to her feet and drag her away.

We run and I hear more shouting in German, and scuffling as I imagine they spill out onto the street — I dare not look behind me. The edge of my vision catches a bright flash of light and, as my foot hits the ground, I feel a vibration rippling beneath it. The sound that follows is so loud my ears hurt with the pressure of it. A hot blast hits my back with a physical force that slams me, face first, to the ground. One hand still clings tightly to Zia while the other covers my head, as pellets of I don't know what drop onto my body.

I try to open my eyes, but dust coats my skin and hangs thickly in the air, and I can see nothing. Dizzy and winded, I blink, still trying to take in what has just happened. But before I can gather my thoughts, Zia's hand is tugging mine, pulling me to my feet. I stagger on wobbling legs, clinging on to Zia even though I can barely see her, my other arm over my nose and mouth as I try not to breathe in the murky air.

Sounds are oddly muffled, but I hear the cleaner nearby and can just about make out his shape through the thick, grey fug. Taking a breath, smoke and grime fill my mouth and I immediately cough to dispel it. My throat rasps and suddenly breathing is difficult. Frightened, I slow a little, but Zia's hand grips me harder and drags me around a corner. I follow, and then I see a doorway loom; as I fall through it, it closes quickly behind me.

The cleaner leans against the door, panting. He is covered in dust, making him look like a curly haired version of the Michelangelo statue Saba showed me in books about the Renaissance. I turn my head to Zia, who looks the same, with traces of ruby shining through at her lips. When she sees me, she pulls me to her and we hold each other.

'What has happened?' I hear an old woman's voice

ask, and we all turn to her. She stands behind a glass counter filled with buttons. Zips, threads and wools are stacked on the shelves behind her.

Zia opens her mouth to speak to the woman, but begins to cough again and I gently pat her back.

'No time,' urges the cleaner. He looks at the woman. 'Is there another way out we can use?'

The woman nods and, nimbler than her years might suggest, leads us through to the rear of the shop, pointing towards a small door that's already half ajar. The cleaner nods his thanks as he ushers us out into a narrow alleyway.

The dust has begun to settle, and we can hear the shouts, whistles and footsteps of the Germans running through the nearby streets.

'Here!' says the cleaner, and we turn into a main street in time to see a bus driving slowly towards us.

The cleaner raps on the bus door and, as the driver quickly pushes the lever to open it, he says to Zia, 'They have seen you. Stay at home – do not attempt to meet me again.'

Zia nods her head at him. Then, blinking, she remembers why she is here. She yanks open her bag and pulls out the sheet of paper. The cleaner takes it and gives her a small smile, before pushing it into his pocket and stepping away from the bus. There is just time for him to dash over the road and disappear into an alley before the Germans are upon us.

There are shouts behind us as Zia and I climb up the step and drop down behind the other passengers. The driver swiftly shuts the door and pulls away, ignoring the undeniable calls of 'Stop!'

Zia and I crouch in the aisle of the bus, hanging on to the edge of the seats as the bus speeds along the road. I look at her and see tears running down her face, leaving black and grey streaks on her cheeks.

'Take this,' says a kind voice, and we both turn to a woman who holds out a clean white handkerchief to Zia.

'Here,' says the elderly woman on our right, 'I have some water. Let's clean you up before you get off the bus.'

As two more handkerchiefs are waved towards us, I look at Zia. Her grey and ruby lips part, and her white teeth appear in a large smile.

PIPPO

1944

The Visitors

Pippo was good at his job. They said he was like a bird in the woods — he had the ability to disappear in plain sight. It was the reason the partisans depended on him to collect their guests from a designated place and take them back to his family home. When their stay in the safe house was over, he would escort them to their next contact, usually someone on the edge of the city who would take them onto the following part of their journey. He did it without causing suspicion, and he'd never been stopped by the police or the Nazis.

He enjoyed his work, meeting all kinds of people — escaped prisoners, spies, partisans — and although he had to clench his teeth, he never asked who they were, what they'd done, or where they were going. He knew his job was too important for childish chatter.

Sometimes they told him. Sometimes they'd been on their own for so long that they just wanted to talk to another human being. Pippo listened, quashing the dozens of questions that popped into his head with every sentence he heard, and nodded. When they were walking the back streets of the city, he had to be on his toes, listening for Germans around every corner, watching for anything out of place. Only when they'd arrived safely at home, and their guest was settled comfortably in the tiny attic room, would he relax.

The apartment felt like home to him now. Being on the third floor gave them the advantage of hearing when anyone came into the central stairwell, and their visitors time to hide themselves in the secret cupboard behind the piles of damp sheets.

When Bruno had come with the news that Donna's name was on a list of known partisans, they had quickly packed up the family's things and moved to an area nearer to the city's centre. There, Donna had started taking in laundry. The Germans took over the best residences in the city, housing officers in smart hotels. Donna worked for a large laundry service that collected and cleaned sheets and towels, tablecloths and napkins, and delivered everything back to the hotel staff. When they had too much work, which was almost all of the time, they sent piles of laundry to Donna.

The apartment had a small, enclosed courtyard where Donna sat, washing and scrubbing every item that came in. Gino and Violetta played with other children from the block of homes, their screams and shouts echoing around the space.

Mario was in touch often, sending messages that he was safe via some of the men and women who hid at the apartment. They knew that he was in the north, and that the Communists had built a strong militia within the partisans. News of their successes were sometimes reported in the paper that Donna read to Pippo in the evenings when the children were in bed.

Now more than ever, Pippo wanted to know what was happening across the country. He would find newspapers that had been discarded and take them back to Donna, who would run her finger along each line, slowly reading the latest news. Pippo often tried to read too, but he read even more slowly than Donna and the two of them became impatient.

Since the Germans had arrived, the brief return to a free press had been replaced by censorship and propaganda. But political and partisan papers could be found easily and, once read, were left in places where others knew to look for them.

Along with the papers, Bruno had kept them up to date. Just a few months after the arrest of Mussolini, he'd spat on the floor as he'd explained that as the Allies advanced from the tip of the boot, the King and Badoglio had fled. 'Like rats leaving a sinking ship,' he had said, pulling a curl distractedly.

'But now we are on the side of the British?' Donna had asked, confused.

'That's the trouble,' Bruno had replied. 'The government has declared war on Germany, but Badoglio left no instructions for the military. Some are travelling to join the British and Americans to drive the Nazis out.'

'And the others?' Pippo had asked.

'The true Fascists have joined the German army.'

'So Italian soldiers will be fighting Italian soldiers?' Donna had asked.

Bruno had nodded.

'What a mess.'

'You're right, Pippo,' the man had sighed. 'You're right.'

They had been lost for words when the Germans had rescued Mussolini from the hotel where he was being held captive and placed him at the head of the government. But soon, it became clear that Il Duce was no longer leader; he had no power at all.

Since then, the newspapers had reported the progress of the Allies. Pippo and Donna had watched the line as it moved speedily up the country, telling them the British and Americans were getting closer with every battle. But then the line stopped. Month after month, nothing changed. Bruno blamed the Germans' military skills, and also the weather.

Pippo didn't know about the Nazis' battle competence, but he could understand the freezing cold and wet winter slowing down movement of any sort.

He was wrapped in all his clothes when he met Bruno one dark morning.

As they exchanged pleasantries, they stamped their feet and tucked their hands into their armpits, their eyes darting around them to see if they were being watched.

'Something is coming,' was all Bruno would say.

Pippo knew better than to press him for more information, but his mind whirled with all the possibilities. Would it be civil disobedience? A national strike designed to reduce the Nazis' ability to run towns and cities? Or a military action — sabotage, an armed attack, a bomb?

He said nothing, but waited for Bruno's instructions.

'The next delivery will be in two days,' the man said.

'One parcel?' Pippo asked, blowing into his own cupped, gloved hands.

'Two,' came the reply. 'Warn your mother.'

Pippo nodded. He never corrected people that Donna was not his mother now. In so many ways, she was.

'Pick up from the university library. Do you know where that is?'

The boy nodded again. 'Inside?'

'Outside. Afternoon. Five thirty.'

The boy was turning on his heel to leave, thinking how a run might warm him, when he felt a nudge on his arm. Looking back, he saw Bruno reaching out a hand. He turned and shook his friend's hand, relieving him of two packs of cigarettes as he did.

Pippo sucked on a cigarette as he waited. From where he stood, he had a good view of the library entrance, the word *Biblioteca* set in stone above the door. The door opened and the boy's back stiffened, but he relaxed when a young man came out carrying some books under his arm and scurried off into the cold wind.

The thought of being a student, reading books and writing papers, left Pippo feeling empty. The country needed academics, of course, but he'd rather be out living life, seeing and doing what those students were reading about.

Clara would have liked to be a student, he thought, an image of his sister unexpectedly coming to him. In his mind, she appeared younger than she really was – younger even than he was now – because she looked exactly as she had the last time he saw her.

He was sure that she would have been drawn to a university like this. A place of learning, but also of history, filled with interesting people and beautiful objects. She had always been fascinated by the trinkets their mother kept — where they came from and what they meant. She was in awe of the paintings in churches they attended, and loved to listen to stories — whoever told them. Not the tales of legend and imagination, folklore and fairy stories that he adored, but real people in real places at real events.

She had been the one who told him their father's story. Pippo knew Clara cherished her few recollections of him, and had quizzed their mother about *her* memories of him, gathering facts as a squirrel scrabbles for nuts on the forest floor.

After his death, their mother rarely spoke of him, so it was Pippo's sister who had told him of their father's dark hair and big smile, his quiet words. How he had loved them all, and how he had always put family first.

The narratives had drifted away now, all apart from one. His sister had painted him a picture of her favourite memory so vividly that he could still pull it easily into his mind.

It had been a celebration, a wedding perhaps, and Clara had watched their parents dance. Their mamma had stepped forward first, her black hair curled and pinned under a pretty scarf. She had stood in front of their father and spun around, her arms in the air, laced sleeves fluttering and jewellery glinting in the sun. Behind her, their papa had stood tall in his best white shirt. Suddenly, she had said, his head began bobbing up and down as his legs kicked and twisted at the knee. Clara said she had danced beside them, twirling and whirling to the music that friends and family played. It was her happiest memory of their old life and, although it was from a time before he was born, it had become Pippo's too.

He dropped the cigarette and tapped the glow out with the toe of his boot. He twisted the red band on his wrist round and round as he tried to picture his sister now. A young woman of sixteen, he could see her dressed in smart clothes like the student who had just walked out of the library. Her hair was still long and dark, her eyes glowing like drops of honey, but she was taller, more elegant, her lips a little pinker.

He hoped that the image of her that he had conjured was close to what she had become. He hoped that wherever she had gone the day he woke up alone, it was a good place. The dream of his mother, which still came to him from time to time, led him to believe that Clara was not with her. And if she couldn't be with their mamma, he wanted her to be somewhere safe, with plenty to eat.

He wondered if she ever thought of him. She'd never forget her baby brother, he decided. What was it Clara and Mamma had called him? A little chatty bird, he recalled with a smile. He wasn't quite as chatty these days.

He gazed, lost in his thoughts, at the library.

'Is there a place I can get washing done?' a quiet voice suddenly whispered in his ear, making him jump.

Annoyed at himself for not being alert, Pippo turned to the person who had crept up beside him. The winter light was starting to fade, but he saw the warm, friendly face of a man in his thirties. Behind him fidgeted a younger man, who pulled his cap down on his forehead, hiding his green eyes.

'I know somewhere,' Pippo replied with a nod. 'Follow me.'

As the three set off through the rapidly darkening streets, Pippo glanced at them again. The one who had spoken to him was obviously Italian, a resistance fighter no doubt, probably a Communist. The other was harder to determine – Pippo wasn't even sure if he was Italian. If he was a fighter, he didn't have the confidence and swagger of a soldier. Instead he was stiff and anxious, uncomfortable in the situation he found himself.

They were silent as Pippo led them down alleys and quiet streets, stopping occasionally when he spotted police or Germans, slinking into doorways or stairwells. It was only when the boy pushed the heavy wooden door of his building closed behind them, clicking the solid latch into place, that he saw the young man breathe out slowly, leaning on the wall to stop himself from falling down.

'What's wrong with him?' Pippo asked the other man.

'First mission,' said the fighter with a grin, adding cheerily, 'he's the bomb maker.'

Pippo wondered if someone so nervous should be in charge of explosives, but shrugged and led them up the stairs to the apartment.

Donna welcomed them quietly, learning quickly that their names were Domenico and Maurizio. Maurizio,

Domenico informed them, was from the south and had been smuggled over the battle line to help the resistance.

As Donna poured them both a hot drink, Pippo saw the young man's pale hand shake as he reached for the cup.

'*Grazie*,' he whispered, bringing the steaming tea to his face.

'Gino, fetch the food,' said his mother, and the boy dashed towards the small kitchen. Violetta leaned on her mother's skirt, twirling an apron string and sucking her thumb, watching the two men with large eyes.

'How long will you be with us?' asked Donna, as the young boy returned carrying a board with a fresh loaf of bread, a small piece of cheese and a knife.

'Two days,' replied Domenico, pulling up a stool and sitting down to slice the bread. 'We're here to do a job — a big one. We'll leave in the aftermath. *Mangia!*' He jerked his head from Maurizio to the food.

The young man did as he was told and sliced a sliver of the hard cheese, before biting gingerly into it.

'A big job?' Pippo was unable to stop himself asking.

'Yes,' nodded Domenico. 'If all goes to plan.'

Maurizio took a sharp breath and, catching crumbs of cheese in his throat, began to cough.

'Don't panic,' laughed the older man, slapping his companion on the back, 'we'll be fine.'

Pippo was admiring the bicycle that Botte had been given by an uncle when the bomb went off. Even though it was some distance away, the sound was unmistakable and they felt the rumble under their feet. It was a big explosion, much larger than the ones Bruno was usually involved in, and as soon as he heard it, the boy knew it was a serious act of subversion.

Most people stopped and turned, looking towards the sound and watching the grey tower of smoke rise above the rooftops, but Botte said, 'Come on,' and Pippo swung his leg over the rack behind the seat. They were off. Peddling hard, Botte steered towards where the explosion had come from, veering around pedestrians and other cyclists.

As they turned a sharp corner, Botte's eyes were on the thick smoke up ahead and he didn't see the horse pulling a cart slowly up the street. Pippo shouted in his ear, and the boy swerved the bike to avoid the blinkered beast, who hesitated, heavy foot raised in the air.

The bicycle missed the horse, but its front wheel caught the cart's large wooden wheel and twisted, flinging both boys against the edge of the cart. Pippo grabbed the oily sackcloth that covered the cart's goods to stop himself from falling, but instead he slid to the cobblestones as the cover fell with him.

The cart's owner shouted that the boys were idiots, and grabbed the cloth quickly to recover his load of sand-filled sacks. He was fast, but not quick enough to prevent Pippo glimpsing two faces nestled amongst the sacking. One looked terrified, green eyes shining with fear, the other only mildly surprised. When Domenico realized who it was, he managed a wink before the cart's owner pulled the cover over his face.

Calling to his horse and tapping its back with the reins, the driver moved the cart away, slowly and steadily leading his load to safety. Pippo checked Botte, who was inspecting a graze through the ripped leg of his trousers, before helping him up.

'Come on,' he said. 'Let's go home.'

Everyone said that the Germans were furious. The blast had killed two senior officers and a number of soldiers, and destroyed an armoured vehicle. People spoke in hushed voices, saying that the Nazis would never allow an incident like this to pass, that there would be reprisals.

Pippo had avoided Bruno since the attack, and he and Donna had gone over the apartment a dozen times, checking for any evidence that guests had stayed. But when there was a loud knocking on the entrance early one morning, a chill ran down the boy's spine nonetheless.

'You go,' said Donna through the curtain that separated where she and Violetta slept from the boys. 'I'm still getting dressed.'

Pippo slipped his feet into his thin, worn shoes and dragged his fingers through his hair, trying to smooth it down.

'Can I come?' whispered Gino from the bed.

Pippo looked at him for a moment, the young boy sitting in bed, his dark eyes earnest and frightened.

'Stay beside me,' he nodded.

The two boys dashed towards the stairwell to see what was happening. They watched as Signora Bianchi hobbled towards the large door, wrapping her black shawl tightly around her shoulders.

'Open the door!' shouted a voice with a thick German accent, and Pippo saw the old woman's hand hesitate for a moment beside the lock. She twisted her head and looked up the stairs to where the two boys stood, watching.

Pippo nodded to her and she turned the heavy lock. As soon as they heard it slide out of its holding, the soldiers on the other side yanked the handle and pushed open the door. The Signora shuffled out of the way as a stream of uniformed men flooded into the entrance.

Peering over the railings, Pippo saw that most of their neighbours were standing at the top of the stairs or in their doorways, just as he was, waiting to see where the soldiers would go. An officer stepped in from the street and snapped his orders at the Germans, who began to run up the stairs.

The first pair of men pushed past Signor Eposito, into the first floor apartment where he lived alone, as the rest continued to climb. Pippo knew then that, while the Germans might have been informed that the resistance had stayed in the building, neither Donna nor he had been named: if they had, the soldiers would have come straight to their apartment; instead they planned to search everyone's homes.

He and Gino looked on as several of the soldiers came closer, boots stamping up steps, over the sound of crashing furniture and smashing glass coming from the lower flats. Finally, two men – surprisingly young, Pippo thought – reached their floor. It was only then that he realized Gino was not by his side.

'Mouse?' he whispered, turning anxiously.

Instead, the boy was in front of the door, saying nervously that his mother was dressing, his arms outstretched as if to stop a football going into a goal. But it was not a leather ball, it was a German soldier.

The Nazi pushed Gino harder than was necessary and the boy, light as a feather, stumbled backwards from the shove, hitting the edge of the door frame. His head bounced once, violently, before returning to its upright position. Pippo shouted Gino's name and dashed towards him as the child slid down until he was sitting, the edge of the door propping him up.

The soldiers ignored them and tramped into the apartment, pushing the table and chairs out of their way as they searched for any form of evidence against the family.

'Donna!' Pippo shouted as he kneeled in front of Gino. The child's eyes flickered briefly before his face relaxed, eyes open but unseeing.

'No,' whispered Pippo as Donna appeared at the door, dragging Violetta behind her.

'Gino?' she said, taking in the limp form of her son propped up on the floor, the smear of blood running down the sharp edge of the door frame.

'Gino?' she repeated, more quietly, sinking to her knees and lifting her child's face in both hands. The boy's body slumped forward, and Donna grappled it into her arms, whispering his name again and again.

'What's wrong with Gino?' asked Violetta loudly, and Pippo pulled her towards him, holding her tightly as they watched Donna keen, rocking the boy in her arms.

It was so easy, Pippo thought. All the bombs and ammunition they used to kill soldiers, and yet to take a life took simply a push; a small shove and a fall.

The family stayed still until the soldiers finished their search and left, with just a fleeting glance towards the mother sobbing into the neck of her dead child. They had found nothing.

Dazed, Pippo helped Donna carry Gino into the apartment and place him carefully on the bed. By then, neighbours had appeared at the door. The boy called in the women he knew would help Donna and asked the others to let them grieve.

By the time Violetta and Donna had been wrapped in the cocoon of hugs and soft words, a feeling was bubbling angrily in his belly. He turned and left the apartment, taking the stairs slowly. He glanced into each doorway where the same sight of neighbours picking up furniture and clearing broken keepsakes was repeated. By the time he reached the door to the street, he felt the gurgling rage settle to bile, a bitter sensation spreading from his stomach up to his heart and lungs.

Stepping out onto the street, he turned away from the group of soldiers who were already pouring into the entrance next door on their fruitless search, and looked up the quiet road.

It was still early, but he was sure he could find Bruno. He would find his friend and ask him how he could use this feeling inside him. This feeling that made his fingers curl into his palms, digging his bitten nails into his own skin. This feeling that made his breath jagged and his teeth grind against one another. This feeling that made him hum a tuneless song to stop himself from screaming with fury.

He began walking slowly, but soon the feeling made

him pick up his feet and carried him forward in an easy run. It felt good – or at least, it helped – so he let the feeling push him faster and faster until he felt he was almost flying.

Driving himself on until he could feel each painful cobblestone under his thinly soled shoes, until his breath burned in his lungs, his nose ran and his eyes watered, he headed to the square without thinking, instinct taking over. Eventually, though, he could run no further and he slowed to a fast walk, his hands resting on his thin waist, his whole body gasping for air.

It was only then that he noticed how many people were going in the same direction as him. It was still early morning and he could think of no reason why people would want to go to the square at this time. He listened to the murmurings of the men and women beside him as he joined the growing crowd. 'The Nazis,' he heard. 'Reprisals,' he heard. 'Executions,' he heard.

When he reached the edge of the square, he ducked past and pushed through until he found himself crouched at the ground, peering towards the square between the legs of two German soldiers.

Another line of Nazis stood in the centre of the square and, past them, Pippo could see more men. An order was issued in German and they raised their rifles. Then he saw the men the guns were aimed at. Men who were blindfolded with their hands tied behind their backs. He ran his eyes over them, looking for Maurizio and Domenico, relieved to see that none of them resembled the two resistance members.

But then he saw the man standing at the far left of

the line. A man in a cleaner's overall with wild, curly hair.

The sound of Pippo crying Bruno's name was lost in the crack of gunfire.

CLARA

1944

The Departure

'Filomena is dead.'

In my mind, I can still hear the Signore's tired voice as he stepped in through the door. I can hear the sound of my own gasp, and Zia's muffled wail as she held her handkerchief to her mouth.

I take a deep breath. It has been months since that dreadful night. That night when the Allied bombing came earlier than their usual night-time raids. When Filomena didn't come home, and Zia pleaded with her husband to go out as soon as the attack had finished.

Once the sirens had wailed its end, he pulled on his coat and hat and disappeared into the darkness, heading towards the train station, where Zia knew Filomena had gone. Occasionally, black marketeers would arrive from the countryside with fresh meat and vegetables, and Filomena would go and chat with the other cooks and housewives as they waited for a train, and possibly food, to arrive.

That night, she had gone in the hope of buying

something for the Signore's birthday the next day. A piece of goat, perhaps, or a rabbit, she said. She had left a meal cooked and warming in the oven, and the three of us had eaten the bean dish, hoping that the next evening's dinner would be something more special.

The bombing started at twilight, when Filomena would normally have been on her way home. But that evening, we discovered later, the passenger train was delayed, and she had stayed to wait for it.

The Allied bombers were more interested in the movement of munitions by rail, and flew up the train line from the south. The station was hit and a handful of innocent people were killed, including our beloved Filomena.

Zia was inconsolable and for weeks barely left the house, drifting from room to room in her pink dressing gown as if hoping to find her cook and friend. For a fortnight I took over the role of cook, having watched Filomena at her work long enough to know how to get the most out of our chicken's eggs, and make our rationed ingredients go further. I didn't know where she bought the black market goods she often came home with to supplement our meals, but the Signore did what he could, asking his fellow workers and tracking down a slab of cheese one day, some slices of pork another.

Despite our efforts to run the house as Filomena had, we couldn't raise Zia out of her depression, and the Signore and I found ourselves working together to find a way to help her.

'Perhaps if she had something to do?' I suggested one evening as we sat quietly in the kitchen. Zia was in the library, smoking and flicking through old magazines without looking at them.

'A job?' he asked, surprised. He had never considered the idea of a wife who worked.

'No,' I replied slowly, wondering how to express my idea. 'She was passionate about her work with' — I dropped my voice, although there was no one to hear — 'the partisans.'

The Signore shook his head.

While stealing information from under the Nazis' noses in his office was almost impossible, he continued to listen carefully to passing conversations and unguarded comments. He passed on what he could, but Zia had continued helping the resistance in other ways. An upstanding woman whose husband was a civil servant was unlikely to be considered a threat, and she knew it. Her elegant handbag carried notes and once, she'd told me in an excited whisper, even a pistol. She had met people in coffee shops to pass on coded messages as she'd raised her cup to her painted lips.

We were out one day when a young man had run past us being chased by a policeman. She had dropped her bag, quite purposefully, at the policeman's feet, tripping him and sending him sprawling across the pavement. I stood aghast as she showered the man on the floor with apologies, trying to help him to his feet but only slowing him down. The poor policeman politely thanked her and limped away, long after the young man had disappeared down a side street. When he was out of sight, Zia had winked at me, and I'd understood she'd recognized the young man as a partisan.

She had seemed so alive at that time. There was a lightness to her step, and her face shone. She'd felt that she was playing her part in the war and, as the Allies crept up the country, she could hold her head high and say she'd done the right thing.

But one day the Signore had come home from work and told us the resistance had let off a large bomb, killing many Nazis. He'd shaken his head wearily and remarked that the Germans were very angry. They were searching house to house for those involved, following any intelligence they had, and they would make a point of punishing whoever they found.

Zia had said nothing then, but I could tell she was pleased with the news of the bomb. I'd wondered if she had played some part in its organization. That night when we were all sleeping, a loud cracking sound woke us. While Zia and I nervously crept down the stairs, the Signore had run ahead. We found him standing in the front room staring at a broken window.

'Be careful,' he'd warned, pointing at our bare feet and peering out, although it was clear that whoever had broken the window was gone. A movement caught my eye, and I turned my head to see Zia bend down and pick up what looked like a rock. Turning it in her hand, she and I had both seen a small piece of paper stuck to it. She'd peeled it off and tucked it into her dressing gown pocket, before dropping the stone quietly onto the rug in front of her.

It was a message for her. But why break a window? Was it the only way they could get news to her quickly? The curfew made it dangerous to be out at night. Perhaps it was the surest way to get Zia's attention.

The drama of it had certainly worked.

'It's me,' the Signore had said, tiptoeing over the glass to join us.

'What do you mean?' Zia had asked, confused.

'It's their way of telling me they think I'm a collaborator,' he'd said, spotting the rock and nudging it with his foot.

'Surely not,' she'd replied, distracted.

'What else could it be?' Recently, the Signore had spoken of the threat more and more. In perilous danger of being caught by the Nazis, he had also become paranoid that the partisans and their supporters, knowing nothing of his help, would see him as a traitor — someone who had worked with the Germans against the Italians.

'The danger is over now,' Zia had said dismissively. 'Let's go back to bed and worry about this mess in the morning.'

But Zia had slipped out early the next morning before anyone was up. I'd wondered what the note had said as I'd lied to the Signore, saying that no, I had no idea why the Signora had gone out so early. All I knew was that she was protecting her husband from the truth. If the Germans asked him, he could honestly say he knew nothing.

He was still questioning me when we'd heard the door open and close, and we'd rushed to the hall to see her. She was pale and had clearly been crying, and I'd held back while her husband had stepped towards her, holding her arms to look at her before pulling her to him in an embrace.

'Where have you been? I've been so worried,' he'd whispered.

Zia had let him hold her, her nose nuzzled in his neck. I'd wanted to leave, let them have their private moment in peace, but I'd wanted to know where she'd been more.

She'd lifted her head, wiped her eyes with the heel of her hand, and said, 'I, ah, I woke early and went for a walk. When I got to the square, the Nazis, they were . . .' She'd glanced at me.

'What were they doing?' I'd asked.

'Last night, they arrested some members of the resistance.' Her hand rose to her mouth as her chin wobbled. 'They led them into the square . . . and . . .' She'd struggled to speak, her breath catching the sobs.

'They shot them,' the Signore had finished.

She'd nodded, her red eyes darting between me and her husband.

'It must have been terrible to see,' he'd hushed her gently.

'There was someone you knew.' The words came out of my mouth before I'd finished thinking them.

Zia had looked at me and nodded, before collapsing again into her husband's arms. And I'd known straight away it was the cleaner. The man with the curly hair. The one who had helped us escape from the bomb. My heart sank and, like her, I'd felt like crying, crying for him and the men and women who had risked their lives to rid our country of our occupiers and oppressors.

'Brave men, all of them,' the Signore had said quietly, leaning his face onto the top of his wife's head.

Zia had never taken another mission for the resistance. She avoided the places she knew they might try to contact her, and it seems they left her alone. She can't have been the only one deterred by the brutal conse-quences of small rebellious actions.

'No,' I agreed with the Signore. 'Too dangerous. But what else is there?'

'There are charities,' he suggested.

'Not more knitting,' I replied.

'No,' he smiled. 'But a colleague told me they need help at the orphanage. There are so many children . . .'

'Perfect,' I whispered.

'You think so?' he asked, surprised and strangely pleased at my response.

'Yes,' I nodded. 'Tell her today, please. I can't wait to see her face. Just . . .'

'What?'

'Well, just remember what happened the last time she found a child with no family.'

The Signore looked at me and blinked. He smiled gently, and I saw the kind man that Zia had fallen in love with.

The next day, Zia was up early to bathe and dress in one of her favourite frocks. She left the house wearing sandals, no hat, and a look of trepidation. But when she returned she was relaxed and chatty, telling us about the children she'd spent time with, her dress covered with grubby finger marks. She had taken a step towards being herself and, in my mind, I praised the Signore for knowing what it would take to bring his wife back.

As I sit in the library surrounded by the books I find most comfort in, letting my mind pass over the events of the past year, I wonder where it will end. Our enemies are killing us, as are our would-be rescuers. It seems no matter what we do or which side we take, and even if we take no side at all, we are in mortal danger every single day. I have no idea if Saba, whose home was this building and its contents, is still alive. An image of him shuffling away in his slippers passes in front of me and I shiver.

I turn my thoughts to Pippo and hope that he has escaped the worst of the war. If only I hadn't broken my promise to Mamma, my promise to look after him. I still cling to the words of the old woman and listen for him wherever I go, but I haven't heard or seen a glimpse of him for years now.

Of course, Mamma appears in my thoughts too. The image of her is blurry these days; only her golden eyes and gentle smile have any clarity. Her voice has disappeared and, while I remember some of her words, her names for us, the songs she sang, her gentle teasing, her sound and tone are all gone.

But her sense of being stays with me. I hold the red wristband between my fingers and recall leaning on her as she told stories of our family and heritage, reminding me of the places we had been and the sights we had seen. I can still feel the softness of her stomach under my head, the resonance of her words vibrating through me. I am only a child in my memory of her, but even now, I feel her beside me. These days, she is an invisible support, a pair of unseen hands that keep me standing during times when I think I will fall to the floor in despair. And yet often it is the loss of her that leaves me feeling so hopeless. I miss her so much. My mamma.

My eyes drop to the book in front of me, tears brimming, and I try to read the words. But they blur, losing their form and meaning, and I rub my eyes roughly.

Enough, I decide. Enough of this reflection and self-pity. I can do nothing to bring all those I have lost back to me. If the blue-eyed woman was right, I will see Pippo again — perhaps even Mamma too. Until then, there is a life to be lived. I close the book in front of me and return it to its shelf, nod to the woman at Saba's desk, and leave the library.

The early summer sun is warm, and I close my eyes and raise my face to feel its heat. I hear a bus rumbling nearby, and the shouts and chatter of the general noise of town. The smell is a mixture of tobacco and the cooking of food. It seems to matter little how harsh the rationing gets; Italians will still find something to cook and eat.

The change in sound is gradual and, at first, I don't notice it, instead enjoying the old buildings around the university, unscathed by the bombs and as full of character as ever. Then I realize that the background noise has died down, and the clatter and shuffle of people moving has replaced it.

Cautiously, I walk quickly towards the end of the street and, standing at the corner of a shop, peer into the main road. Nazi cars and the occasional lorry filled with troops are filing steadily in one direction. A long, black saloon near me sounds its horn impatiently, and I can see its officer occupants fidget with annoyance. Soldiers walk quickly; some even run alongside the cars, and people move aside to let them pass.

I edge my way onto the pavement and stand by my fellow Italians, watching the exodus.

'They're leaving?' I ask the woman beside me.

'Yes,' she replies simply. I glance at her face and see it is pale and stern. A young girl stands next to her, watching from behind her mother's skirt.

'Does that mean the British are coming?'

'The British, the Americans . . . I don't care who it is, so long as they drive them into the depths of hell.' She speaks quietly through her teeth with a venom that can only come from unimaginable pain.

I nod in agreement, but she doesn't look at me. She takes the child's hand tightly and leads her away.

The little girl turns her head and gives me a charming grin. I am about to wave in reply when I feel a jolt of electricity run through me, from my head down into my heart and body and even to my toes. I stand stock-still, the current freezing my muscles in spasm, and the child stalls to stare at me.

'Come on, Violetta,' her mother chides, pulling her to follow.

I want to stop them, to say I feel a connection to this child, and now, I suddenly realize, to the woman as well. But my body's reaction to them won't allow it. As my tense muscles begin to relax, I wonder how I could explain it to them – a physical reaction to two strangers.

The girl turns her head and skips to catch up with her mamma, and they disappear into the crowd that is growing by the moment.

I watch them go, feeling that I have just lost something but having no idea what. Shaking my head, I suddenly want to be at home. I turn against the tide of Germans and start to weave my way between those departing and those watching. The crowds are silent. I am sure that inside they are cheering but, until these vile visitors are gone, no one feels safe.

A few streets away, gunshots are fired, and the pavement clears slightly as people instinctively press back against walls and doors. But not a single person leaves. They want to be sure the Nazis go — words on the radio or in newspapers are not enough.

Suddenly, a woman in an apron, her hair bouncing in wild curls, strides in front of me towards an open-topped car. She steps close to it as it drives slowly, and its SS officers turn to her. As quick as a hare, she jerks her head back and throws it forward, launching a glob of spit. It lands on the shocked man's neck as, too late, he raises his arm.

Others see the woman's action and, in a wave, it spreads. Jeers, shouts, swearing, spitting . . . I even see people try to cuff the heads of those who pass. I remember the crowds who raised their arms to salute Il Duce — a friend of these Germans — and for a moment, I wonder if we will ever remain loyal to anyone.

But who would have known then, when all we heard about was Mussolini's successes, his prowess and power, that we would be reduced to starving paupers, beaten into submission by friends and foe? I forgive us our weaknesses; our passions that rise and fall like the sun. I cannot forgive the Germans. With them true evil lies, and we Italians have been witnesses of it.

More shots are fired, into the air from what I can hear, but I decide to take the side streets home. I pass women hanging over balconies, having conversations with their neighbours about what is happening. I pass children playing with bits of shrapnel and pretend grenades, driving imaginary Nazis out of their street.

I call Zia's name as I walk through the door into the peaceful house, and she replies from the kitchen.

Opening the door, I see she is sitting with the Signore. They are sipping red wine from two of their finest glasses.

'Clara,' says Zia, pulling another wine glass towards her husband, who picks up the aged bottle and pours the dark red liquid into it. 'Isn't it wonderful?'

I nod and accept the drink from the Signore.

'A toast,' Zia cheers. 'To the future!'

'To the future,' we concur, although somehow we don't quite match her enthusiasm. In my case, it is uncertainty about that future – and I suppose it's the same for the Signore.

Zia looks down momentarily. 'I'm sad that Filomena isn't here to see it. She would have been the first to go onto the street to see the Germans go.'

I think of the woman spitting at the officers and can instantly imagine Filomena doing the same thing.

'Of course,' the Signore says gently. 'She would have cheered as they left. And we're all pleased to see them gone. But . . .' He pauses for a moment. 'I don't know what will happen now. We must prepare ourselves for the chance that those of us who worked for them, or were even associated with the Fascists, may be seen as collaborators.'

'That's stupid,' retorts his wife. 'Everyone will want to begin again. Start fresh. We'll be too busy getting our lives back to normal – building new homes for all those who've lost theirs, making pasta instead of guns, finding families to care for the children at the orphanage . . .'

The Signore looks at his wife, into her eyes shining with hope.

'You're right, my love,' he agrees. 'You're right. It is time we took care of each other.'

PIPPO

1945

Donna's Tears

When they'd heard that Mussolini was dead, Donna had wept. It was as if the pain of all the years of the war had finally been released, and she'd sobbed. Pippo had watched for a while as she cried and keened, then turned to Violetta, tears for her mother pooling in her eyes. He'd picked up the girl, as light as a doll, and taken her into the bedroom, whispering to her that her mamma was fine – they were happy tears, the news meant that Italy was free now.

'Let's give her some peace,' he'd said, and Violetta had nodded, pulling a strand of hair behind her ear. Pippo couldn't remember the last time Donna had brushed Violetta's hair, and he'd asked the girl to find her hairbrush. She'd climbed under the bed and, after a few minutes of scrabbling, returned with the dusty brush.

He'd wiped it on his shirt, then, settling behind her, gently started tackling the knotted and tangled hair. Violetta had squirmed and yelped, but soon her brown hair lay long and straight down her back. It needed cutting, Pippo had thought, running his fingers through his own shaggy fringe.

Since Gino's death, Donna had changed. She seemed to have no energy for anything. The once spotless home was now dirty and dank. Pippo tried to keep it clean, but when the laundry had complained that their washing was returned late and filthy, he had taken over the work from Donna.

He had scrubbed and wrung the sheets and tableware, hanging it out to dry as he'd seen Donna do. And when he delivered the carefully folded laundry, he had taken Violetta with him, letting her help carry the large basket. Together, they'd collected the payment, then visited shops and found black marketeers to buy bread, rice, vegetables, and sometimes even pasta.

He had let the child help with the chopping and cooking as Donna weakly attempted to wash dishes or, more often, sat in her chair, staring into a distance with dark, impenetrable eyes.

Pippo had tried to bring her back to them, urging her to come outside to see friends or enjoy the sunshine. He'd brought her newspapers, which she had read slowly, before folding and placing them under her chair.

Violetta had more success, pulling her mother up from her seat to take her out or help her with her letters and numbers. Donna would look at the girl, cupping her chin in a trembling hand, before nodding slowly and agreeing to go wherever she wished, to help however she could. But her muted enthusiasm never lasted long, and she would soon bring Violetta home, saying she was tired, or put down the pencil, rubbing her eyes, telling her daughter she had to rest.

The day Mussolini was announced dead was the first time since they had buried little Gino that Pippo had seen Donna cry. He had been to see Bruno's contacts, the few who were still alive, to find out if there was any news about Mario. He had asked them to pass word to him months ago, in the hope that he would return home. But that day, as with all the rest, no news was the only news.

Pippo knew that Donna was wondering if her husband was dead too. If he were, Pippo thought it might kill her. This war had taken too much as it was, and her love for Violetta might not be enough to see her through.

As he had been walking home, he'd heard the excited chatter of people in the street.

'He's dead.'

'Are you sure?'

'My sister heard it on the radio.'

'How?'

'Killed, by the Communists.'

'Are you sure he's dead?'

'I told you, it was on the radio.'

'I would spit on his dead face.'

'I would do worse than that.'

'He's dead?'

'He's dead.'

By the time he'd reached the heavy wooden doors of their apartment, he'd heard enough people talking about the news on the radio for him to believe it.

From all he'd read in the papers, and what his well-informed friend Botte had told him, it seemed that the end was near. The Nazis were retreating, the Allies were in Germany, and they were bombing the Germans now, not the Italians.

When her tears had dried, Donna had asked a few questions and seemed interested in the news for a while, but then shook her head and went back to her slow, distracted life. Pippo knew that until Mario returned, she would remain this shadow of a woman. He hoped with all his heart that her husband would be able to find the wife and mother they knew and missed.

But today, just a few days later, came the news that Hitler was dead and everyone knew the war was over. Donna mumbled that it would change nothing. The boy knew that she meant it would not bring Gino back. He also knew change wouldn't happen overnight. They were still hungry all the time. Reports of diseases spreading across a country with no medicine and few functioning hospitals were frightening. There was still an anger between people — those who dared to support the Fascists and those who had either never supported them, or who now felt they needed to prove their absolute rejection of their previous beliefs.

'Perhaps Mario will come home soon,' he said to Donna.

Sitting in her chair, her thin frame hunched, the woman who was almost his mother allowed him a small smile.

'Perhaps,' she said quietly.

CLARA

1945

An Invitation

'They are coming home,' says the Signore.

'Who?' I ask.

'Those who were taken away,' he replies. 'The ones who survived,' he adds quietly.

'The Jews?' My thoughts immediately go to Saba and I wonder how, as I have so often over the past few years, an elderly gentleman would manage in a prison, or a camp, or wherever it was the Germans held them. I asked the Signore if he knew where my friend had been taken, but he always shook his head, and I knew it was not that he hadn't seen reports in his office, it was that he couldn't bear to tell me.

Perhaps his telling me of their return is his way of saying there could be the smallest chance that Saba may be coming back.

'Is it . . . only the Jews?' asks Zia.

I frown at her, not understanding her question.

'Anyone who was taken,' repeats her husband. 'The camps have been liberated.'

'Camps?' I ask. 'Do you know—'

'Please don't ask me,' says the Signore, closing his eyes and shaking his head as though he is trying to dispel his thoughts.

'I see the partisans have begun to return,' says Zia, changing the subject, and I am inclined to let her. 'And even soldiers.'

Her husband nods his head. 'There is little information. Since the Germans left and the British and Americans arrived, our office has been in a state of confusion. I would like to arrange the movement of people, ensure that the trains transport people home, reunite the lost with their families, but it is so hard.'

'Keep trying,' says Zia gently, rubbing his hand, which rests on the kitchen table. It is Sunday and we have had a late breakfast. The Signore and I are dressed, but Zia still wears her dressing gown, her hair hanging in unravelling curls around her face.

He tries not to look at me, but his eyes flicker to my face before returning to his wife's hand on his. 'Even if . . .'

'Yes,' she nods.

I am unsure if they are still talking about my friend the librarian, but I know that she is willing him to do the right thing — whatever it is.

I remember a time when the Signore would have put Mussolini's wishes above his wife's, when he acted on orders with relish. But the years of war, seeing firsthand the actions of the powerful and how they destroyed the ordinary, have changed him, and he has, I think, returned to the man Zia fell in love with all those years ago.

In the meantime, he has tried to make amends in his

own small way. The Fascist books have disappeared from his library, along with the pins and badges he used to wear with pride. He is quieter now — more reflective and thoughtful. He tells us that his duties at work include ensuring hospitals and orphanages have food deliveries; he tries to pass on information about returning troops to their families, and provides support to those who have lost their homes.

He and Zia have talked many times of him leaving his job. Zia has always said she would be happy to work. She would clean or take in needlework — do anything — but the Signore says whatever she earned would neither make ends meet nor allay his discomfort.

I have offered to find work too, but he is adamant he will stay. 'When it is over, I will help to rebuild a better Italy,' he says. 'Now, I understand I work for the people, not the government or whatever political party will take charge next.'

But there is anxiety in his voice, because nobody, not even those working within the civil service, has any idea what will happen now.

'Clara,' says Zia, interrupting my thoughts. 'Clara, if your . . . friend . . .' She pauses.

'Signor Leone?'

'Yes.' Her eyes drop. 'Him, or anyone else. If they return, and you want to help them, our home is open.'

'I could invite Saba here?' I ask, surprised. Zia has never met him, and I only told her about him after the Nazis took him away.

'Yes.' She looks me in the eyes. 'If someone is important to you, they are important to me. To all of us.' She glances at the Signore and he nods his agreement.

'Thank you,' I say.

'But,' adds the Signore, 'I think you must prepare yourself for disappointment. You have seen for yourself how brutal the Nazis were, and your friend was . . . is an elderly man.'

'I understand,' I say, but a memory of his last words to me echo in my head: 'I speak German — it will help me.'

I hope he was right.

PIPPO

This time, it was different. It seemed more real. He could hear the words the crowds shouted: 'Kill them!' 'Fascist bastards!' 'Murderers!'

He could see his mother standing high up, turning her head towards him, her eyes glinting gold. She looked at him and, although he could not hear her speak, he knew the word she said.

'Pippo.'

Suddenly there was a loud sound, a crack, near his ear.

It woke him from sleep with a jolt, his insides fizzing as if charged with electricity. Breathing slowly, he tried to relax but, as he lifted his hand to wipe the perspiration from his top lip, he saw it was shaking.

He could feel the warm mound of Violetta sleeping beside him, wrapped into herself like a snail. The bed next to his was empty, but that was not unusual. Donna often slept in her chair, or slowly paced the room, as though she were looking for something to do.

Quietly, he slipped out of the bedroom, careful not

to wake the child. He was surprised to find the other room empty. Perhaps Donna had gone for a walk. Checking his pocket for money and grabbing a glass bottle, he pulled the door gently closed behind him and started down the stairs. Violetta would have fresh milk this morning.

On the street, he found the milkwoman and held the bottle out as she lifted the large urn and measured his milk, before pouring it deftly into his bottle. He paid and thanked her, and was just turning back for home when he caught sight of a man. He was thinner and his hair was dotted with grey, but he knew immediately that it was Mario.

His heart leaped, and he was about to wave and call his name when he saw that Mario's arm was around Donna, supporting her as they both walked slowly. Pippo slipped down an alleyway and ran through the side streets back to their home. Taking two steps at a time, he raced up to the apartment and inside, where he left the milk in the kitchen and went to wake Violetta.

Confused, the child let herself be dressed and her hair quickly brushed before being led out of the bedroom. There, the two of them stood listening to the footsteps on the stairs. When the door opened, Pippo beamed and Violetta smiled nervously.

'Mario!' the boy said, unable to stop himself a moment longer. He lunged towards his old friend and wrapped his arms around him. Donna peeled herself away from her husband and reached out to their daughter.

Mario held Pippo in a tight embrace, before placing a heavy hand on his head and looking into his eyes.

'Thank you, Pippo. Donna has told me how you have

kept this family together. I will always be indebted to you for taking care of them.'

'It's what you did for me when I had no family,' the boy said with an embarrassed smile.

'You have a family,' Mario said, touching his forehead against Pippo's.

Still unsettled from his dream, the words warmed him and, when he heard a small voice say, 'Papa?' he had to will himself to let go of the man and make way for the child.

'Violetta,' said Mario gently, dropping to his knees and opening his arms.

Nervously, the little girl stepped towards the man she barely knew. But she let him take her in his arms and nuzzle his nose into her neck, smelling her hair. Standing, he lifted her easily, and waved Donna and Pippo towards him. They stood for a while, holding each other, knowing that one member of their family was missing.

'Let me make you some breakfast,' said Pippo eventually.

'No,' said Donna firmly. 'No, let me.' She gave the boy a grateful smile and turned to the kitchen. Violetta loudly insisted that Papa meet her toy bear, and Pippo leaned against the wall, feeling the fluttering in his chest becoming a little less noticeable.

After a simple breakfast, Mario announced he would like to take a walk. He had been away for years, and now the war was over he wanted to see the city again.

'You will find much changed,' commented Donna as she buckled Violetta's shoes.

Pippo realized that he had become used to seeing

rubble on the streets, shells of burned buildings and craters where homes had once been. Roads had changed and there were fewer functioning railway lines than before the bombing. As they walked, he tried to remember the city as it was when he'd first lived here, but he couldn't.

All the while, Mario talked quietly. He told Pippo that he had returned as soon as he could. He'd heard about Gino and his old friend Bruno while he was with the Communist partisans in the north. He said the news had driven him to fight the Germans and the Italian Fascists with more ferocity than he knew was in him.

And when the war was finally over, it had taken weeks to travel back to them. There were people everywhere, he said. British and American soldiers trying to bring a sense of order to wherever they were based, still recovering from the exhaustion of battle. German soldiers, surrendered but still in their uniforms, trying to get home to whatever waited for them there. Prisoners of war, released from wherever they'd been held – prisons, concentration camps, working gangs. He'd even met Jews, he said, cautiously coming out of hiding. So many people criss-crossing the country trying to find their way home, and he was just one among them.

He had arrived in the night and fallen into the arms of his beloved wife. As soon as it was light, she had taken him to where Gino was buried. He was not ashamed to say he sobbed like a baby beside the small stone memorial Pippo and Donna had somehow found the funds to pay for. 'A child,' he said, shaking his head. 'Just a child.'

The boy saw Donna wipe her hand over her face as she listened, her eyes red-rimmed. She looked down at her feet as Mario swore through his teeth that he would never forgive them. Not just the Germans, he said. His own people had killed his son. Befriending the Nazis, working with their occupiers — they were all guilty of murder, he said as they crossed the piazza, the cafe's radio playing a cheery song loudly. The Fascists and those who worked for them were as guilty as those who lifted a gun or raised a hand.

'But what of Communism?' Pippo quietly asked.

Frowning, Mario said firmly, 'Communism is an economic solution to create equality in society.'

'But isn't it also a way of bringing people together?' pondered Pippo out loud. 'A community of all people, working together for the common good? Isn't now the time for us to work with everyone, even our enemies, to rebuild Italy?'

Mario's frown hardened into a scowl that darkened his face. 'Those who joined Mussolini and Hitler are beyond redemption. We must show them who is in power now, and the only way to do that is with the violence that they inflicted on us. They will never understand anything but this.' Mario pushed back his jacket and his hand settled comfortably on the wooden handle of a gun.

CLARA

Loud knocking at the door stalls our quiet breakfast conversation. Zia looks at her husband, who rises slowly from his chair.

These are fearful times. We are all aware of the venom directed at anyone who was a known Fascist. Neighbours denounce neighbours, colleagues inform on colleagues. Zia says it's as if everyone wants to blame someone for their hunger and their tragedy. But we have all suffered. No one has escaped without pain — and now that Hitler and Mussolini are dead, we should be finding ways to be more like our liberators.

When the Americans drove through the city, we cheered. I stood on my tiptoes, watching from my bedroom window feeling elated — at last we were free. But are we? Too late, when we realized we had chosen the wrong side, made friends with the wrong people, we turned to those who had been our enemies. Now they have freed us, and to convince them that we were secretly on their side all along, we turn our self-loathing on anyone we can point a finger at and say, 'Them. It was them.'

The Signore's chair scrapes the stone floor as he stands.

Zia and I watch him walk out of the kitchen, along the hallway and to the front door, where the knocking has started again. He opens the door, but we can only see his back, not the man who says loudly that his presence is required — is demanded — at his place of work.

'Why?' we hear him ask.

'To defend yourself and your colleagues on a charge of collaboration,' comes the reply.

Zia's hand jerks to her mouth and, jumping out of her seat, she cries, 'No!' But it is too late. The door is pulled shut and the Signore is gone.

'Help me, Clara,' she says, grabbing my hand. 'Help me get dressed. I must go with him.'

Together we run up the stairs, and I pull open her wardrobe doors to find her trousers.

'No,' she says firmly as she sees me unhooking a hanger. She reaches past the dark slacks and pulls out her green suit. It is her favourite — a classic cut in a shade that complements her colouring. It is the outfit she was wearing when she found me.

PIPPO

Pippo glanced at Donna and saw her face pale at the sight of the weapon.

'It is for the community to decide the fate of others,' she said, as Mario slipped the flap of his jacket back over the gun. 'If there's one thing you taught me about Communism, Mario, it's that the people's power comes from unity. One man cannot make decisions that affect the lives of others. Otherwise, it would be no different from—'

'Maybe Italy is not ready for Communism,' retorted Mario.

'Perhaps not,' agreed Donna, gently placating him, 'but it is ready for kindness. We all need some time to heal. And while we do, there is a chance we may find a small amount of hope.'

Mario stopped walking abruptly and turned to his wife. Pippo and Violetta looked up at him. 'You want to be kind to the people who killed our boy? Kind to those who told the Nazis where to find Bruno? No!' spat the man in fury. 'No!'

Donna gazed at her husband as if looking for someone she once knew. Tears began to well in Mario's eyes, and he angrily wiped the back of his hand across his face.

His wife reached for his hand, grasping it in hers and raising it to her lips. 'I will love my husband until the end of all days,' she whispered to him.

Pippo waited for him to reply – 'I love my wife more than life itself' or 'My wife is the most beautiful woman in the world' – but Mario just stared at Donna, unable to let the rage leave him.

'They will have their day,' he said quietly, with a calm that sent a chill through Pippo. 'Just like Il Duce.'

CLARA

Quickly, I help dress her and arrange her hair. I scrabble for my shoes and, before we know it, we are slamming the door behind us and dashing up the street.

'Hurry, Clara,' Zia says, puffing a little. 'Such dangerous times,' she mutters, and I can hear the fear in her voice.

Will there be a time when they are not?

She takes my hand in hers and together we continue to rush along the pavement.

As we near the building where the Signore works, the street becomes busier. Up ahead, a crowd is gathering, and I look to Zia. She hesitates a moment before hitching her handbag onto her arm and, still holding my hand firmly, leading us into the thickest group of people.

Passing through, I hear people talking and snippets of their conversation.

'You know they helped the Germans – and Mussolini before that.'

'Well, of course they did. Anyone who worked for the government is complicit.'

The street widens up ahead, and to the right is the building where the Signore has worked since long before the war. The stone steps to the entrance are hidden by a dense throng of people, but we can see a small gathering standing outside the main doors looking down at the crowd.

I scan them and my heart skips a beat as I see the Signore among them. Zia sees him too and pushes more determinedly through the people.

'We used to trust these people.'

'They have blood on their hands.'

'They're murderers.'

At these words, I turn my head and see a young woman, her face red with anger. I wonder what has happened to her, and who she believes the Signore has killed. I wish I could tell her that he is not the one she should blame – yes, he was a Fascist, when most of the country believed it was our future, but now he is on the side of right. He has helped the cause more than anyone knows but us. I know she will not listen. She has made her decision.

PIPPO

Pippo was looking at Mario, still shocked by the venom in his words, when loud shouts made them all turn their heads to the left. Up ahead he saw a crowd gathering around a government building, a group of men being jostled onto the top steps of the entrance.

'Let's go home,' said Donna quickly, grabbing Violetta's hand.

But Mario ignored her and strode towards the building. Pippo saw Donna hesitate for a moment before following her husband. He followed, too – like her, he had waited too long for Mario to come home and didn't want to let him out of his sight.

'What's happening?' Mario asked the crowd, with the authority of a military officer. Pippo had never heard him speak like that before, and wasn't surprised when two men immediately responded.

'It's the officials,' one said.

'The ones who ran the city for the Nazis,' said the other.

'Fascists,' said the first.

'They say they're not political,' said the second. 'They say they were just doing their job.'

The first snorted.

'What kind of job?' asked Mario.

'Moving troops,' said one.

'Helping them find Jews,' said the other.

'And partisans.'

As he listened, Pippo watched ten or twelve men and a few women standing on the steps looking down at the crowds below them. Civilians with guns blocked their way into the building. Some were obviously frightened – he could see them trembling, even from this distance – while others tried to defend themselves to the shouting mob.

Mario pushed forward, and Pippo saw his eyes gleam with anger. He and Donna, who held her daughter tightly beside her, followed in his wake as the people made way for him. As they moved through the bodies, Pippo felt them part, then fill the space behind them again like water. It made him nervous, fearful of finding an escape should things turn nasty. But Mario ploughed on, even though the crowd became denser and nastier.

It was harder to see over the heads of those in front of them, and Pippo lost sight of the government officials. When Mario finally stopped walking, Pippo pushed in front of him to get a view of the accused, and saw that their numbers had swelled.

Now there were three times the number, and more were being bundled up the steps to join them. There were more women too and, from their dress and the way they clung to the men, Pippo realized they were the officials' wives.

Were they guilty by marriage? he wondered. If so, what of their children, their employees? What about whoever sold them their bread or milk, or fixed their telephone, or did their laundry?

No, he decided, and turned to Mario.

'This is not right,' he shouted over the noise. 'Not the women. Not their wives.'

But Mario couldn't hear him over the noise of the braying crowd.

'Mario!' Pippo seized the man's sleeve and, blinking, his friend looked down at him.

'This isn't right,' shouted the boy again, shaking his head fiercely. 'It's not right.'

Mario glared at him.

'Not right?' he spat. 'Not right? My baby boy buried in the ground. That is not right. Bruno, shot like a dog in the street. That is not right. All the men I've seen killed, fighting for what is right, while those cowards helped send more to their deaths.'

The boy didn't know how to argue against Mario. The man had lost too much, seen more than Pippo could ever know.

Donna stood beside her husband, frowning. Violetta hid in her skirts, frightened by the clamour and crush of the people around her.

The crowd seemed to become louder, shouting and waving their arms, pushing into him. '*Va vai!*' shouted Pippo in anger. 'Get lost!' And for a moment, he heard himself saying those words before, an echo of another time and place.

He tutted at the thought and reached up onto his toes to get a better view.

CLARA

Glancing about at the bitter, spiteful faces, I suddenly understand Zia's fear, and a well opens in the bottom of my stomach.

If Zia is afraid, she doesn't show it. Her face is calm but determined as we march through the throng. People push and shove to get a better view of the men, and a few women, at the top of the steps. Some begin to call out and shout, swearing and accusing.

Frightened, I pull back on Zia's hand. She turns and looks at me sternly.

'What are we doing?' I ask.

'We're going up there,' she replies.

'But how will that help?'

'I'll tell them,' she shouts over the din of the crowd, 'tell them I worked for the resistance, that he helped me pass secret information.'

'I don't think they're listening,' I say loudly, trying to be heard.

'I'll make them listen,' she says, and suddenly I see the panic in her eyes.

'Let's find the police,' I say hopefully.

'There are your police,' she replies, pointing to a group of uniformed men, watching the situation with a disengaged interest.

Suddenly she turns back to me, puts her hands on my arms and lowers her face to mine. 'Clara, you're right to be afraid. Go home. Wait for us there. We'll come home when this situation blows over.'

'No,' I shake my head violently. 'No, I won't leave you.'

'Go home, Clara,' she says firmly, standing upright.

I shake my head, tears rising. 'Don't go up there, Zia,' I beg. 'Please.'

We both look up to the group of people on top of the steps. They are trying to talk to the people beneath them, but there is no single person to hold a discussion with, only a braying crowd.

'I have to be with him,' she says simply.

Of course. Of course she wants to be with her husband. She loves him. I am not her daughter. She cares for me a very great deal, I am sure of that. But she will never love me as she loves him. Or as she would love her own child.

I nod.

Zia pulls me to her and squeezes me. 'I'll be back soon,' she says into my ear. 'We'll all be together again soon.'

She gives me one last look before turning away and pushing through the throng again.

My head spins a little. The people around me jostle and shove, and I turn to go home.

Then I catch my breath as a bolt shoots through me.

It starts in my heart and, in a flash, spreads down my arms and legs to the ends of my fingers and toes. My body feels electric, zinging and fizzing while a sound fills my ears, blocking out the noise of the crowds around me.

I listen. For the most part, what I hear is silence. An absence of sound but with the solidity to deafen me to all other noises. And then I hear him.

My brother.

PIPPO

Wavering on his tiptoes, he looked at the government officials and their wives, and something about the way they stood, helpless in the face of such anger, reminded him of trapped animals. As he watched, two more women were pushed onto the top step to join those who already stood there. One of them, dressed in an elegant green suit, lifted her head high as she took the hand of a man and spoke a few words to him. Pippo thought he recognized her.

The shouting grew, further fuelling the crowd's rage. He heard words thrown with as much ferocity as the spit that flew through the air.

'Fascist bastards!'

'Collaborators!'

Pippo glanced around and saw Donna, standing silently as tears ran down her cheeks.

A chill tingled along the boy's spine. He wanted to leave, but his feet were rooted to the spot. There was something so familiar about this moment. As he looked forward again, the woman in green turned, sunlight flashing on her ruby red lips. And immediately he knew. She was the woman at Don Orlando's house. He saw her in his mind's eye, tucking an envelope into her bag. He remembered the pistachios, and how Bruno had sent him to Don Orlando's house when Violetta was so ill. He had saved Violetta's life, and Pippo and Donna had repaid every lira.

He turned to tell Mario that one of the accused was someone who had worked with Bruno, but he was shouting along with everyone else.

'Traitors!' he hollered. 'Murderous traitors!'

CLARA

It is not his voice. He is not talking. But it is him. If my brother were not a being but a sound, he would be what I can hear. It is a buzzing energy, a force of life, a somersault in the air, a zigzagging kite, a giggling laugh.

The woman with the blue eye said I would hear him, and I have. I blink, suddenly seeing the sky, the clouds, the buildings, the people around me. He is here. He is here in this crowd.

I turn my head, scanning everyone standing around me. But I cannot see more than a few people in front of me. I need to get higher. I push past people, looking for something to climb — a lamp-post, a windowsill — anything.

When my eyes fall on the group of people at the building entrance, I start heading towards them. I will climb the steps and turn towards the mass of people, and I know I will see Pippo. I do not think this; I know it. I know to my very core that I will look out and he will be there. And maybe he will see me. Maybe he will remember me and he will wave his arms to say, 'Here I am, Clara,' and we will fall into each other's arms. And it will be as if we were never apart.

The furious people have become a wall, and I push hard to get past them. I don't say 'excuse me'; words like *scusi* are unimportant to me. I shove, I pull, I barge — anything to get past them and onto the raised steps. My body is still crackling with electricity, and I barely feel the pavement beneath my feet, the skin of others against mine, the breath in my open mouth.

At last, the toe of my shoe hits the stone step and I stumble, putting my hand out to regain my balance. My arm scratches against an iron railing, and my wristband catches on its rusty edge. I pull at it, trying to free myself, but the red band breaks. I watch it fall to the floor, quickly disappearing under someone's foot. I am about to bend to retrieve it, when the fizz of energy reminds me of my brother. I will find the bracelet later.

Quickly I turn and climb the stairs. Looking up, I see the shocked face of Zia staring down at me. I know she is frightened; I see her clasping her husband's hand tightly. I want to speak to her, but I must look for Pippo.

I turn and, climbing the final steps backwards, look out across the faces, searching for my brother. In the energy coursing through my body, I try to feel a magnetic pull towards him, but the sensation is too overwhelming, too confusing. I hunt through the men, women and children in front of me, desperate to see a face that has changed but is so familiar to me it is like looking at myself.

Hands gently pull me back from the edge of the step. Zia guides me between her and the Signore, then leans forward in front of me. At the edge of my vision I see something hit her left cheek and, with disgust, she wipes a gob of spit away with the sleeve of her green suit.

A tall man wearing a black hat seems to be reading from a paper to those standing around me. I cannot hear his words, but he seems to be accusing them collectively of atrocities and collusion. Some are arguing with him angrily; some, like Zia, stand silently, terrified. The Signore seems to be trying to defend his colleagues, suggesting they continue their discussion somewhere quieter, in a place of safety.

The man in the hat ignores him and continues reading, while screams and abuse shower everyone. I ignore it. None of it means anything to me. All I care about is finding Pippo.

PIPPO

'They're not collaborators!' the boy shouted as loudly as he could. 'That woman' — Pippo tugged on Mario's sleeve and pointed to the woman in green — 'she worked with Bruno!'

But the boy's voice was drowned out by the shouting and jeering all around him.

As he looked back at the couple, the woman's husband seemed to be trying to negotiate with his accusers. She, however, stood still, holding his hand, looking out over the crowd in front of her. Terror had frozen her to the spot, and Pippo willed her to move, to get away.

He must try to help again. He had heard the authority Mario's voice carried — if he spoke in her defence it might make a difference.

As he turned his head and made to grab Mario's arm, he heard a terrible howl. The beast-like sound came from somewhere deep inside the man who was the closest thing to his father, travelling up through his throat and exiting his mouth through bared teeth.

Pippo stopped in shock and could do nothing but

watch as, with a single movement, Mario drew his gun and took aim.

Following the line of the glinting metal, Pippo saw what — who — it was pointing at. The man next to the woman in green. Her husband.

CLARA

My eyes scour the choppy waves of faces below me, resting briefly on each brown-haired boy before continuing their search. The clamour around me starts to fade again. Silence falls into the space it leaves and, alert, I let my head turn as though guided by someone's hands. The faces below blur, becoming a blanket of pink and grey.

And there, in the middle, I see him.

My brother.

I see a boy; the baby he was, the man he will be. I see the child and I see his father. I see myself and I see our mother.

PIPPO

Pippo saw a glint of light and his dream was broken. There she was, standing next to the woman in green — her dark hair falling around her high forehead, a long, straight nose and eyes of golden honey.

Mamma.

The moment he saw her, she turned her head towards him. He watched as her eyes widened and shone with light, and her face was transformed by a smile so large it felt like the sun was beaming onto him. And then she spoke.

He could hear nothing except the crowd around him, but he saw the word that came out of her mouth.

Pippo.

CLARA

His eyes turn to mine and we look at each other. He sees me, his sister, his friend and, until we find her, his mother. At last, I know can fulfil my promise to Mamma. The promise to look after my brother. After all these years, we are no longer lost. We will be together again.

I say his name.

PIPPO

Suddenly he recognized the loud sound he had heard so often in his sleep, the noise that had woken him that morning.

'No!' screamed Pippo, grabbing at Mario's arm.

The gun fired and the sound echoed Pippo's dream.

He looked back to his mother, only to see her fall: a flash of gold disappearing.

CLARA

A crack breaks the silence, but it does not cut through the energy that fizzes inside me. Joy spreads through my soul and I am happier than I have ever been in my life.

My head snaps back but the smile on my face feels as light as my heart.

I am falling. But I feel no pain. I am filled with pleasure, with a bliss that is pure.

I am with my brother again.

PIPPO

The Sister

As the crowd hushed to a stunned stillness, he saw that his mamma was gone. Instead, there was only the woman in the green dress. He watched as she turned her head down towards the ground. And then he heard her scream.

Pippo yelled too. He noticed briefly that the sound echoed over the silence of the crowd. He pushed and shoved his way through a solid body of people, looking for but unable to see his mother.

When he reached the stone steps, he felt hands helping, guiding him upwards. Climbing to the top, he slowed, seeing the woman in green hunched over a fallen figure. A man was bending over her too, clinging onto her side as if to keep them both from collapsing.

Pippo took a step to the side, and then another, until he saw the woman lying on the ground.

For a moment, he saw his mother and a pain stabbed at his chest, gripping his lungs so tightly he couldn't breathe. Then he noticed that Mamma looked younger than he remembered, the tone of her face lighter, her skin smoother.

One more step took him to her and he kneeled by her shoulder, a gasp catching as the truth clutched his heart.

'Clara.'

The word escaped him as a whisper.

Her eyes were still open, still golden, but the flash of light was gone from within them.

He watched his hand reach towards her, one finger touching her cheek, running down towards her chin before gently making its journey up the other side of her face and along her forehead. Just as he remembered Mamma doing to him.

'Clara,' he said again, taking in his sister. She was the same girl he remembered, but she was also his mother. He could see an elegance that was not there before, youthful cheeks replaced by a slender bone structure, and a pinkness to her lips.

He was unable to move or think. He simply looked at his sister, absorbing all that he could. He studied her face, then his eyes followed a line down her body, taking in the height of her, observing her well-cut clothes, her slightly chewed fingernails.

And finally, he made himself turn his eyes to the wound in her chest, a large glistening circle of red on her cream blouse. Beneath her body, a puddle of almost black liquid slowly grew.

He closed his eyes quickly, pinching them tightly shut, calling up an image of his sister, the girl he remembered, the laughing, serious, caring child he knew. Then, just as fast, he opened his eyes again, aiming his gaze at Clara's face; the pale skin, the lifeless eyes.

'Pippo?'

He heard his name and, without looking up, nodded. 'Pippo, I am Carolina.'

For a moment, he dragged his eyes away from his sister to look at the woman in green. Tears lined her cheeks and fell unheeded from her chin. Her hand rested protectively on his sister's shoulder.

'Clara calls me Zia. She lives with us.' As she spoke, she gestured at the man standing beside her. 'She has done from the time that she . . . you lost each other.'

The man cleared his throat but did not try to talk.

Pippo tipped his head down, an acknowledgement that he'd heard her words, before turning his gaze back to his sister.

'She's dead,' whispered the woman.

He nodded a tiny nod. He understood.

'Pippo,' continued the woman softly but anxiously, 'are you with your mother?'

The boy shook his head.

'He is with me,' said a voice.

Pippo recognized Donna's voice, and a strength in it that he had not heard for many years. Blinking, he turned to face her. She stood beside him, an arm around Violetta, flanked by Mario, who wiped his face with his hand anxiously.

'Pippo has lived with us since the day he lost his mamma and sister. We tried, but we couldn't find either of them. And so he became a part of our family. Now I think of him as nothing else,' said Donna.

'Of course,' replied Carolina, her voice shaky. 'That is how we feel about Clara.'

Watching his sister's face while listening to the women talk, Pippo noticed the hubbub of the crowd again. After the shock of the gunshot they had fallen silent, an audience watching the act play out on the stage in front of them. But now, discomfort and perhaps a sense of culpability was settling over them and, murmuring to one another, they slowly started to disperse.

'We must find out who did this.' Carolina's husband spoke for the first time. There was no rage in his voice but a sense of bafflement, a need for clarity in the confusion.

There was a pause, and Pippo's mind raced. A part of him knew it had been Mario's gun that fired the shot, but the link between his adoptive father and his sister's murderer refused to form.

'It was I.'

Mario's gruff voice shocked him. As the words sank in, a fury rose in Pippo that he had never felt before. He jumped to his feet, turned and, pushing Donna aside, threw himself at the man, arms and legs thrashing.

Mario did not try to defend himself, but let the punches and kicks come. He winced as a fist struck his nose, and bent slightly as a knee thudded into his groin, but he accepted every strike and hit that came at him.

The rage disappeared almost as quickly as it had come, and Pippo fell onto his knees, exhausted. His breath rasped and he choked in more air, only to hear an anguished cry escape his mouth. And then Donna was kneeling beside him, her arms wrapped around him, hushing him and rocking him as he wept, just as she had done in that empty room when he had lost his sister the first time.

Eventually, Pippo's tears died away, and he became aware of his surroundings again. He saw Carolina's husband quietly talking to two policemen, one of whom was looking down at Clara's body, the other at Mario, who stood in front of him, a thin line of blood trickling from his left nostril.

Slowly, Mario pulled his jacket open and, very carefully and deliberately, took the gun out of the inside pocket. Both policemen stood alert, but Mario turned the pistol over and passed it to one of the uniformed men, gently laying it in his open hand.

The Signore continued talking, as if trying to explain who the characters in this tragedy were. Carolina stood beside him, tears still running down her face.

Finally, the Signore seemed to run out of words and he stopped abruptly. One of the policemen nodded, replied briefly, then spoke curtly to Mario. The man nodded in agreement before turning and lifting up his daughter. He hugged her tightly and kissed her, whispering a few words in her ear before returning her to her feet. Then he nodded and put a hand on his wife's shoulder.

Donna lifted her head, and she and Pippo looked up at Mario.

'I am being arrested,' he said calmly. 'They're taking me to the police station now.'

'Pippo needs me,' Donna said quietly. 'I will come later.'

Mario nodded and Pippo saw the remorse in his face and, as he allowed himself to be led down the steps by the policeman, a calm acceptance of his actions and the consequences. But when he reached the bottom, he turned and looked up at Pippo, who was sitting, leaning against Donna.

'I don't have the words, Pippo . . .' he said quietly, shaking his head. 'I do not deserve your forgiveness, but please . . . please know that I have always loved you. Ever since you, just a tiny boy, stood up so proud and sang "*Bandiera Rossa*" . . . you stole my heart. I shall hope with all my being' — his voice dropped to a whisper — 'that I have not lost another son.' He coughed huskily, and Pippo saw the tears in his eyes.

'*Dai*,' said the policeman, nudging him forward, and Mario turned and walked into the dispersing crowd.

Pippo sat back on his haunches, looking down at his hands that lay in his lap. He saw his fingers pulled into fists but, unable to find the strength to hold them clenched, watched as they relaxed open.

Then he noticed the red band on his wrist. The bracelet he had worn, knowing his mother had made it to protect him. A magic link between him and his sister and her, she had told him. And all these years he had been apart from them, he had twisted it, every turn a prayer sent up to the heavens, calling for his mother and sister to come back to him.

His fingers wrapped around the fabric and he yanked it. The wristband dug into his skin, but he pulled it hard and the old strips of cloth ripped. He let it drop to the floor, then stood, holding Donna for support. Turning, he looked at his sister once more, surprised again to find her face new to him, and yet also undeniably the person he had never been apart from until that day when he was seven.

Pippo took a deep breath before casting his eyes to the woman in green.

'Tell me about my sister,' he said.

EPILOGUE

1958

Two Red Wristbands

'And that,' he said, a trace of weariness creeping into his voice, 'is how I lost my sister.'

Pippo sat back from the microphone and paused for a moment, thinking. Leaning in again, he said, 'The times are good, friends, but never let us forget where we have been and who we have lost along the way. Whether we saw them fall or they disappeared into the night, we must hold on to our love for them, and speak of them often. That way, they never truly leave us.

'And now, kind listeners, I shall say goodbye. Join me, Pippo the Chatty Bird, again tomorrow morning. Until then, *Buongiorrrrrrno a tutti!!*'

He waited until his colleague nodded his head before he let out a long sigh. Rubbing his eyes, he wondered how he had stumbled onto the subject of Clara during his radio show. Yes, he loved to talk, and was open and honest about his life and loves, but he always kept his chatter happy and cheerful.

Perhaps, he thought, Clara was on his mind more

than usual. He still visited her grave regularly, and most days he walked past the place where she was killed, but recently, memories of his sister had popped into his mind often, and when he least expected it.

Eating breakfast with his wife just this morning, a memory of Clara sharing her bread and wild berry jam with him had appeared with such suddenness and clarity that he'd felt his eyes prickle with tears.

Even so, his job was to entertain his listeners. To bring them smiles and music that would cheer them through their mornings. Although Pippo knew his show's audience was not huge in number — after all, a morning programme was still something of an experiment — he thought of the salesman driving to his next appointment, or the housewife sitting down for a coffee between chores, or the craftsman in his workshop using his hands to create, and he wanted to feel like a friend sitting beside them.

Who, he thought with a sigh, wanted a friend telling them about a mother who walked out on her two children one night, and a sister killed by a misfired bullet after the war?

No, he shook his head, tomorrow would be fun and laughter the whole show long. Decision made, he stood, pulled his jacket from the back of his chair, and left the studio for his meeting.

Dino's cafe was busy with couples sitting at tables and young people perched on stools at the bar. Modern and light with vinyl flooring, it had metallic furniture and an enormous machine that hissed and sprayed with every new order of coffee. It was so different from when it had been Ferrari's trattoria that he could barely remember how it used to look, but Pippo liked its new vibrancy and life.

A flash of emerald green across the room caught his eye, and he crossed to the table as the woman raised a hand in greeting to him.

'Zia,' he said, taking the hand and leaning over to kiss her on both cheeks. 'It's good to see you — and looking so well.'

The woman ran her hand over her short wavy hair. There were strands of frost in the chestnut now, and he noticed faint brown blemishes on the back of her hand as she pushed her cup towards him, but Zia smiled at Pippo comfortably.

'Another?' He lifted an eyebrow and, when she nodded, he turned to the bar. Putting the cup on the counter, he pointed at it and raised two fingers at the young man, who flung a tea-towel over his shoulder and turned to the large coffee machine.

Settling into the seat opposite her, Pippo asked after her husband.

'He is well,' Zia said, 'busy with the town council, but he enjoys it.'

Pippo was pleased that Signor Salvadori was happy. He had a great deal of respect for the man. At the moment when he should have been vengeful at the pointless killing of Clara, he had been nothing but compassionate. Through his own terrible grief, and supporting Zia in hers, the Signore had visited Mario in prison. He had seen the man's remorse and asked him to put it to good use: if Mario would use his influence and connections to stop the violence, to talk of forgiveness not retribution, if he could halt the attacks and accusations against so-called collaborators, then Clara's death would not have been in vain.

When Mario had accepted the request, the Signore, as his sister had always called him, had used his acquaintances in the police to have him released. Mario had been true to his word, attending meetings determined to damp down the fervour, to redirect energy towards planning a better future and leaving the bitterness behind.

Yes, Pippo smiled to himself, Clara had been lucky to live with a good man like him.

'And how many children do you have now?'

'Only three,' said Zia with a smile. 'Three, five, ten – however many, and whatever age, they are a blessing.'

Pippo shook his head in admiration. After losing the closest thing to her own child, Zia had turned to other people's children to ease her grief.

With Mario's aid, she and her husband had fled the city, where accused collaborators were in such grave danger. Pippo's adoptive father had used his contacts in the country to help them find a sleepy village where no one was interested in politics and retribution. The Signore had taken a job as a postman but, as the village had grown into a small town, he'd found his way back into an administrative role, spotting opportunities for local businesses to expand and building stronger connections with nearby cities.

After a few years of tending to her home, her garden and her grief, Zia had sat her husband down one evening and talked to him. He had nodded solemnly, listening to everything she said. And when she had leaned back in her chair, tears brimming in her eyes, he had reached for her hand and said, 'Of course, *Amore.*'

The next day, he had made enquiries at orphanages and children's homes and, by the following week, meetings had been arranged. Zia busied herself preparing the house and, when the time came, she welcomed the officials into her home. Impressed and relieved to be offered a solution to their problem, they quickly agreed that a few children could come and stay for a week or maybe a fortnight. When they'd left, Zia had shut the door quietly, sunk to her knees and sobbed.

The first children arrived on a hazy autumn morning. A brother and a sister, both under ten years old. Timid and frightened, they had clung to each other in the doorway as the priest who had brought them drove away. Hunching down to their level, she had smiled gently at them.

'Welcome,' she'd said quietly. 'You can call me *Zia*. Aunty.'

Those first two children had stayed for three years. And just weeks after their arrival, they had been joined by four more. Zia asked the village for help, and the community, relieved to encounter a gleam of hope, sprang into action.

The carpenter had made bunk beds to line the small rooms, the old ladies knitted jumpers and socks, and the baker's son delivered unsold bread most evenings.

Over the years, children had come and gone, and Zia had thrived. Devoted to each child, she would quietly get to know them, then build up their confidence with love and support.

Her husband had unconsciously been drawn in the

children's care too, reading a story to this child while Zia put another to bed, cleaning sticky fingers after a particularly messy breakfast, and snapping his arms as an ever-hungry crocodile chasing screaming prey.

Pippo looked at Zia's face as she talked about the children in her care, and decided what he saw was contentment.

When he had first met her on that terrible day, the only thing he could remember of her afterwards was her matching red lips and nails. These days there was no make-up, no painted nails, no tailored clothes. Today she wore trousers, flat shoes and a woollen cardigan in her favourite shade of green.

He preferred this woman to the one he had discovered had been Clara's carer. This lady was relaxed and at ease, and he felt a pang of sadness that his sister hadn't seen what she had become — the mother she was to Clara had become a mother to many. How lucky he was, he thought, that she was his friend.

Through Zia, he had a connection with his sister and the years of her childhood that he had missed. Though they only met a few times a year when Zia came to the city to shop — usually for one of the children's birthdays — he enjoyed their time together. They chatted easily about his family. How doting a grandmother Donna was to Violetta's baby Gino. And why Mario was leading the changes in the trade union where he worked. 'We're moving towards a freedom from politics,' Pippo quoted him with a wry smile.

'Zia,' he said when there was a pause in the conversation, 'I talked about Clara on my radio show this morning.'

The woman in green took a slow sip of her coffee. Putting her cup down carefully, she asked what he had said. He explained that he hadn't planned it, but suddenly he was telling anyone who would listen about how he had lost his sister.

'She has been in my thoughts too, lately,' nodded Zia. 'Memories of our time with her come to me almost by surprise. When I see a book I think she would have liked to read, or,' she smiled to herself, 'trying to teach one of the girls how to knit. All of a sudden, she's there, those amber eyes, that serious look on her face . . .' Her voice drifted off, carried away with the memories.

Pippo nodded. 'But why now, do you think? Why did I feel compelled to talk about her to people who never knew her?'

'Maybe your listeners each have their own Clara. Someone they lost and want to remember.'

'Perhaps.' Pippo gently twisted his cup in a circle.

Zia reached out a hand and patted his, noticing, as she did, a thin red wristband.

'You still wear it,' she said, touching it lightly.

'I never take it off,' he replied, as they both studied the faded fabric.

'See you tomorrow,' Pippo said, waving one hand to the receptionist, pleased that today's show had returned to its usual upbeat tone.

'Pippo,' the young woman said urgently, before he had the chance to open the door.

Turning to her, he saw her smile and nod her head towards an elderly gentleman sitting on the edge of one of the seats.

'Signore?' said Pippo. He was tired. He'd woken throughout the night dreaming of Clara. Every time he went back to sleep, she had appeared; sometimes talking to him as she had when they were children. Sometimes she was hurriedly following after Mamma, who carried him the first night they arrived in this city. And sometimes she simply took a single step forward and, for that moment, he truly believed he was looking at Mamma.

The old man rose slowly from his seat, his back so bent he had to tilt his head towards Pippo as he shuffled towards him, hand outstretched.

'May I call you Pippo?' he asked with a trembling voice.

'Of course,' Pippo replied, gently taking the wrinkled hand, partly in greeting and partly to support the gentleman. 'But, Signore, you are at an advantage . . .'

'My name,' said the old man, grinning to reveal missing teeth, 'is Signor Leone.'

'*Piacere*, Signore,' said Pippo, patting the hand he held. 'A pleasure.'

'I heard your programme yesterday,' the old man nodded. 'Very good, young man, very good.' Pippo lowered his head, accepting the compliment. 'And,' he continued, 'I wondered if I might talk to you . . .' He glanced at the woman sitting behind the desk, who was following the conversation. 'In private.'

'Of course,' replied Pippo, intrigued. 'Come this way,' he said, leading the man towards a door where a meeting room lay empty. He settled him comfortably into a chair and offered him a drink, which the Signore politely refused.

'So,' said Pippo, perched on the edge of his chair, 'how can I be of service?'

'I think,' replied Signor Leone, peering with faded brown eyes at the younger man, 'that I may be of service to you. I'm afraid I haven't heard your radio show before, but my granddaughter is staying with me at the moment, and she was listening to it while we sat together yesterday.

'I have to say, she was ready to turn the wireless off when you were talking about your family, but I refused to let her. As soon as I heard Clara's name, I knew it was the girl I met all those years ago.'

Pippo leaned forward and asked quietly, 'You knew my sister?'

The old man nodded, his bald head catching the light that shone through the window.

Pippo's lips curled into a smile. Now he knew why he had spoken of Clara. Somehow God, the universe – whoever – knew that this elderly gentleman would be listening.

'How did you know her? Please, tell me everything.'

'I worked in a library. She came in one day and we started talking about books.'

'She liked books?' Pippo remembered Zia had said she did, and thought of the lack of books in his childhood.

'Oh, she loved them. She visited often after school and we read together and talked. We were friends,' the old man nodded his head, 'she called me Saba – Grandfather.'

'Go on,' said the younger man.

'She . . .' Saba's voice quivered a little more noticeably. 'She tried to warn me the Germans were coming for me.'

'Did she succeed?'

The old man shook his head.

Pippo stared at him. 'You were taken . . .' He searched for a word and decided on, 'away?'

'Yes.'

'But you made it back.' It was more of a statement of disbelief than a question.

Slowly the Signore nodded. 'A long time ago, I was a professor of languages. I speak German. And Yiddish, and Polish, and whatever language they needed me to speak. I worked for them. And it saved my life.'

Pippo saw the old man lift his head a little higher.

'I also speak Romani,' he said, looking for a reaction in the younger man's face. When there was none, he carried on. 'Romani is the language of the gypsies. The gypsies who were rounded up first by Mussolini, and then by Hitler.'

Pippo nodded slowly. 'And what has that to do with Clara?'

'It is not of Clara that I speak now.'

Pippo felt a faint tingling in his chest, as if a tiny bell was ringing to warn him of some unstoppable freight train approaching fast. He twisted the red band round his wrist.

Saba looked down at the bracelet and smiled, as if receiving confirmation to continue.

'The place where the Germans took me, that was where I met your mother.'

Pippo's breath caught in his mouth. For what seemed like a very long time, he didn't breathe in or out.

His lips began to move, trying to form the questions that crowded his mind, but no sound came so he stopped, simply blinking at the Signore.

'Your mother was taken the night you arrived here,' he explained, 'by Blackshirts. The Racial Laws had just been passed. They were acting beyond the word of the law, some local official trying to impress their boss. But when they saw your mamma out late at night on her own – her colouring, her eyes, her headscarf and lots of gold jewellery – they stopped her. They asked her – was she a gypsy? She replied that she had been, but that she had left the community. They said, "Once a *Zingara*, always a *Zingara*."

'They took her and dozens of others; Roma, Sinti, whoever they could find who was different, and held them. Eventually, they transported them to the far south of Italy and put them in a camp. That's where she lived, Pippo, for years. All that time you and Clara were growing up, she was working and suffering.'

Pippo shook his head; the words that formed seemed either inaccessible or unsuitable.

'When the Germans came, they took the gypsies and the Jews and every other "undesirable" they could find to their concentration camps.

'Pippo.' The old man reached out a quivering hand and the younger man took it, holding it in both of his. 'Pippo, your mother helped me. I could barely walk – they had marched us for miles, and I had been taken wearing only my slippers. Your mamma let me lean on her and, when we stopped for a rest, she bound my feet with the fabric of her headscarf.

'By the time we got off the train in Poland, I had

convinced the guards that I would be useful to them as a translator. And I managed to persuade them to give your mother a job too. She worked as a seamstress, fixing uniforms and making dresses for the officers' wives.'

'And . . .' Pippo finally found his voice. 'Did she speak to you of me? Of Clara?'

'Of course,' nodded the old man with a smile. 'As soon as we began talking, we discovered the incredible coincidence — that I knew her daughter. She wanted to know why you both were not together, but all I could tell her was what Clara told me.'

'What was that?' Pippo's voice was a whisper.

'That you were sleeping. She went out to look for your mother and when she came back you were gone.'

Pippo nodded.

That he remembered. Waking up on his own and deciding to go and look for his sister. If only he had stayed in the room. What would have happened to them if he'd stayed? Would they both have been taken in by Zia? Would they have been put in an orphanage? Whatever, they would have been together. And maybe Clara would still be alive. Tears welled in his eyes.

Saba studied the man sitting opposite him and could see the boy he had once been. The child that Clara and their mother knew. He tapped Pippo on his leg to get his attention, drawing him out of his thoughts.

'I have some news that may raise your spirits,' he said when Pippo looked up at him. 'Your mother is alive.'

Pippo gasped and his fingers went to his lips, where they pulled at his skin anxiously, unable to tease the question he so wanted to ask out of his mouth.

'Yes,' the old man nodded happily, 'I know where she is.'

Pippo put his head in his hands and let the tears come.

He lifted his left hand to the twisted iron door knocker, and paused. What would he say? What would he ask? What did he want to hear?

He grasped the black metal ring and dropped it against the wooden door.

Bang.

The sound was like a gunshot. He closed his eyes and was a boy again, tearing off the red band around his wrist and throwing it to the ground in fury.

Bang.

Lost in the memory, he saw a plaited strip of red, an exact replica of his own, on the ground before him.

Bang.

With the final knock, he saw a memory that was not his own, but one that Saba had shared with him. On the day that Clara died, when her wristband had been torn from her and Pippo had ripped his own from his wrist, their mother had fallen to the ground. In his mind's eye, he could see the old man rush to her aid, but it was too late, the damage was done.

Pippo breathed out unevenly and waited. After a few moments, the heavy door was pulled open by a nun. After a brief conversation, she nodded. Yes, his mother was here, and yes, she was waiting.

As they walked down a cool white corridor and up a flight of wooden stairs, Pippo took in the place where his mother had been taken care of since the hospital administrators and Saba had brought her here.

'She was convinced you were both dead.' The elderly man had shaken his head as he'd told Pippo of her collapse. 'As soon as she could speak, she told me. She didn't want to come back to the city, didn't want to see where you had died. She didn't want to live,' he'd added quietly. 'But her body had different thoughts on the matter.'

'Or perhaps' – he'd looked into Pippo's face – 'something deep inside her knew you were still alive. Perhaps it told her to wait.'

And so she had waited – for more than ten years. She had waited here in this institution that smelled of lilies and polish, where Jesus and Santa Maria gazed down with serenity and grace on all who passed by. It was, Pippo decided, a pleasant place. It was quiet and calm, sheltered from the reconstruction and modernization that had shaped all aspects of Italian life outside.

At the end of another long corridor, they stopped by a door. The nun gently rapped on it twice with her knuckle. On hearing a response from inside, she gestured towards the handle, smiled and turned to leave, walking silently away.

Pippo paused only momentarily, not wanting to give himself the time to hesitate, before pushing the handle and opening the door. Stepping into the room, he found it just as Saba had described it. The right-hand wall was lined with shelves filled completely with books of all shapes and sizes. More books were piled on a small table beside a single bed in the corner of the room, and another stack stood beside the door, a vase of red geraniums placed carefully on top.

'Your mother collects books,' the old man had told him. 'I told her how Clara loved them and, when your mother was moved to the hospice, she began to fill her room with them. She says it makes her feel that your sister is close.'

And as Pippo breathed in the musky smell of the books, he felt, or perhaps just wanted to feel, his sister's presence. His sister who, through her love of books and friendship with a Jew at a time when such relationships were so dangerous, had brought him here.

He turned his head to where a figure sat by the window. Sunshine sparkled on the glass, casting the shape of the woman into silhouette. Outside, dazzling red and orange flowers swayed in the garden below, and beyond a small wall lay a field of wheat which the wind swept through, creating gentle golden waves.

As he took a step forward, his mother's form became clear. Dressed in a long dark dress, sitting with her hands resting in her lap, she turned her head towards him. The sun flashed on her black hair, revealing a single stripe of pure white running down the right side of her face.

And there was his mother. As he stared at the woman he hadn't seen since he was a small child, he knew her. Her high forehead and long nose, skin the colour of ground cinnamon, the eyes of gold that still shimmered with an internal fire. It was the face of the person he had laughed with, had endlessly chatted to and had adored entirely.

His mother looked into his face and smiled at her son.

It was only when his mother smiled that the condition the Signore had described became obvious. The left side of her mouth rose and her left eye wrinkled as the muscles pulled taut, but the right side of her face remained emotionless.

'It was clear from the moment I reached her as she lay on the floor,' Saba had told him, 'that one side of her had died. Paralysis, the doctors said; a stroke.'

As Pippo stood waiting for the words to come, the first greeting he would give his mother after so many years, Mamma looked past him, her eyes drifting to the right. She leaned forward, her lips parted and, in a voice that was as familiar as if he had heard it only this morning, she uttered a single word.

'Clara.'

Pippo smiled. Turning his head, he looked down to the child who stood hiding behind his leg. He squeezed her left hand which he held in his right.

'Don't be afraid,' he said softly.

Hesitating a moment, the girl looked at him with eyes the colour of rich, deep honey, then back to the woman sitting by the window.

Taking small steps, she crossed the room. Pippo watched as his mother held out her good hand, and the little girl, her brown hair turned chocolate by the light, reached to take it.

As she did, the sun caught a flash of red. A braided strip of red fabric was bound tightly round the girl's right wrist.

Unconsciously, Pippo's fingers reached for his own left wrist and turned the band, remembering how he had found his sister's bracelet on the ground the day she had died. At the time, he had tucked it in a pocket next to his own, knowing he could not bear to lose them. Now his daughter wore her aunt's.

'Clara,' his mamma said again, reaching to his daughter's face and stroking it.

'*Buongiorno*, Grandmamma,' said Clara.